MARY K. SAVARESE

The Star Writers Trilogy

THE GIRL IN THE
TOILE WALLPAPER

Book 1

of the

Star Writers Trilogy

The Girl in the Toile Wallpaper

Mary K. Savarese

© Copyright 2021 Mary K. Savarese

ISBN 978-1-953278-20-3 Hard Back
ISBN 978-1-953278-21-0 Soft Back
ISBN 978-1-953278-22-7 E-Book

This is a work of fiction. The characters are both actual and fictitious. With the exception of verified historical events and persons, all incidents, descriptions, dialogue and opinions expressed are the products of the author's imagination and are not to be construed as real.

Published by

INDIGNOR
— HOUSE —

INDIGNOR HOUSE™
Chesapeake, Virginia
www.IndignorHouse.com

It is written in the stars!

"Savarese is skilled at contrasting medieval and modern worlds, flowing between them in a manner that is enlightening and creates no confusion in the transition process, which creates a seamless story based not just on one or two main characters, but a host of special interests and objectives. Fantasy fans of high school age and older who look for a blend of mystery, history, and spell-binding intrigue will relish the journey and discoveries which defy time, space, and death. Complex story that comes alive and is satisfyingly unpredictable, and firmly rooted in strong characters. A story that is hard to put down."

Diane Donovan, Midwest Review

"Savarese's novel is an inventive and original portal fantasy that avoids the genre's most overused clichés. At moments the story evokes Doctor Who and A Wrinkle in Time (Tyler is a brainy kid with a love of physics), though the plot is unlike anything the reader is likely to have read. Savarese piles incident upon incident, and readers who enjoy a quirky science fiction story with magic and a hint of romance will find much here to entertain."

The US Review of Books

For

Katherine & Walter

And

Elaine & Andy

TOILE (TWAL)

I give you my toile. My flight of fancy, my visual narrative, my contrast in bold colors, depicted as scenes of bucolic life on cloth and paper. I incorporate whimsy, far-away places, tranquil pasturals, animals, even historical figures. In other words, I bring present-day to life …

— Christophe-Phillipe Oberkamf,
on creating Toile de Jouy

Prologue

It is said, "Where evil rages, hope prevails." This is not about evil for hope shall find a way ...

He watched as the dark shadows swirled across the room. A wind, as strong as a summer tornado, spun and yet moved nothing. Dante hid in the shadows and the sound of squalls raged through his ears. He inched his way toward the massive windows and darted behind the heavy drapery. His heart raced and he gasped when shards of light flashed through the room and threatened his reality. When a lightning bolt shattered, he winced and stepped deeper into the folds of the fabric.

Standing in the middle of the study, a boy held tightly to a girl in his arms. Dante wanted to help them but how? The evil man's robe glimmered with each wave of his arm. Dante watched in horror as the man threw the sheets of paper onto the floor. His long, golden fingernails glowed in the dim light. As the pages floated, each piece crawled toward the couple as if alive.

Awkward sounds filled Dante's ears while ghost-like buildings hovered through the air as if they were nothing more than a whisp of smoke. Now, a medieval scene flashed before his eyes, and the curtains vibrated in his hands. A flicker of an olive tree and then a farmhouse and then a vineyard ... *are those sheep?*

1

Dante tried to inch closer but his feet refused to move. He was glued in place behind the drapes. The ghostly objects disappeared into the paper and he trembled in terror. The shadows formed into a miniature print, each arranging itself according to the direction of the evil man. The man was painting a distressing scene through the movements of his symphonic hands.

The wizard swiped along the floor and the girl was jerked into the air. She hovered for only a moment before spinning as easily as a spinning wheel. Then, as if no friction ever existed, the girl screamed and the wind sucked her into the cloth paper … *the girl was gone.*

Chapter One

It is said, "Some loves are linked through times." This is not such love but it could be ...

Present Day

Sprinting to the most romantic bridge in all of Italy, the Ponte Vecchio, Tyler stopped to catch his breath. He didn't have much time. *Gotta get to the middle.* Handsome and dressed in a black tux, the young American pushed his way through the daunting crowd. Tyler scanned across the anxious eyes of the loving couples. Men were smiling at women and the women glaring back as if their hearts were being silently stolen.

Tyler spotted a single head of silver. There didn't seem to be anyone standing next to the old man. Leaning into the tangled mass of arms and legs, Tyler pushed his way through. Each step took him closer to the wavy, silver lines that were only a few feet away. An old, Italian man leaned cautiously over the stone railing and stared out at the swirling and darkening water. His yellow eyes seemed to reflect the world as if they'd seen more than they had ever wanted to.

Tyler peered through his fingers that shielded his eyes as the bright sun threatened to cloud his vision. The man, dressed in a creamy linen suit, looked frail but content. His thin frame allowed his clothes to drape across his body as if they were several sizes too large.

Could that be him?

Tyler Charles checked his watch. It was just a little after three on that bright Saturday afternoon. He sighed. *Phew … made it.* He squeezed between two couples and pushed forward. To divulge his secret to a complete stranger felt outrageously crazy. His stomach tightened and his hands shook.

"Scusi me." Tyler sighed and brushed his dark hair from his eyes. "I … I'm … I'm supposed to talk to you?"

Glancing around at the loving couples, Tyler's heart pounded. He adjusted his pants before looking down at his tux. Shaking his head, he thought about *her*, then pushed the thought from his mind.

"I'm no stranger to love," Tyler said now also looking at the water. "I never felt loved before. Well … from my mom … but when it comes to women … yah know what I mean?"

The man remained quiet.

Probably doesn't understand a word I'm saying. Tyler pushed back from the railing. "Okay … I'll admit it … had a couple of girls throughout the years … maybe several."

The old man nodded at Tyler.

"Fine … five. Had a total of five lovers. Thought that maybe, just maybe, I could stay in love this time."

The old man looked over at a couple who were kissing.

"At least one should have lasted … was more of a *like*, actually …"

The old man yawned.

"Umm, well … I convinced my fiancé that we should marry here … in Florence." Tyler shifted his stance. Again, he tugged at his pants. "Not my fault … I thought I had it this time. You know, the real deal …"

The old Italian smiled.

Tyler glanced across the river at the Florencian buildings. All seemed calm and inviting. However, Tyler felt anything but invited. "Now …" Tyler sighed. "Now … she's my ex-fiancé."

Again, the man looked over at a kissing couple.

"My God … I just left her standing there in that room … all by herself. I couldn't face her." Cupping a hand over his mouth, Tyler moaned. "Uhh … I let her down. I let everybody down … my family … our friends …"

Their gaze locked and Tyler felt something odd race through him. *Does he even understand me?* The old man looked deeply into Tyler's eyes. Tyler couldn't move.

"Uh." Tyler grinned. "I wear contacts."

The old man squinted.

"Maybe my brown eyes give me a brown disposition?"

The old man turned his attention back to the water and rested his arms on the railing.

What the hell? He shook his head. *I'm making a fool of myself.* Tyler glanced over his shoulder as several couples passed giving him a birds-eye view of a metal gate that was covered in locks of various shapes and sizes. Tyler wiped the sweat from his brow and frowned. He had seen those locks years earlier, fifteen to be exact. He was only twelve.

"Damn." A tear fell and a memory flooded his vision. "The more things change, the more they actually stay the same." A waiter had said that to him once and now the words flew past Tyler's lips. "Those locks are for lovers. They toss the keys into the river to seal their fate."

Lyly's beautiful eyes flashed before him. Tyler took a step back. His heart pounded and the pain from losing her filled his soul. Only once had he ever truly felt in love, and he was only twelve. Way too young to understand the why's. Reaching out, Tyler touched the edge of the old man's linen suit that rested on the old brick. The touch felt real, subtle. He jerked away his arm.

"Maybe it was the curse," Tyler said, holding back a sob. "Fifteen years ago. That's when I first met *her*. I was just a kid. But I grew to love her." Tyler raised his hand and pushed his hair from his eyes. "I know what I must do."

The old man glanced at him.

"I've got to find *the girl in the toile wallpaper*. I have to go back."

The old man's suit glinted in the afternoon sun.

"Back to the beginning …"

Standing together, the man wearing cream and Tyler wearing black, stared out together at the ancient architecture. The air cooled as the clouds rode across the sky.

Loosening his black bowtie, Tyler cringed. "I was only twelve and …"

The old man rested on the stone bridge and frowned.

"… I had come here with my aunt. Was supposed to be at camp …"

Chapter Two

It is said, "Too many cooks spoil the broth." This is not about the cooking but rather the brothing ...

Fifteen Years Ago

Standing in the kitchen of her Massachusetts home, Elysse Charles scowled at her younger sister. Both women with long dark hair, flawless skin, and brown eyes could practically be clones of each other. Only their personalities distinguished the two. Elysse with her anxieties always seemed to grow tense whenever Megan was around. And Megan, with a more practical outlook on life, always seemed to be either ignoring or antagonizing her older sister.

"He's a nerd like his dad, so what?" Elysse laughed. "He'll probably be working in the scientific community someday. All nerds work in the scientific community, don't they?"

"Tyler's obsessed with computers," Megan replied. "And he's a bookworm."

Elysse shoved her passport into her travel bag and frowned.

"You know that's not what I mean." Megan smirked.

Elysse grabbed her bag and dropped it on the floor.

"He has no friends," Megan added. "Why? Because he'd rather be with a book ... and he never leaves his room. Why? Because he's always on that stupid computer!"

Elysse turned away. "Your point?"

7

"I'm just saying it's not healthy. And … it's probably not safe having a computer in his room. Who knows what he's doing on it? Could be researching bombs or something worse."

"What are you talking about?" Elysse turned and glared at her sister. "You know something I don't?"

Megan took a step back. "No."

"Then don't be ridiculous." Elysse felt her face flush. "He's just deep into physics right now. And we've already blocked the inappropriate sites."

"I don't know —"

"And that's why, my dear sis, Tyler's going to camp. For the next two weeks, he'll be forced to make friends. And … he's in the fresh air and away from his computer."

Megan shrugged.

Forcing a smile, Elysse launched into her rehearsed speech. "That's why you're the best little sister in the world. I can't tell you how much I appreciate you driving him to camp. Maine's not a short trip. I'd never catch my flight in time."

"Danny will be surprised," Megan said.

"I can't wait. Besides, I need a vacation. We've been working nonstop, and we could use some alone time."

"Will the conference be over by the time you get there?"

Elysse shook her head. Her thoughts bubbled and if she said anything more, she'd probably start a fight. Keeping her mouth shut was usually the best choice. *Who are you to tell me how to raise my only child? You're not married or in a relationship.* Elysse mumbled through her thoughts and chanted her mantra: *She's doing me a favor … she's doing me a favor …*

Wrapping six of his dad's physics books inside his t-shirts, twelve-year-old Tyler shoved the disheveled clothing into his backpack. His camp trunk had already been picked up several days ago, and of course, his mom had found the books and pulled them out.

'Ty, get those outta there!' His mother had yelled. Never before had he seen her so angry. 'You're gonna have a ball,' she said. *Yeah right!* he thought.

His stomach churned at the idea of having to make new friends. He had none here, so why would he have any there? Camp Wamptucket, a place secluded somewhere in northern Maine, was not a place he wanted to be. Girls were not a part of his life and neither were boys. Keeping his nose inside a book was much safer.

Physics was his comfort zone, not to mention, it was fun. Someday he would discover something new and then his name would be displayed to the world. However, something else had his name on it right now and not something he wanted. Peeking out his window, his muscles tightened. There stood his nemesis, Kevin Smitters — the boy who wore oversized-red sneakers as his trademark.

Kevin bullied him all through gym. Always seemed as if the teacher turned her back at just the right moment. No one ever came to Ty's rescue. Everyone feared Kevin just as much as he did. But it was Tyler that Kevin had chosen as his punching bag.

Yesterday, the last day of school, Tyler finally fought back. Needing to use the bathroom, Tyler froze when he spotted the big and barely tied, red sneakers poking out from under the stall. Now, it was just the two of them … *mano-a-mano.*

Kevin stepped out and cracked his knuckles and laughed. "Well, well, poopie-head. Gonna be cool givin' you a proper farewell. Then we'll start all over again next year."

Tyler balled up his fists and waited. A little voice whispered, *hit him first*. Tyler swung at the huge boy. Instead of his knuckles hitting skin, his fingernails slid across the now startled face.

Kevin fell back on his butt. "Ass! You're mine, dude!" Kevin yelled, wiping the blood from his cheek.

Tyler ran and smiled all the way home. However, he wasn't smiling now. Kevin was pacing, panther-like, in front of his house. Taking in a deep breath, Tyler snickered. In half an hour, he'd be on his way to some place unknown. Therefore, he could dip down in the front seat of Aunt Meg's car, and Kevin would never see him. And the idiot would probably pace the block all night.

Sitting at his computer, Tyler waited. His document had to finish downloading and printing before he left. Time was running out. The site had been blocked by his parents but Tyler knew how to break through the firewall.

"Okay, Meg," Elysse said, dropping another bag at the door. "It's a three-hour drive. You should arrive around noon. Then two and a half hours back to the airport. Even with traffic, there's plenty of time."

"I'm just dropping him off, right? Nothing else? I can't miss my flight in Boston."

"You'll be fine. Mine leaves in three hours. Yours isn't until tonight."

"My boss made the arrangements." Meg sighed. "It's an important project. I can't be dealing with head problems right now."

Elysee stared at her and frowned.

"Okay … I'll just drop him off."

Elysse drew an imaginary X on her heart just like she did when they were kids. "I promise. His camp counselor will be waiting for you."

Meg sighed again.

"Honest!" The doorbell rang. "Now who could that be?" Elysse asked.

Megan picked up the newspaper from off the counter and laughed. "This is front page news? *Pig Flu Making Its Way Through the Northeast.* Is this a joke? Am I missing something about pigs getting the flu?" She raised her voice so Elysse could hear.

"Apparently it is. Making the front page and all." Elysse opened the front door.

"I'm missing a lot lately," Megan yelled back.

Elysse dragged a husky-built boy with taffy brown hair into the kitchen. He smiled and the red scrape on his cheek darkened.

"Meg, I want you to meet Tyler's fra-end." Elysee smirked. "From school. His name's Kevin."

"Hi, Kevin," Megan said. "Nice to see Ty has a friend." She leaned over and whispered to her sister, "At least one."

Kevin nodded.

Frowning, Elysse coughed. "You can go right up. Tyler's room is the first on the right."

"Thank you, Mrs. Charles," Kevin replied, making a fist.

Shutting down his computer, Tyler was already missing it.

'It's all about comradery and the great outdoors, Ty, not about computers,' his mom had said every time he protested.

He shook off the odd feeling that was suddenly creeping up his back and glanced out his window. No sign of Kevin out front. He probably went home. Tyler shoved the printed report of the downloaded article into his backpack. He smiled knowing where he had hidden the physics books.

His mother's words echoed up from downstairs. "Ty! Your friend, Kevin, is on his way up."

Tyler's mind twirled. Watching the knob turn, Tyler held his breath. His heart raced. He jumped at the door just in time to push it closed. Kevin pushed back from the other side.

"I know you're in there!" Kevin whispered. "Open up. Get what's coming to yah."

Elysse and Megan flinched when a loud thump grabbed their attention.

"What's going on?" Elysse peeked out the living room window. Everything appeared quiet. "I'll get Ty ready to go."

"I'll wait in the car," Megan said. "Have a wonderful vacation with Danny."

"I owe you one," Elysse replied.

"No problem. What else are little sisters for?"

"Ty, where's Kevin?" Elysse asked.

"Umm … he had to go."

"Really?" Elysse glanced around. "I didn't see him leave."

That's because he didn't leave; for Kevin had forced his way into Tyler's bedroom. The boys danced back and forth tossing insults at each other.

"Hold still so I can belt yah." Kevin lunged at Tyler.

Tyler reached for his only weapon — his backpack. He flung it at the boy, and it landed near the opened window. Tyler ran to grab it for another pass. Kevin reached out for him, and instead of taking a step, Kevin's foot entangled in the strap of the heavy bookbag. Tyler's old physics books helped to fling the boy through the window.

"Heyyyyy!" Kevin yelled and flailed as he dropped toward the hardened ground.

Jumping up and down, Tyler yelped. "Yessss!" Tyler peeked out the window and stared down at the panting Kevin Smitters. He waved and laughed as the boy slowly rolled off the crushed bushes.

Tyler sat his backpack on his bed.

Elysse closed the window and smiled. "Okay, time to go. Aunt Meg's in the car."

"Why can't I go with you, Mom?" Tyler lowered his head.

"Because you can't. You'll have a great time at camp."

Tyler frowned.

Handing him the required paperwork, his mother hugged him in tight. "Love you, Ty. Dad and I will pick you up in two weeks." Mom kissed him on his cheek, steering clear of his rimless glasses.

"Love you too, Mom." Grabbing his bookbag, he shoved the documents into a side pocket.

As his aunt drove down the street, Tyler stared out the window.

"Hey, Ty … there's your friend Kevin. Want to say goodbye? I can pull over. Looks like he's limping."

"Uh … no. We already said our goodbyes." Tyler waved at Kevin. He smiled when he noticed the new, red scratch on the boy's face. Then he thought of the seventh grade and his smile disappeared.

Elysse left with suitcase and travel bag. She smiled at the thought of surprising her husband. Since they hadn't parted on such good terms, she prayed that their private time together would change everything.

Chapter Three

It is said, "There is no destination without a beginning." This is not about destinations but rather the mode of travel…

Megan Brandt was all about her job that left no extra time for a routine family life. A man was the last thing on her mind. She worked in the Boston division of one of the most prestigious wallcoverings and fabric houses in the world, Tighe & Randall, and Megan worked hard. Elysse constantly tried to match Megan with one of Elysse's husband's friends. To Megan it was just another annoying dinner party.

'What's up with your sister?' a potential suitor had once asked. 'She's cute and all but she's always too busy.'

Therefore, none of the blind dinner dates ever called Megan back or asked for her phone number.

But for Megan, something better was right around the corner. She was just handed a new project. A secret project known only to her and her bosses. Her goal was to create a new division. And then … she would be the boss.

Elysse thought of nothing except for her vacation. She glanced at her watch and smiled. In thirty minutes, she would board the plane.

Then in a few hours, she would step onto the island of Bermuda. Danny was a speaker at the International Scientific Conference for his lecture on molecules. Danny had no idea she was coming. A romantic get-away should help their strained marriage. Her stomach churned. After thirteen years, all couples had issues, right? Just some alone time and everything would be better she had told Megan.

Then again, many couples divorced, right? What would make her marriage any different? Being a single mother wouldn't be all that bad ... Elysee walked past a large window and stared at her reflection. She shook her head. No, she didn't want a divorce. She still loved Danny very much.

Besides, her son and sister were driving to the camp right now and life was wonderful. Checking her phone for the last time, she smiled. No missed calls. Shutting it off, she shoved her phone into her purse. No need to turn it on for a week. Emergency contact was now Meg, not her. Everything was set. Everything was perfect.

With such a close call with Kevin, Tyler wanted nothing more than to be left alone. Feigning sleep seemed rude but to have to endure answering random questions about mundane life was just out of the question. 'Bet you can't wait to get to camp, huh, Ty?' The answer would have been ... 'No.' 'Bet you're anxious to make some new friends, huh, Ty?' The answer again, would have been ... 'No.' In reality, his shoulders would shrug and his eyes would roll. Better to fake sleep than be bombarded with doubts.

"Dag-gon-it!" Aunt Meg pushed the buttons on the radio.

Tyler stretched and coughed. "Something wrong?"

"No signal. Probably almost there." Megan turned off the noise. "Excited? You should make lots of new friends at camp."

"Maybe." Hearing the word *camp* sent chills up his arms. He shivered. Pulling down the visor, he stared at his partial reflection in the small mirror. Running his fingers through his dark messy hair, he sighed as his glasses swayed crookedly on his long skinny nose. He glared at his eyes. He didn't like his eyes. One was a dark brown and the other was more of a tan. He pushed his glasses up and laughed. His mom said one was from her and the other from his dad.

Ever since his first day of school, he hated others looking too closely at him. A girl once dragged him to a sand box to build a castle. All was great until she stepped a little too close. Then she screamed. 'Freak!'

After that, Tyler avoided direct eye contact whenever possible. Again, he sighed. The invisible band that practically glued his glasses to his head tickled his neck. He had lost his glasses twice, and his mom warned that she'd never buy another pair if he didn't wear the band.

"Are you okay?" Megan asked, turning onto the camp's road.

He cringed as they passed the *Welcome to Camp Wamptucket* sign. Below the bright yellow letters, he laughed at the line that read: *Where Dreams Are Made.*

"More like nightmares," he mumbled.

"What?" Megan asked.

"Nothing."

"We made good time. Place looks a little empty."

"Really?"

"I wonder where the camp workers are. Keith is your counselor."

Tyler glanced around the empty parking lot.

"Get you settled and I'm out."

"Boston, right, Aunt Meg?"

"Yep."

Megan parked and stepped out. Tyler strained to lift his heavy backpack.

"Looks like a lot of fun," he mumbled.

"Oh, Ty, you'll have a great time."

As they walked down the dirt road, the breeze carried the leaves across their path. The birds chirped but everything else remained quiet … too quiet.

"Where is everybody?" Megan asked. "Are we early?"

Tyler shrugged.

Dozens of trunks heaved into a pile gave them reason to pause.

"Those should be in the cabins," Megan said, pointing.

Tyler shrugged again.

"Hi!" A young girl wearing a green camp shirt popped out from between the bushes.

Megan and Tyler jumped back.

"Sorry," the girl said. "Didn't mean to startle you. Name?"

"Tyler … Tyler Charles."

"I'm his aunt. His counselor is Keith."

"Keith? He's the sickest of 'em all." She pushed her hair behind her ears.

"I'm sorry to hear that. Then who's Tyler's counselor?"

"Counselor? We don't have any. We're closed." She chomped on her gum, blew a bubble, and then popped it.

"Closed?" Megan's eyes widened.

"Yes, ma'am. We sent a fax. Everyone is sick … except me." She popped as she chewed.

"Sick?" Megan repeated.

"Started last week," the girl said. "The cook was first. Some guy at the Board of Health said we had to shut down." Not stopping to take a breath, she pointed to the large pile of trunks. "Yours is in there somewhere. Just grab it."

A huge grin decorated Tyler's face.

"And then you can leave," the girl said.

"Leave?" Megan repeated.

"You don't want pig flu, do you, ma'am?" the girl replied.

The term *ma'am* infuriated Megan. *I'm not a ma'am. Ma'am's for old ladies.* She watched as Tyler fumbled with his trunk.

"What do you mean by closed?" Megan asked.

"Closed, as in not open," the girl glared at her. "Pig flu … I didn't catch it. I'm not sick, therefore, I'm here. The sickos are at home … in bed." The girl popped another bubble.

"I just drove three hours! His mother's on a flight to Bermuda. And I have a plane to catch. I can't bring a twelve-year-old with me to Italy. I'm working!" Megan shouted. "Did you call anyone about being closed?"

The girl shrugged. "Just the fax. Phones hardly ever work up here anyway. We *are* in the boonies, yah know."

"I read about the pig flu in the papers." Megan softened her tone. "I just need to know, what's the new plan."

"New plan?" the girl asked.

"What's your name?" Megan asked.

"Missy." She smiled again. "Camp Wamptucket will mail you a full refund."

"That's not what I mean. Where does Ty go now? There must be another camp that's free of the flu where I can drop him off?"

"Yes, there are."

19

"Great." Megan sighed. "I'll take him to one. Address?"

"They're full."

"Full?" Megan repeated. "Then what do I do with Ty?"

Tyler grinned.

"Um, he goes home … with you," Missy said.

Megan frowned. "I'm leaving for Florence tonight."

"Sounds   cool."   Missy   furrowed   her   brows.   "Florence, Massachusetts is just a few hours from here."

"Not Florence, Massachusetts. Florence, Italy!"

Pointing in the direction of Tyler's trunk, Missy checked off his name. "Tyler, you're good to go." Missy shrugged and turned to another family. "Name?"

"Com' on, Ty. Grab an end. I'll have to figure this one out."

"Sorry, Aunt Meg."

"Not your fault." Lifting one end of the trunk, Megan's insides fumed. Whenever her sister crossed her heart, Megan should know better. She always seemed to grab the short end of the stick — or trunk in this case.

Sitting in the car Megan fumbled with her phone. "No service, I guess we *are* in the boonies. Can you stay with your friend, Kevin?"

Tyler shifted in his seat and rubbed the back of his neck. "Uh, no. He's leaving for camp tomorrow."

"Obviously, that one doesn't have pig flu."

Tyler shrugged.

"You understand that I'm supposed to leave for Italy … tonight?"

"Can I go with you?" Tyler asked. "I'll be good. I promise. I have loads of books to read. You won't even know I'm around."

"I thought of that Ty but you'd need a passport. I can't just drum one up at the last minute."

Digging into his backpack, Tyler pulled out an envelope. "You mean this?"

"Why do you have a passport on you?"

"Camp had a field trip to Canada. Mom told me to keep it in case I needed it."

"Then …" Megan sighed. "Tyler Charles is going to Italy."

Tyler's face lit and he sat up straight. "That's the country that looks like a boot!"

Megan laughed.

"All right! Never been to Europe. Just Canada and Mexico."

Megan pulled out of the empty parking lot. "I need cell service. You need a ticket."

"Too cool!"

"Haven't seen you this happy in a while. It's warm in Italy. Glad you have your camping clothes."

Tyler pulled the duffel bag from his trunk and filled it with shorts, t-shirts, and underwear. "Aunt Meg … I have to tell you something."

"What's that?"

"I didn't want to go to camp."

"Then … your wish came true."

Now, she wished her dream would come true — the start of a new toile division under her charge. So far, today was nothing but a nightmare.

"I pray this isn't an omen of things to come," she whispered.

"What?" Tyler asked.

"Nothing," she replied.

Megan lovingly accepted the task of taking Tyler to Italy with her. Afterall, she was the *good* little sister. Not that taking him would break the six o'clock news or anything but Elysse still needed to know where her son was and with whom.

"Hey, sis … no emergency. Just an FYI. Tyler's not at camp. That stupid pig flu. So, camp's closed. Ty's going with me to Florence."

Megan hated leaving messages. But she knew her sister would power *off* for the week and not check it even once. But a short note was better than nothing.

Should I leave the same message for Danny? Megan thought it over. *No … my sister would kill me. Blow her whole surprise. Fine, she owes me a bigger one now.*

Megan glanced at the flights. Alitalia Airline was on-schedule for eight. She considered the time difference and length of flight and sighed just knowing that, for the next eight hours, her legs would cramp. As they followed others down the walkway, Megan glanced over at Ty. He looked way too happy. Not normal for a twelve-year-old.

"Our seats are 16A and B," Megan said.

"Business?" Tyler asked, glancing around.

They stepped onto the plane and waited. As they inched toward Business Class, she had to laugh. Ty was checking out everything.

"I think these are ours," Tyler said, dropping his bag on the floor.

"I believe you are correct."

Their seats proved to be quite roomy and comfy. Tyler sat by the window thrilled over everything. After takeoff, the attendants passed out the dinner trays. Tyler seemed to be enjoying his Italian meal of antipasto, lasagna, and salad. Megan shook her head and chuckled. Two cannolis sat on Ty's tray. His as well as hers.

"Thanks, Aunt Meg, this is great." Tyler yawned. "Can't wait to get to Italy."

"Glad you're happy." Megan rubbed her stomach. She wasn't feeling well. Perhaps it was just her nerves.

With the cabin lights dimmed, a warm cookie, and a glass of cold milk in his tummy, Tyler soon fell asleep. Megan covered him with a blanket. Still feeling a little queasy, Megan nibbled on her meal.

"Signorina Brandt, is the food not to your liking?" the attendant asked with a strong Italian accent. "May I bring something else?"

"Oh, no, everything's fine. My nephew ate enough for the both of us." Megan laughed. "I'm just not hungry."

"Don't hesitate to ring if you need anything." The attendant smiled before walking away.

"Grazie," Megan whispered, practicing the only Italian word she knew.

Megan sipped on her glass of red wine and her mind twirled. Perhaps once they arrived at the hotel, she could find a small room for Ty. If not, her room would be a little crowded. Megan needed enough space to spread out her work.

I'll have to hire someone to take him on a few tours.

Megan thought about the most wonderful opportunity that was handed to her just a few days ago. A new toile division under her leadership.

I deserve it. Nobody works harder than me.

Megan sat back and allowed the conversation with Mr. Tighe to flow through her mind.

"Megan," Mr. Tighe had said while tugging at his trousers, "I know you know that Tighe & Randall is one the most prestigious wallcoverings and fabric houses in the United States."

"Yes, sir and —"

"Don't interrupt me now ..." Mr. Tighe raised his hand. "We bought the rights to a secret collection of toile wallcoverings."

"Toile?" Megan repeated and her heart pounded. She expected a promotion but nothing this exciting.

"Paper and fabric," he said.

"Yes, sir. I understand toile." Megan smiled.

"You don't understand, child. This paper was locked away for over two and a half centuries!"

"What?"

"I thought that would grab your attention." Mr. Tighe chuckled. "Originals, possibly purchased from Jouy, France."

"Where the famous Toiles de Jouy originated?" Megan asked.

"By the famous Christophe-Philippe Oberkampf himself." Mr. Tighe rocked back and forth on the heels of his feet.

Megan's mind flew through the possibilities. Secret toile wallcoverings that included everything from basic life, historical events, royal courts, ancient architecture ... the possibilities were endless.

"Toiles tell a story," Megan whispered. "Where are they?" She glanced around.

"They are not here, child. Still on the walls at the Italian estate. And they are ours!"

"Who are you sending?"

Mr. Tighe laughed. "Why, you!"

"Me?"

"Yes, you. A whole new division for us." Mr. Tighe held out his hand.

Megan pulled her warm blanket around her neck. She closed her eyes and thought about what she would find. Toile paper that had not been seen in over two centuries. *Wow, what a secret.*

Chapter Four

It is said, "What often determines a man's legacy is not what's seen." This is not about what a man sees but what he is missing …

"Catman! Catman!" A group of tourists, gathering in the crowded piazza that overlooked the River Arno, chanted. "Catman! Catman …!"

The mid-day sun was hot, and a scrubby skeletal of a man wearing a black t-shirt and jeans waved his tattoo-ladened arms through the air. A daily duty to bring attention to *The Catman of Italy*.

"Com'on now," Tino yelled out with broken English. "You clap louda and scream louda if you wanna bring 'em out." Tino pointed to the boards that hid the miniature performers from the anxious crowd.

The chanting and clapping grew louder. "Catman! Catman! Catman!"

Three wooden boards, covered in various types of fabric, hid what the excited crowd wanted, and thirteen cats waited patiently without making a sound.

"Soon, my little ones, soon," Fabrizio Gattomo whispered.

Fabrizio, a thin, middle aged Italian of small stature, stood tall and proud. He brushed back his graying hair and scratched his slightly crooked nose. He sighed. Wearing a red-striped shirt and beige cargo pants, Fabrizio excelled at being The Catman Extraordinaire. Even his

God-given sir name, Gattomo, meant *cat* in Italian. Ever since early childhood, Fabrizio loved his cats and his cats loved him. Since he never married, his cats were his family. They were his children. Thirteen strays, his lucky number, were his whole act. He took better care of his felines than himself. Just a few more seconds and he would release them to perform their show.

Tino shivered as a breeze caressed his face. He glanced at the boards and the material rolled with the wind. *More wind and we are in trouble.*

Fabrizio jumped out from behind a colorful board and bowed. He raised his eyes to the heavens as if in prayer. Running into the crowd, he slapped hands with as many people as he could reach. Cupping his ear with one hand, he touched his heart with the other. When he waved his hand through the air, the crowd went wild.

"Catman! Catman! Catman!"

He summoned silence by lowering his arms. The crowd hushed. Standing in front of the three fabric-covered boards, Fabrizio remained silent. Behind the boards, his nephew, Tino, cautiously opened the crate, and thirteen felines of different colors formed a straight line.

Out front, Fabrizio meowed. The sound was as real as the cats he had raised. The crowd roared. Fabrizio had them right where he wanted. He meow-ed again and seven males, gray and black, walked proudly to the front of the boards.

"Mushmellow!" Fabrizio yelled out. "Fabio, Curry, Harry, Asti, Georgie, and D'oreo." He pointed to each as they formed a line. Fabrizio ordered, "Sit." And the cats sat.

He turned to the crowd and bowed. The crowd clapped and cheered. Again, he lowered his arms as a signal for everyone to quiet down.

Raising his arm up and down, Fabrizio meow-ed and said. "Allie, Belle, Cherie, Gigi, Minnie, and Trixie … come!" Six felines ran to the front of the board. Fabrizio gave out the order. "Sit!" And the cats sat.

The crowd chanted their favorite name. "Catman! Catman! Catman!"

Fabrizio raised his finger to his lips. The crowd hushed. After a quick hand jester, Fabrizio clapped. "Okay my little ones. Up!"

The thirteen cats dashed to the middle board and disappeared behind the chutes of colorful fabric. Each clawed to their assigned position and then waited. Shadows from the bright sunlight helped to create the imaginary scene. A pastural view with trees, sheep, and flowing blue water instantly materialized before the crowd. The three-dimensional affect dazzled anyone not blocked by a hypnotized viewer. A small black tail waved suddenly under the hem and the crowd roared with laughter.

Laughing and making another quick hand gesture, Fabrizio yelled, "D'oreo, your tail. Up!"

On cue, D'oreo's tail disappeared.

Fabrizio meowed and the cats emerged from behind the fabric and formed a line. The crowd cheered. Fabrizio meowed again and pointed. The cats obeyed and climbed behind the curtain of the first board. Instantly, an underwater scene of fish, crabs, lobsters, and seaweed waved in the sunlight. After a few minutes, Fabrizio used his hand gesture and meowed. The cats climbed down and formed another line. They accepted their applause, and following Fabrizio's orders, entered the third board. A city skyline with a full moon came alive. During each of the cats' performances, Fabrizio had to yell out, "D'oreo hide your tail!" And right on cue, the tail disappeared.

It seemed as if the howling crowd could not get enough of the cats and their amazing performance.

"Momento!" Fabrizio said to the crowd. "Eh … like you and me my cats need a break." He laughed. Walking by the boards, Tino handed Fabrizio a small bucket. Pulling out a few sardines, he tossed several onto the ground and the cats crawled down to eat.

Tino turned each board around to reveal new potential scenes. Outer space with a sun, laughing children on a Merry-Go-Round, and the finale … *The David*. White fabric on a black background. The thirteen cats snuggled within their assigned spaces to create the statue of a man. A man that was first sculpted by Michelangelo.

"Scusa," Fabrizio said. "If you are interest, the actual statue is on display in the Accademia Museum. Notta far from here. You will find impressions all around our great city. But no. Is this not the best, how you say, creativity?" Fabrizio laughed.

Tino frowned. Although, The Catman's show was complete, Tino's job was just starting. Moving quickly before the crowd dispersed, Tino ran through the tourists holding out a white bucket.

"Paper? No, no coin. Too heavy, eh, you understand?" He moved his hands in all directions.

The cats formed their line and stared at the crowd.

"You may pet 'em if you'd like … gently now!" Fabrizio said. "They no scratch. I will tell you of a tale of the most famous of all cats."

After motioning the smaller children to the front, Fabrizio started his story.

"His name was Celestial KittyCat, or in Italian, Gattino Celestiale Gatto. Two and a half centuries ago, a young man arrived in Siena." He smiled at the children and nodded as their parents dropped the paper euros into the bucket. Fabrizio knelt and petted a cat. "And what happened in Siena, you ask?" Cupping his hands across his heart, he pumped it open and closed. "Love is what-ta happened. But something went wrong. The young man was turned into a black cat. An immortal cat." Fabrizio pointed to the children. Hearing a chuckle, he continued. "I speak-a the truth! A mystic from the far east turned the young man into a black cat."

Fabrizio hesitated as more euros fell into the bucket.

"On one side of the black cat are three golden brands. A sun, a star, and a moon!" Fabrizio glanced around before continuing. "You know of the alignment that I speak?"

The crowd leaned forward begging for more.

"In two nights time, our sun and Venus and a full moon will be in perfect alignment!"

Fabrizio waved his arm. The crowd stared into the bright afternoon sky and shielded their eyes.

"For the first time in over a century, our planet of love will sit between the sun and the moon. I tell-yah what this means. Catch Celestial KittyCat and he must grant you a wish. If he does, then he will once again become a man. As the alignment is on his fur, the alignment will be as above!"

The crowd laughed.

The Catman of Florence bowed. "Grazie," he said. As he clapped, he pointed to his cats. "They-a the real stars." Then he pointed to Tino, his nephew, who quickly held up the large bucket.

Once the crowd dispersed, the cats followed Fabrizio behind the boards. He helped to guide them back into the cage. Petting each one, Fabrizio handed out more treats. Now alone, Fabrizio reached into the white bucket and pulled out a small handful of euros. "Go pay those suckling pigs their share."

"Si, Uncle Fab."

"Then, put the boards into the truck." Fabrizio turned his attention to his cats.

"Si, Uncle Fab."

The start of the Italian summer announced the arrival of more tourists. Tino had watched as The Catman made a decent living with his strays. A percentage he shared with the town's polizia, and a pittance he shared with Tino. Tino marched to the corner of the piazza and reached into his pocket. He pulled out several euros.

"Crowd control is not cheap," a polizia on duty said. "Good crowd today. Looks like Catman made out with his cats." The polizia laughed before splitting a wad.

"Yeah, the rats did good." Tino frowned.

"Tino no like-a the rats?" another officer asked.

"I wish them dead," Tino replied. "Hate 'em. Always have."

Tino never completed school. He was now twenty-two and jobs for him were scarce. Instead, he worked for his uncle cleaning the litter boxes, filling the food bowls, and whatever else his uncle required. It was Tino's job to keep thirteen cats happy. Smiling, Tino felt the euros he had held back. He tapped his pocket. *Beer money!*

After returning to his uncle, Tino locked the crate and hissed at the cats. He pushed the boards closer to the truck and dismantled them. This was a daily routine — three times a day, seven days a week.

"Soon, my children," Catman said. "You will-a be-a home to play and play we will. First, we rest as we still have two more shows to perform."

Tino cringed every time he heard his uncle meow, and he was even more tired of hearing that stupid story. *Tale of Celestial KittyCat!* Because of the alignment of the three celestial bodies, his uncle had spiced up the legend. Everyone from Florence was talking about it. Just the other day, he saw several children's books on display at a local bookstore. All about a blonde-haired man turning into an immortal pussycat.

As a child, Tino worshiped his Uncle Fab. He would stand at the end of the dirt driveway and wait until he could see his truck. Then Tino would race home to tell his mother. When his mother died, Tino was only twelve. Just old enough to understand that she would never come home. It was Uncle Fab who drove down that dirt road to rescue him. Tino had waited years for his father to show, but the man never did. To this day, Tino had no idea where his father lived or even if he was still alive. He loved his uncle, however, love only extended out so far. After that, sanity seemed to take control.

Tino was sick of Uncle Fab only paying him twice a month and not enough to live on. Working with his uncle was not the best life. At least he had a roof over his head. This morning was a nice start to a good collection, and the polizia were happy. When they arrived at their first floor flat, Uncle Fab released his children.

Stupid rats. Tino glared at the vermin.

Fabrizio played with them all evening. They feasted on wonderful morsels ... but only Uncle Fab and his thirteen babies. Tino ate a sandwich. Not to mention that it would be Tino's job to clean up their mess. Again, he patted his pocket. Tonight, he would treat his friends to a beer.

Chapter Five

It is said, "Our fate is written in the stars." This is not about the stars but the people who walk in their light ...

Megan squealed as their flight touched down in Florence. Her first visit to the famous Italian city. Today she'd be inspecting the secret collection of toiles in Florence. First on her list ... make sure that Ty was settled in.

Unfortunately, Italians were never in a hurry. After grabbing their luggage and tackling customs that seemed to take forever, Megan sighed when she saw the heavy traffic. Through the taxi's window, she took the time to enjoy the scenery. Orange rooftops rose in the distance sending chills all through her.

"Ty, check out those buildings," Megan said. "Lotta history here."

Tyler glanced up and nodded. "What's that big dome?"

"That is the Duomo," replied the taxi driver.

He must be used to gawking tourists, Meg thought. "I guess you have lots of visitors?"

The driver nodded.

"What's that?" Tyler asked.

"A cathedral." Megan made a mental note that the cathedral would make a great tour spot for him.

After winding through cobbled streets and open-air markets, the taxi finally stopped at the Grande Hotel. With the help from a bellhop, Megan and Tyler gathered their luggage from the trunk.

"Look, Aunt Meg!" Ty pointed across the street.

"That's the River Arno." Megan glanced around. "It's beautiful here. So green."

"Grazie, signorina," the hotel attendant said with a wink. "Florence is beautiful, just like you."

Megan giggled.

Boom!

Megan and Tyler jumped. An old and rickety green truck with the logo, The Catman and His Amazing Cats, rolled slowly past the hotel.

"Check out the cool truck. Some kind of a cat show." Tyler chuckled.

The bellhop pushed the luggage cart and shook his head. "Every morning, The Catman of Florence puts on the same show in the piazza." He laughed. "And his truck makes that same sound when he leaves." He waved his hand through the air.

"Maybe we can watch the show tomorrow?" Tyler asked his aunt.

"Just you, Ty. I'll be working." Megan stood at the hotel door. The marble architecture and the hanging Italian paintings mesmerized her. "Wow!"

"Wow what?" Tyler asked.

"Just look at this place … postcard … wish you were here!" Megan stepped up to the counter and glanced at the attendant's nametag. "Bon giorno, Mr. Mazzello." She was quite proud of her pronunciation. She had practiced on the plane.

"Good morning signorina and young man. Please, call me Vincenzo." His English was excellent, and he paired it with only a slight Italian accent.

Tyler dropped his heavy backpack.

"Vincenzo, I'm checking in." Megan smiled. "Megan Brandt. I'm with Tighe & Randall. This is my nephew, Ty. I was hoping that you had a small room close to mine?"

"Certainly, Signorina Brandt. We had a last-minute cancellation. We have a small room right next to you. It overlooks the garden courtyard."

"Oh, that's great, Vincenzo." Megan smiled again. "Any suggestions on tours for Ty while I'm working? I left a message."

After staring at his computer screen, Vincenzo looked up and frowned. "A tour for today would be too late. I could possibly find one for tomorrow?"

Tyler leaned against the marble counter. "Aunt Meg," he whispered, "I don't have to go anywhere today or tomorrow. I have my books."

Vincenzo chuckled. "Ah, an excellent studente, I am sure."

"He's the best." Megan hugged Tyler. "Tomorrow is fine. I need to be at work today by two. We can grab lunch before I go."

Megan pulled an envelope from her purse. She handed the sheet to Vincenzo. "Is this very far?"

"Ah, yes. I know of it, Signorina Brandt. It is not in Florence but in Siena."

Megan eyes widened. "Siena? Are you sure? How would my company make such a mistake?"

"We have a driver that can escort you. It is only an hour's drive."

"Maybe we should stay in Siena? I have so much work. An hour each way?"

"Oh, Signorina Brandt, but the festival. All rooms are booked."

"Festival?" she asked.

"Yes, the horse race. The Palio. Our rooms have been booked for months. Especially in Siena. Many will stay here and travel to Siena for the festival. Perhaps that is why your company booked you with us."

Staring at Vincenzo, Megan's mind whirled. *What else can go wrong?* "I don't have a choice."

Vincenzo handed Tyler a small, stuffed, black cat. On the side, and emblazoned in gold, was a sun, a star, and a moon … all in alignment.

"Cute." Ty glared at his aunt.

"Throughout Florence we will celebrate the alignment. First time in over a hundred years," Vincenzo said.

"Alignment?" Tyler asked.

"Yes, the sun, Venus, and super, full moon," he explained. "That cat is from the tale of *Celestial KittyCat* … Gattino Celestiale Gatto."

"Celestial what?" Tyler repeated.

"A love story that took place in Siena during the 18th century. The star is Venus. The star of love … their love." Vincenzo placed his hand over his heart. "Something big will happen that night!"

"Oh?" Megan glanced at Ty.

"An Italian love story. We celebrate everything here."

Megan laughed. Tyler nodded. They aimed for the elevators. When they found their rooms, Megan felt relieved when she discovered that they had adjacent ones. Ty sat on his bed and Megan watched as he stuffed the Celestial KittyCat into a side compartment of his backpack.

"Ready for lunch, Ty?"

"Starving."

"We passed a lot of restaurants that overlooked the River Arno. We'll eat and then I can get busy with my reason for being here." *My job. And my love story is with those toiles*. She giggled.

Chapter Six

It is said, "Live, learn, and let go. You may house their bodies but not their souls." This is not about letting go but housing a soul ...

The sun had just crest the ruins of the Roman Coliseum that was over two thousand years old and still standing. Enclosed by a daring stillness, he stretched before beginning his daily ritual. First the ancient Celtic prayer, *Breastplate*, taught to him as a child by his Irish mum. It was a protective prayer. Never forgetting a word even after all these years, he recited it daily at the crack of dawn.

This morning was special. He had dreamt about a dark-haired foreign boy. This boy held the key to the undoing of *their* demise. He had carried his curse for too long but soon it would be over. If only he could locate the dark-haired boy. Time was short, the alignment was coming. The vivid dream had spoken to him about Florence. Perhaps he could hitch a ride on a worker's truck?

As the sun overshadowed the top of the open-air coliseum, the light briefly hit his three golden symbols. He would need to cover them before he was spotted. Glancing around, he found what he needed. He rolled through the mud until he was coated.

On the outside, he was Celestial KittyCat — a black, scrappy, alley cat with a golden brand on his side. A brand of a sun, a star, and a moon all in alignment. On the inside, he was still Patrick, and his heart still yearned for CallaLyly. He scowled as he thought about the curse that was planted by a mystic from the Far East over two and a half centuries ago.

As he contemplated on how he would find her, a mouse ran along the brick wall. He hated eating them raw, but his body gave him no choice. As his claws tore into the flesh, he growled. Patrick ate the pieces with his paw carefully placing each bite gingerly into his mouth. Then he sat back and licked his fur clean.

Snuggling between the pallets of fabric, Patrick snored. The truck dodged in and out of traffic, and the cat slept soundly in the back of the truck. Dozing throughout the four hours, the trip to Florence seemed to take no time at all. Screeching brakes alerted Patrick to his stop. He waited and listened. When the driver slammed his door, Patrick jumped out, leaving only his muddy footprints behind.

"Bruno!" the driver yelled. "Where did this mud come from? You sleepin' on the job again?"

As the frightened young Bruno stood near the truck scratching his head, Patrick laughed before glancing around for another mud puddle.

"Clean this up before they subtract the damage from our bill!"

Patrick rolled through a small puddle before running for the nearest building. After navigating the city via rooftops, Patrick stared down at the River Arno and the Ponte Vecchio Bridge. The same bridge he had dreamt about.

"The boy should be around here somewhere," Patrick said.

Screams and shouts and loud clapping grabbed his attention. Catman and his troop of Amazing Cats were performing.

"Impressive," Patrick said to himself. "They could come in handy."

Patrick normally avoided real animals. Since he couldn't communicate with them, coming face-to-face with one usually ended up in a brawl. The Amazing Cats seemed different. They were well trained, which meant they were probably easier to manipulate. He stared at The Catman and his stringy assistant with the tattoo-laden arms. He watched as they loaded the crate and boards. He couldn't make out what was written on the side of the truck. Therefore, Patrick jumped to the next building to note the address. Perhaps he could put them to good use, if needed.

For now, it was time to look for the dark-haired foreign boy. The one from his dream. Maybe he was at one of the touristy restaurants along the River Arno. Patrick's tummy growled. The search would have to wait. It was time to hunt for lunch.

"That's it. It's over, Mario!" a young woman screamed out. "I don't ever want to see you again!"

Megan glanced at the next table and frowned. When the woman glared back, Megan turned her head.

The woman abruptly stood and her chair fell over. Tyler jumped to pick it up for her. He nodded as the woman screamed one last time at her date before flinging a small lock and keys onto the table.

After dropping a few euros, the young man stood and darted after the woman. "Marcella wait! You are wrong. I love no one but you."

"Geez." Megan shook her head and laughed. "Even in Florence, the love capital of the world, they fight."

Tyler chuckled.

"One second they fight and the next they make love," the waiter said. "That is true love — Italian style. Maybe you find for you, signorina, no?"

"No." Megan frowned. "I can't even find true love back home. Why would I find it here?"

"A woman as beautiful as you always has a chance at true love in Italy," the waiter replied.

Megan felt her face warm. "Strictly business this trip. No time for romance."

"Aunt Meg," Tyler whispered. "I think he likes you."

Megan shook her head. "Just working for a bigger tip." Megan giggled.

A flock of pigeons flew by the large window. Megan watched as they soared over the water before disappearing into the afternoon sun. The Italian waiter placed the lock and keys on their table. When Megan glanced up, he replied, "They leave behind. For you, signorina."

"What —?"

"I am a romantic," the waiter said, winking. "It is written in the stars for each of us. True love never finds by chance."

"Yuck!" Tyler said, shaking his head. "Girls won't even talk to me."

The waiter laughed.

"They'll be all over you someday," Megan replied. She glanced at the waiter and smiled. "Thank you."

Tyler picked up the lock. "This looks like one of the locks we saw chained on that gate."

"Why *do* people put locks on that bridge?" Megan asked the waiter.

"Custom," the waiter replied. "Lovers bring a lock and two keys. After professing their undying love, they clip the lock to the bridge and throw the keys into the river. Then, their love endures forever." He smiled. "It is the reason Ponte Vecchio Bridge is the most romantic bridge in all of Italy."

"Really?"

The waiter frowned. "The sad truth ..." the waiter glanced around before whispering, "... maintenance clips them off every month." He walked away.

Megan shrugged. "You take it. Maybe you'll have some use for it. I certainly won't."

Tyler tossed the lock in the air before catching it.

"Maybe you'll meet a girl here."

Placing the small lock and keys into his pocket, Tyler scowled.

Once finished with their lunch, Megan handed the waiter several euros. "Grazie."

"Prego," the waiter replied.

"Prego?" Tyler repeated. "Isn't that a spaghetti sauce?"

"Yes, it is." Megan laughed as she gathered her things. "Here it means, you're welcome."

As they left, Tyler glanced at the waiter and laughed. A scraggly black cat had darted inside and made a beeline for their table. The waiter tried to shoo the stray with a tablecloth.

"Get-ta outta here! Too many of you cats all over Florence."

Watching the waiter clear the table, Patrick sensed something special about the dark-haired boy. He felt an overwhelming urge to follow him. But a similar overwhelming urge to eat was just as strong. As he devoured the last few scraps that the boy had dropped, Patrick watched the boy and his companion leave. After the last bite, Patrick stole a peek to see where the boy had gone.

"Get-ta outta here!" the waiter yelled again, flinging a large white cloth at him.

Patrick darted out from under the table and aimed for the open doors. It was time to find the dark-haired foreign boy from his dreams.

Tyler grabbed his backpack and dropped it on the bed. Bouncing on the hard mattress, he chuckled. *Better than a camp bunk.* Glancing around his small room, the high ceiling felt a little overwhelming. He walked over to the glass doors and pulled them open. He stepped out and looked over the railing. He admired the flourishing garden courtyard. Then he shut the doors and aimed for his backpack.

Tyler cleared his throat. It felt scratchy. Maybe the Italian meat he had for lunch didn't agree with him. It tasted terrible anyway. Good thing no one saw him tossing the pieces under the table. Tyler wanted to study the document he had downloaded and printed yesterday before Kevin had interrupted him. He pulled out the paper and stared at the article, *What Actually Occurs When a Bomb Explodes.* He couldn't read it while sitting next to Aunt Meg on the plane. She would have asked too many questions. Questions he was not yet prepared to answer. Glancing through the pages, his heart raced. Tyler was in his own private world of reading and he was happy.

Still licking his paws, Patrick sat just inside the plush courtyard. *Prosciutto,* Patrick thought to himself, *the best I've ever eaten.*

After two and a half centuries of living as a cat, Patrick's sense of smell and taste could challenge the best of most dogs. Sniffing the ground, Patrick had followed the trail left behind by the dark-haired boy. He sat below the six balconies and enjoyed the rays from the warm afternoon sun. The foreign boy was close. He glanced at the large glass doors and frowned. *Which one?*

"I'll start with the opened one on the right."

Patrick glanced up. The railing was just a little higher than he could jump. He climbed into a tree and carefully walked along a lower branch. Loving the feel of his graceful agility, he aimed for the small veranda. Just as he landed, a large brown shoe soared from the bedroom just missing his head. Feeling the breeze from the leathery item, he jumped backwards and meowed as he landed on all fours into the soft grass. The shoe now rested at his side.

"Won't use that door!"

After living as a cat for the last two centuries, nine lives had nothing on him.

Chapter Seven

It is said, "A wise man gains more freedom from their enemies than a fool from their friends." This is not about making friends but making a fool ...

Megan arrived in Siena on time just as Vincenzo had promised.

"Florence and Siena fought for centuries," the driver said as he slowed to stop for a light. "Now, they are great cities. You need to walk Florence ... very historical."

Megan studied the ancient buildings that surrounded them.

"Siena," he said. "Just look at this beauty. You feel as if you have fallen back in time a thousand years ... no?"

"It is beautiful."

"People here do not like change," he said.

He drove slowly as they passed the circular-shaped main square, the Piazza del Campo, similar to an amphitheater that is surrounded by colorful flags.

"I am from here. My lifeblood is of Siena." He glanced at Megan in the rear-view mirror. "We have many festivals in the summer. Now, we prepare for the big race."

"And what race is that?"

"Horses!" He nodded as he turned a corner. "For centuries we have our races. People come from all over the world. Siena is a wonderful place to live."

"I heard a little about your town," Megan said. "You're driving me here cuz all the hotels were booked."

"All the villas are rented too." He laughed. "We very busy."

Megan sighed. Her heart raced as they maneuvered through the tight streets, past the ancient buildings, and distinct water fountains.

"How old are these buildings?"

"Old," he replied.

"What are they made from?"

"Stone," he said.

"You are blessed that no war destroyed them."

"Yes." He nodded. "We are very blessed."

As she tucked the tour information that Vincenzo had given her into her work bag, the car stopped. "We're here?"

"Yes, Signorina Brandt. We have arrived."

"Thank you."

"Call me when you are ready to return," he said. "You have my number?"

"Yes."

Megan glared out the window and stared at the building before her. The gray travertine-stone, shaded from the neighboring buildings, was adorned with quaint arched-windows and darkened stained glass. A large oak door stood in the shadows to greet visitors. A huge metal knocker that reminded Megan of something evil glared at her. She frowned and wondered if it was an omen of things to come. The scaffolding covering the front of the building resembled a spider's web.

"Where are their workers?" Megan asked.

The driver chuckled. "Maybe they eat, Signorina Brandt. This building will be ... how do you say ... renovated? Turned into a museum."

"Museum? With statues? Or what?"

"Oh, Signorina Brandt." He laughed. "No, no, a bank museum."

"Bank museum?"

"Centuries ago, this building belonged to a very rich Sienese family. As with most prosperous families, they fell into ruin. A Florencian family bought it and left it empty."

"How sad."

"Yes, very sad. Since my grandparents' days, maybe even their parents' days, this building has seen no love or attention."

The driver opened the door and Megan stepped onto the ancient brick street. She tugged on her bag. "Grazie," Megan said as she stepped onto the stone stairs.

"Ciao, Signorina Brandt. Be safe."

Megan waved as he drove off. She turned and studied the ancient arch that was covered in moss. The darkened walls gave the place an eerie feel. The air cooled as she climbed the aged and cracked stairs. The old door had stood strong against the winds of time, and when she reached out and touched the iron knocker, it felt bitter and unwelcoming.

She glanced around and shivered. Who would greet her? Hopefully, someone from the living and not someone from the other side. She reached up again and lifted the old lion's head before letting go. The metal banged against the ancient wood and the sound echoed past her and down through the ancient arch. Again, she shivered. Butterflies swarmed in her stomach, and she now wished that the driver was still by her side. She took a step back, and the gothic, oak door creaked open. A middle-aged man with graying hair and a trimmed goatee smiled. His light business attire instantly set her nerves at ease.

"Signorina Megan Brandt?"

"Yes." Megan replied. "Tighe & Randall?" She extended her hand. "Please, call me Megan."

He rubbed her hand and nodded. "Welcome, Megan, welcome. Please come in. It is chilly in the shade."

Megan stepped into the vast lobby.

"I am Alberto. We have been expecting you." Alberto spoke in perfect English with only a slight Italian accent. "You Americans always tend to be right on time. We Italians have a very bad habit of running late."

Megan slowly glanced around the huge room that was filled with tall scaffolding. "Thank you, Alberto. I am quite excited. I can't wait to see the rare toiles."

"I guarantee, you will not be disappointed."

The vast lobby made Megan hold her excitement in place. Colorful pastels of pink, peach, and green filled her view. A marble floor, depicting a scene of baby angels and cherubs in flight surrounded by heavenly stars, encased her.

"My God, look at this floor!"

"It is impressive, is it not?" Alberto said.

The marble staircase to the second floor raised forward as if heaven's clouds awaited her. The only thing pulling her from the beauty was the metal scaffolding. The cream-colored walls were water-marked and dark mold now followed along the ancient cracks. In several places, plaster had already fallen, revealing the ancient stonework beneath.

A man, dressed in jeans and a dark blue shirt, sat on a makeshift work bench. His folded arms and legs announced that he was waiting for someone. *Let me guess*, she thought to herself, *on break. Who works around here? No wonder everything takes so long.*

"The tools your company requested are inside the main room adjoining the collection," Alberto said.

Megan shook her head. "What?"

"I am sorry." Alberto frowned. "Your tools?"

"Oh, yes." Megan giggled. "Yes, please. I'm ready to begin."

Jumping up from the bench, the man walked forward and extended his hand. "Signorina Brandt ... nice to meet you. My name is Roberto Cavelli. Please, call me Robert. I understand we'll be sharing the toiles." Robert's English was as fluent and clear as hers.

Refusing his jester of friendship, Megan glared at the man. Her mind flew in all directions. Maybe, Alberto's employer hired him to help her, albeit no one said anything? *Did he just say sharing?* "Did Tighe & Randall hire you to help me remove the toiles?" Megan asked.

Alberto shook his head. "Signorina Brandt, your company and Mr. Cavelli's company have equal rights to the rare find of toiles."

"Excuse me?" Megan's voice echoed through the cavernous lobby. "What are you saying?"

"Signorina Brandt —" Robert started.

"No! Can't possibly ... we ... *my* company purchased the sole rights to the toiles." Megan glanced back and forth and wondered what type of con game they were playing.

Robert took several steps back.

Megan took in a deep breath. "Alberto and Mr. Cavelli —"

"Please, call me Robert," Robert said, smiling.

"Fine, sorry, Robert." She glared at the man. "We ... Tighe & Randall are *clearly* under the impression that we had the sole rights to the paper."

Alberto pulled a document from his jacket. "According to the papers I have, you are sharing the find." He handed Megan the papers.

She read through the words and her world fell apart. Two company names were written in bold across the top of the page — TIGHE & RANDALL and CAVELLI TEXTILES & WALLCOVERING — and they were signed by both parties.

"This is a mistake!" Megan held back her tears. "One moment. I need to make a call."

"Si, of course, Signorina Brandt." Alberto bowed and stepped away gently. "Please, take all the time you need." He moved over to speak to Robert.

Glancing at the time on her phone, Megan calculated the numbers. Six hours difference. It was a little after eight in the morning in Boston. Mr. Tighe should be in by now. As the phone rang, she walked toward the stairs.

"Ronald Tighe —"

"Mr. Tighe." Megan sighed as her stomach churned. "We have a problem. A big problem."

"A problem?"

"We're sharing the papers. Another company is here." Megan tried to keep her voice low.

"Not that I am aware. Who is there?"

"A man named Alberto and a man named Mr. Cavelli?"

"The names are not familiar. Megan, we are not there. You are. I need you to be strong for us. Can you do that?"

Megan's hands shook. Trying to hold the phone was not easy. "Yes, I'm listening."

"We trust your judgement and expertise. Something like this would take a lifetime in an Italian court to fight. You understand?"

"Yes."

"I need you to be professional and cooperative. See what you can get for us. I'll contact our negotiators and see if I can find out what's going on. Can you do that, Megan?"

Megan's mind fell blank. She never had to fight for anything before. The last two days ran through her mind. First, she took her nephew to camp and there was no camp. Then she arrived in Italy and discovered that her work was in another town. Now, she was told that her work was not just hers, and her company was expecting her to take charge. Feeling pangs of guilt, Megan had the urge to call the hotel. Time to check in on Ty. Maybe she could take a few moments to call.

"Megan … you still there?" Mr. Tighe's tone pulled her from her thoughts.

"I'm no lawyer, Mr. Tighe," Megan whispered.

Mr. Tighe chuckled. "Do your best. We're counting on you. We'll call when we have more information."

"More information," Megan repeated, shaking her head. "Yes, sir."

Megan clicked off her phone and stared at it. After a few seconds to regain her composure, Megan approached Alberto and Robert. She stood silently as their heated debate about horse races came to an end.

"Okay," Megan said. "I just spoke to the owners and they have no knowledge of this. Therefore, they have a few calls to make. But they want me to move forward." Frowning at Robert, she continued. "I suggest a coin toss." Megan smiled and winked at Alberto. "Winner receives first crack at choosing." Megan held her breath.

"Fine by me," Robert replied and chuckled. He pulled out a two-dollar euro and held it in his hand.

Megan glanced at the coin and smiled. "I choose the Dante side. I might as well play the female card and choose first."

Again, Robert chuckled. "You toss?"

Megan gently picked up the coin. She stared at it for a moment before kissing it. Then, she tossed it in the air. Not wanting a debate, she allowed the coin to fall to the floor. It rolled and they followed it as it aimed for the stairs. It landed on the hand of one of the baby angels. Megan grinned as she stared at the wonderful face of Dante. Alberto laughed.

Robert sighed. "Looks like you win."

"Hmm." Megan shrugged.

"May I call you Megan?" Robert asked. "We *will* be working together … friends perhaps?"

"I don't see why not." Megan turned and frowned. "Let the games begin," she whispered.

"Excuse me?" Robert said as he reached down to retrieve his coin.

"Nothing," Megan replied.

Chapter Eight

It is said, "You will never be wrong by doing what is right." This is not about doing what is right but being wrong ...

Alberto and Megan walked into the large and ornate side room. She glanced out the gothic windows that overlooked the garden. The garden no longer showed life or color. Instead, dead shrubs and vibrant weeds filled the grounds. The room was vacant except for Megan's tools that sat near a corner — cardboard tubes, a ladder, and a folding bench. Off to one side, Megan noticed some older tools and a ladder.

Must be Robert's.

Megan turned and studied the disaster that greeted her. A wall, bare to the wooden lath, reminded her of the old buildings in Boston. Plaster that once covered the walls was now splattered across the floor. She coughed, not from the dust, but more from the memory. It was obvious that the room had been sealed off for a very long time. And beyond that, a smaller and more colorful room that was hidden by a thick film of sliced plastic. No door, just a rectangle hole that probably used to house a door.

She took several bold steps toward the smaller room, or maybe, a closet. "I'm ready to see and hear the story," Megan said.

"Watch your step please," Alberto replied, blocking her way to the closet. "This room was shrouded in darkness for over two and a half centuries."

Megan pushed a small pile of plaster with her foot. "Don't want to bring up the dust, do we?" She sighed.

Robert snickered.

Alberto stepped up to the entry. Heavy plastic hid most of the room from Megan and Robert. Megan glanced at Robert who appeared to be drooling. Megan shook her head.

"Megan and Roberto ... behold!" Alberto pulled back the heavy plastic as if announcing a Broadway play. "The toiles are ready to speak to you."

And I'm ready to answer! Megan glared at Robert who only grinned.

"There was a false wall here," Alberto said still blocking their way. "We discovered it during renovations. A leak in the roof." Alberto pointed to the damaged ceiling. "The door is missing. No windows in this room." He stared silently up at the ceiling as though incased inside a private thought. "The secret room had sheltered the toiles from aging. Hid them from the light."

"Who would do such a thing?" Megan asked. "Why lock them up in a room like that?"

"We believe that was the owners after the Montevellis," Alberto replied. When Megan blinked, he added, "Centuries ago."

Trying to peek around Alberto, Megan gazed past the door and into the color. "I hope we have appropriate lighting," she said. "We definitely want to avoid disintegration."

"Of course," Alberto replied. "LED." Alberto pulled out a cord from within the doorframe.

Glancing at Robert, Megan frowned. She raised her hand and sighed. "I have first dibs!" She paused. "Alone."

Robert laughed. "I just realized how much I miss your American slang."

Megan furrowed her brows.

"I'll just check on my tools," Robert said.

"I'll wait for you out here," Alberto added, grinning. "Should you have any questions, I'm right here."

Megan nodded and her heart pounded. She stepped through the frame and gently pushed aside the heavy plastic. The fourteen-by-fourteen square foot room, with an equally high ceiling, overwhelmed her. Feeling slightly light-headed, she allowed the plastic to close. She moved slowly. The panels were about four feet in width. One was of a Tuscany vignette, another a house, another a girl, and another of several buildings. All different in color, size, and shape. It was amazing.

"What in the world?" Megan's eyes darted from paper to paper. For a moment she felt as if she was in a hardware store looking at a display. But no. She was in a single room in a very large house. Megan expected many rooms with many different toiles. Not one room with several different panels. And the room had been sealed and hidden. Why? What for?

"Okay, Megan. Get a grip." Megan took several large deep breaths. "This is not normal. But you're here to do a job, not psychoanalyze the dead."

Megan shook her head, which didn't help to soothe her nerves. With her hands shaking, she pulled her plastic gloves from her pocket. She stepped up to the first panel. Taking a small tape recorder from her bag, she spoke slowly. "The room is covered with panels ... looks like about six basic designs. The first is an indigo medieval house ...

wonderful shade of blue. No words to describe it. The backdrop is of a bright fiery red. A young girl is sitting on a bed. How odd."

Gazing over at the next two panels, she couldn't believe what she was seeing. The room was covered. All with different panels. She stepped up to a black and white toile with a cream background.

"A scene from the City of Siena ... the Campo, Mangia Tower, and the Duomo or a cathedral." Again, she breathed in deeply. "Simple, but effective." Next, she studied another vignette. "Tuscany countryside with farmhouses, dirt roads, river bends, olive trees, forests, farm animals, swings, lanterns, and ... the same young girl with the long, curly locks sitting on a swing." She paused. "No people were in the black and white one, how odd." She reached out and froze. Oh, how she wanted to touch the green and yellow one, touch it all. "This is the brightest blue-green I've ever seen. A sun-yellow background. Wait ... it can't be! This paper looks, three-dimensional? What type of cloth is this?" Megan raised her hand. She reached out and touched the amazing scene. When her hand disappeared, Megan jumped back and gasped. "What is this?"

Feeling dizzy, Megan stepped over to the heavy plastic. She pulled it aside and walked out. Taking in a deeper breath, she watched as Robert arranged his tools. Alberto was on his phone talking in Italian. Taking in another deep breath, she felt a little better. She stepped back into the room. Not sure on how to proceed, she walked up to the next paper.

"Oriental," she said into her recorder. "Faraway lands."

Megan paused as she glanced back at the green and yellow paper. She wanted to touch it again. She felt drawn to it. Shaking her head, she moved on.

"A royal court that almost resembles a deck of cards."

Stepping up to the last toile, she paused. The paper had once covered the entryway. It was now leaning over and falling away from the opening. She reached out and pulled it up.

"A seafaring motif," she said. "Blue-green with opal coloring. The bottom corner piece is missing."

She glanced back at the panels. Only two had a person and both were of a young girl. Unusual ... toiles usually had many people. Maybe it was too expensive back then or too complicated. She stepped back. That green and yellow paper still haunted her. It was almost as if it was talking to her. But that could not be. Paper didn't speak or did it?

Megan nodded. "It's okay," she said to the girl in the paper. "You're coming with me."

Megan laughed. Now, she knew she was losing it. Maybe the flight tired her more than she realized. Stepping through the heavy plastic, she stood straight and said, "Robert ... I'm taking the first three, two have a young girl in them."

From her professional work tools, she grabbed a small jeweler's eye loupe and followed Robert as he stepped inside.

Alberto, still on his call, waved at her.

"Interesting." Robert stared at the vignettes.

"Very," Megan said, staying close to the man.

He chuckled. "I can see why you chose the ones you did."

Megan placed the eye loupe onto the green-yellow paper. Staring into the small circle, she hovered above the young girl. Behind the girl was a Tuscany farmhouse.

"See anything?" Robert asked.

"Hoping to decipher the texture detailing and composition of the cloth." Megan mumbled as she spoke. She moved the loupe ever so meticulously. "This is so detailed!"

A blue green eyeball suddenly stared back at her and blinked.

Megan gasped.

"You said something?" Robert asked.

Megan glanced back through the loupe and blinked several times. Again, someone or something stared back.

"Holy crap," Megan whispered, loudly. She took several bold steps backward.

"Everything okay?" he asked.

"I'm fine. Thanks."

As Robert moved to the other side of the room, Megan stared at the young girl. She was sitting on a swing. Was the swing moving? No, it was not or was it? Megan's heart raced. An illusion, that was what it was. But an excellent illusion. How could something so small as an eye be so detailed? It looked real.

"Perfecto!" Robert said. "Thank you, Megan. The three that are mine are exactly the ones I would have chosen. We will get along just fine. I will begin by the door."

Megan nodded. He was annoying her. He was trying to get her to believe he had the better of the lots. *Did it really matter?* She just needed to remove her paper and leave. She stepped out of the room and sighed. "You are right, Alberto, they do not disappoint."

"Ah, good, good, did I not tell you?" He handed Megan his card. "When you are finished for the day, I will need to lock up. You work tomorrow, no?"

"Yes, I will be here. It will take a few days to remove them all."

"Then until tomorrow, ciao."

"Ciao, Alberto." After reading over the card, Megan placed it into her work bag next to the driver's card.

Megan had about four hours left to work. Using a special solution, a steamer, and a spatula, she meticulously lifted and trimmed the toile paper. The process was slow and tedious. But to her surprise, the paper was somewhat accommodating. It came off in large strips, which she rolled and placed into special tubes.

Purposely staying clear of Robert who worked on the other side of the room, Megan noticed that he wasn't using gloves or a mask. He was working with an old steamer that hummed as if protesting at being disturbed. At least with all the noise he was making, there was no need for small talk.

She was so emersed in her work, Megan didn't notice when Robert left the room. Feeling sweat run down her back, Megan too stepped out of the heat and steam. The cooler air felt refreshing. She placed her tubes next to her work tools. Strips of toiles lay rolled up next to a large crate where Robert was sitting.

Careless fool.

"Megan," Robert said. "Just in time. Please join me."

Pulling items from a backpack, Robert handed her several waxed papers that were filled with bread and cheese. He pointed to his plastic containers that he had left opened on the crate.

"Please help yourself to some antipasto." Robert placed salami and provolone on his crusty bread. Taking a bite, he hummed. Then he pulled out a bottle of red wine.

Megan removed her work gloves. The cool air again felt wonderful against her sweaty skin. She eyed the rolled toiles that were taped shut.

Shaking her head, she sighed. "Antipasto? Wine? Next to the toiles? A little careless?"

Robert glanced at the paper. "They are fine."

Frowning, her stomach rumbled. "Maybe I'll have a little. No wine, thank you. Do you have water?"

"Wine is our water."

"Not while I'm working."

Robert pulled a water bottle from his backpack.

"Thanks. Some spread you have here. I'll remember to bring a sandwich or something tomorrow."

Pointing to the food, he smiled. "Eggplant ... artichokes ... mushrooms."

Placing a little on her plate, Megan ate quickly as she needed to get back to the toiles.

"I work better without gloves," Robert said. "I'm old fashioned perhaps compared to you Americans."

The toiles laying on the floor seemed to bother her. "I have extra tubes if you'd like to use them?"

"No need. These are fine."

Tossing her plate and plastic utensil in a trash bucket, Megan walked away frowning.

They're fine! First and last time I offer you anything.

Agreeing to call it quits in an hour, Robert phoned Alberto while Megan called her driver to schedule a pickup. She returned to the toiles and placed her mask on her face. Then she took it back off. Stepping up to the green and yellow paper, she blinked several times.

"What in the world?" Megan stepped back and then up to the paper again. "Where did she go? I know she was here a minute ago." Megan glanced around the room. Then she smacked herself in the head. "I'm losing it." She shook her head and glanced back at the yellow and green paper. Megan held back a scream. The girl was now standing by a sheep and wore a pure-blue dress, exposing a purple sash. "No!" Megan whispered. "You were sitting on that swing and wearing a green dress!"

"All good?" Robert asked, stepping into the room.

"All good," Megan replied definitely feeling the jetlag.

It was time to return to the hotel, check on Tyler, and enjoy some much-needed sleep. After carefully placing a sixth tube near her boxes, she wiped her forehead.

"Maybe back then the color blocker was used as an illusion," she said to no one. "That would explain it."

Chapter Nine

It is said, "When you stop dealing in reality you achieve greatness." This is not about achieving greatness but dealing in fiction ...

Megan dashed into the hotel lobby and the chiming of the antique grandfather clock grabbed her attention. She had to jump over another guest's suitcase before stopping to catch her breath. Nine o'clock on the dot. Exhausted and needing a shower, she aimed for the front desk. Wanting to keep her nephew busy, Megan picked out the busiest tours. Shifting her workbags to her other shoulder, she passed several guests conversing in Italian. Megan stepped up to the counter and nodded to Vincenzo.

"Still on duty?" Megan asked.

"Angelina is ill," Vincenzo replied. "As you American's say, I am having double duty."

Megan giggled. "You mean pulling a double shift."

"Ah, yes," Vincenzo laughed. "Pulling double shift. I guess I lose a little in the translation."

Handing Vincenzo a tour brochure, Megan dropped her workbag by her feet. The canvas sack that protected her toile tubes she kept hanging on her shoulder. "This should work for Ty. Can I book it for tomorrow?"

"Ah …" Vincenzo sighed. "Popular one. Let me check." He picked up the phone.

Megan turned and watched as a young mother struggled with a sleeping toddler. The mother was conversing with her friends when the sleepy little girl opened her eyes. Megan smiled. Hearing Vincenzo, she turned back to the counter.

"Mama!" the little girl screamed. "Mama! Mano! Mano!" The child squealed from her mother's shoulder.

Megan turned around and smiled at the frowning woman.

The little girl struggled in her mother's arms. "Dita, mama! Dita!"

Megan glanced at her hands. "My hands are very dirty. I'm sorry."

"No mama, sacca … dita!"

"She's overtired," the mother said, patting the young child on the back.

Megan glanced down at her feet. *Maybe I have something on me?* "Oh, I see." Megan knelt and picked up the top to one of the tubes. Holding it, she showed the mother and child. "Is this what you're trying to tell me?"

The little girl shook her head and again pointed to Megan's bag.

"Yes," Megan said, pulling her bag forward and replacing the top. "See, it fell off."

The little girl shook her head before nestling into her mother's neck.

"Scusami," the mother said.

"No problem," Megan replied. "We're all tired."

"Your nephew is all set," Vincenzo said.

Megan turned and smiled at Vincenzo.

"The tour was fully booked but the owner is a friend of mine."

"Grazie," Megan said, taking the ticket from Vincenzo. "May I place an order for tomorrow? Breakfast and lunch for Ty, and a box lunch for myself? I'll need mine before I leave in the morning."

"Of course," Vincenzo said. "My pleasure."

Megan grabbed her bag and stepped away from the counter.

"Mano! Mano!" the young child yelled still pointing at Megan.

"Scusami," the mother said again. "I don't know why she is so upset."

"Maybe she just had a bad dream." Megan's body ached. She was ready for a hot shower and a soft bed. And ready for the day to be over.

The birds in the courtyard were distracting Patrick, and he hated to be distracted. It was important to remain focused. He had to find that dark-haired boy, and he knew that he was just behind one of those glass doors. He had seen him, he was sure. He tried the first door and a shoe was thrown at him. When he landed on the second balcony, he glanced through the glass. An old woman was sleeping. Only four glass doors remaining, and his life depended on finding that boy.

The alignment of the sun, Venus, and the moon would happen soon, and that boy held the secret. His dream told him such.

Focus, Patrick. Focus!

His cat instincts were stronger and harder to ignore. He kept finding himself chasing after stupid birds or rats or mice. Unfortunately, with his age creeping up, the birds were just too fast. A mouse or rat, now they were easier prey. Patrick had lived for two-hundred and seventy years, and only twenty of those had he lived as a human.

As Patrick watched the trees sway in the wind, a double glass door opened, and bits of prosciutto with meatballs landed near his feet. Patrick watched as the door slowly closed.

Aiming for the delicacy, Patrick nodded. The leftovers smelled of the boy. Savoring the tiny morsels, Patrick waited. The opportunity to capture the boy would soon present itself.

Megan dropped her bag at the foot of Tyler's bed. Sitting against the headboard, Tyler looked flushed.

"Spaghetti and meatballs?" Megan picked up the dish.

Tyler nodded. "Good day?"

"Yes." Megan sat the dirty dishes outside the door.

"Aunt Meg, I think there's something in the meatballs making my throat hurt."

"Oh?" Megan sat next to Tyler and felt his forehead.

"Lunch made my throat hurt too."

Megan tried to fluff the pillows but Tyler kept shifting back and forth.

"My back doesn't hurt," Tyler said, pushing Megan's arm away. "Just my throat."

"That meat was an Italian ham," Megan said. "You don't have food allergies do you?"

Tyler shrugged. "I still think that meat is giving me a sore throat."

"You may be coming down with something. Hope it's not pig flu. They might throw us out of the country." She placed her hand on his forehead again.

"They'll throw us out?"

Megan laughed. "No, I'm joking. You do feel a bit warm."

Tyler tried to smile. "It hurts to swallow."

What else can go wrong? Megan stood and shook her head. "I'll call downstairs for a doctor."

Tyler watched as she spoke into the phone.

"Thank you, Vincenzo." Megan hung up and looked at Tyler. "They're sending up a doctor." Megan closed Tyler's book and placed it on the dresser. "Reading? I booked a tour for you tomorrow. Surprise!"

"Guess I won't be going, huh, Aunt Meg?"

"Not with a fever, Ty."

"I have plenty to read."

"I'm sure you do. I was hoping to introduce you to some Florencia culture."

Tyler shook his head.

Megan opened one of the outside glass doors. "The doctor should be here shortly. I think you could use some fresh air."

Tyler watched as Megan fidgeted with the French doors. He pulled out the folded papers he had hidden behind his pillow. She had come too close to finding them. He shuffled to the side of his bed and dropped them next to the nightstand. If she found the bomb information he had downloaded at home, he would be in big trouble.

"I can only get this one door to stay open." Megan sighed.

Trying not to look as guilty as he felt, Tyler smiled. "How was Siena?"

The cylinder top made only a slight pop before falling to the floor. A small, greenish-tinged hand reached out of the cardboard tube and felt through the air.

Megan grabbed the bag and moved it closer to the glass doors. "Don't need the doctor tripping over these now, do we?"

Again, a thin greenish hand reached out, only this time, it felt around the top of the tube. The other green arm soon followed and reached down to touch the wooden floor. Slowly, the roll of paper inched its way out of the tube.

"Vincenzo said the doctor would be here soon." A light rap on the door and Megan stood.

The paper rolled up to the glass door before coming to rest on the thick rug.

"That didn't take long," Megan said, opening the door. "Hello?"

"This is Doctore DaLucci," Vincenzo said. "And this is Megan Brandt and Tyler."

"Thank you for coming, Doctor …"

The green arms and leg, still attached to the roll, scurried out past the glass door.

Patrick sat and watched as the toile paper struggled to move. He had already listened to the conversations with the doctor. The boy was in there, and just a few feet away. Patrick watched as the hands and one foot scaled the iron encasement. After reaching the railing, the roll weaved back and forth.

"Oh, no!" Patrick screeched. "We need the boy! Won't work otherwise." If a human were to see that roll ... now that would indeed cause trouble. Patrick screeched out, "Mrowww, Mrowww ..."

The toile, still precariously balanced on the railing, froze.

Again, Patrick yelled out. "No ... mrowww ... go inside ... mrowww ... get the boy!"

The roll slowly moved back down the railing and scurried into the room. The curtained door closed and Patrick listened to the click of the lock.

"Ah," Vincenzo said, glancing out the window. "These cats are all over Florence!"

The doctore checked Tyler's ears, chest, and throat before taking a swab. "We have a fever," she said. "I suspect strep. Plenty of rest and fluids. I will prescribe antibiotics. Give him acetaminophen for the fever." She handed Megan a small package. "Anesthetic gum to help with the soreness. After a couple days' rest, he'll be just fine." She placed her stethoscope in the medical bag and pulled out the medication.

"Just when he's better, it will be time for you to go home," Vincenzo said.

"Just my luck," Megan replied, walking them to the door. "Thank you, Doctor and Vincenzo."

Turning to Megan, Doctore DaLucci said, "This antibiotic is strong. Allow him to sleep. He may experience vivid dreams. If that happens, just keep an eye on him. Rest is what he needs."

"I'll have his meals delivered to the room," Vincenzo said. "If he's sleeping, we will leave it on his nightstand. I will cancel tomorrow's tour."

"Grazie," Megan said. "I don't know what I'd do without you, Vincenzo. You've been so wonderful with everything."

"My pleasure," he said with a smile.

After she closed the door, Tyler laughed. "I think he likes you Aunt Meg. Remember what that waiter said? *'It's already written in the stars, signorina.'* Maybe Vincenzo's your star."

"Seriously, Ty?" Megan giggled. "He's just doing his job. I'll owe him a fat tip when we leave. Now, let's go over your meds." Megan grabbed some paper and a pen.

Patrick wanted to help CallaLyly but there was nothing he could do. Not now. A heavy-set man, several doors down, peered over his railing. *That's the old fool that threw the shoe at me!* Keeping an eye on the toile and trying to hide from the man, Patrick jumped onto a leafy branch. The man turned and spoke to someone inside.

"Did you just hear that caterwauling, Lovey?" The man spoke with a British accent. "We're being invaded by wild cats. I saw one earlier on our railing. Took care of him with my shoe."

"Come back to bed," the woman replied. "We have a full day tomorrow."

"Can't see my shoe." The man disappeared behind the door.

Hearing the glass door shut, Patrick leaped onto the grass. He needed help and knew where to go. As he took a few steps, the breeze from the other brown shoe kissed the top of his head.

"Time to get out of here!" Patrick hissed.

The boy would have to wait.

"Not again!" Megan reached down and picked up the circular tab that was laying on the floor. "What is it with these popping tubes?" Megan hammered the lid back onto the cardboard. "That won't fall off now!" Giving Tyler a kiss on his forehead, Megan avoided his rimless glasses.

"Night, Aunt Meg."

"Good night, Ty. I'll check on you in a few. I need a shower."

After grabbing her toiles and workbag, Megan headed to her room. It was time for a bath. Tomorrow was another day, another day with the toiles.

Tyler reached over and picked up his bomb papers. He read and chewed on the cherry flavored anesthetic gum. As he fought off sleep, a noise grabbed his attention. Sitting up, he glanced around. Everything looked normal. He stood and the room spun. He grabbed for the bedpost. *These pills are making me dizzy.* He walked into the bathroom and held onto the door. Reaching down, he picked up the basket and spit out his gum. After relieving himself, he struggled back to bed. Snuggling under the blankets with a flashlight, Tyler fell back into his happy place reading his secret papers about bombs. His urge to sleep was strong and he closed his eyes. Within moments, Tyler was asleep.

The toile inched its way out from under the curtain. It moved toward the bathroom and the waste basket. The little green arm reached out and pulled on the trash bin. As it stole the chewed gum, a soft giggle echoed through the room.

The rolled toile slowly climbed up the bathroom wall. Tearing the chewed gum into pieces, the little green arms and hands secured the toile to the wall. Soon, the two-foot by five-foot, green and yellow, Tuscany toile was displayed for view. Only a small tear was missing from one of the corners. Now, the toile just had to wait for the boy to wake and step a little closer.

Chapter Ten

It is said, "That no matter what happens, or how bad it seems, life goes on and will be better tomorrow." This is not about what is getting better but what is happening tomorrow ...

Patrick arrived within the hour at the residence of The Catman. City rooftops were a blessing to him now for he was less likely to be spotted from up high. Finding a fire escape, Patrick slowly made his way down to the streets. He waited for a car to pass before darting across and into some bushes. Patrick watched as two men struggled with The Catman who was lying on a stretcher. A bony dark-haired man stood on the steps and waited.

"Momento, per favore," The Catman said to the two men dressed in white. He motioned for the bony man to come forward. He grabbed the man's tattooed arm and said, "Promise me, Tino ... take excellente care of my babies. My precious children."

Pulling his arm away, the bony man scowled. "Si, Uncle Fabrizio. I promise." The man glanced away.

Patrick's excitement grew. *Easier for me with Fabrizio gone.*

Patrick watched Tino through the window.

Wearing thick gloves, Tino pushed a large crate into the room. Tino laughed. After grabbing a cat that was sitting on the couch, Tino laughed again. "Now, to take care of you stupid rats one-by-one!"

The cat hissed. Tino threw the cat into the crate and slammed the side shut. Tino knelt and peeked under the couch.

"So much for the promise you made to your uncle," Patrick said. His cat ears turned back and burned with each of the trapped cats' bellows.

Tino disappeared into another room. Patrick looked for a way to enter but the door was locked. He sat on the windowsill and watched. Tino returned carrying a little black and white cat that was not much bigger than a kitten. He also held a water gun. Tino tossed the little cat into the crate.

"Get in there, D'oreo. You rat!" Tino tossed in another one and sighed. "Let's see. Allie, Georgie, Cherie, Gigi … Curry, Minnie, Mushmellow, Harry, Asti … Trixie, Fabio. One more. Belle! Where are you?" Tino searched the room. "Come out, Belle. If you know what's good for you!"

Tino held the water gun as if he held all the power. Crouching, he smiled and sprayed under the couch. After a few moments, a drenched orange and white tabby scurried out.

"Gotcha!"

After grabbing the cat, Tino tossed the last one into the crate. He shoved the lock shut and threw the key onto the table. Tino laughed. He dropped the gun and walked out the front door.

Patrick needed to find a way in. He needed their help and they couldn't help from inside a locked crate. In about twenty-four hours, the celestial alignment would begin, which was his only opportunity to become human and to release Lyly.

He tried a window and it was locked. Jumping to the next, he sighed. A piece of cardboard that was taped to a side window gave way when he pushed it. Patrick slipped through and jumped down. He was now inside a bedroom.

"Meow." The cats were crying.

Patrick slipped into the living room and jumped onto the table. Picking up the key with his mouth, Patrick jumped to the floor. Thankfully, the lock was near the bottom of the crate. Carefully, he maneuvered the key into the small hole. He stopped and looked over at the door.

This was a lot easier when I had fingers!

Using only his paws and teeth, the key slowly turned and the lock popped open.

The wet, orange and white cat stepped out. Her name was Belle. She was followed by the grey tabby that Tino had called Harry. He couldn't remember the other names. The last to step out was the tiniest. A black and white kitten. D'oreo? Patrick shook his head.

The cats purred and stared at Patrick.

"I need your help," Patrick's cat language was not the greatest. "It is time. I am the Celestial Kitty and I need the dark-haired boy. He is at the Grande Hotel behind a glass door."

The cats continued to stare at him.

"I can help you … *oh, what's the word* … I can get you out of here."

"Yes, help us," Belle said. "We will help the Celestial Kitty if you help us. Fabrizio tells us to honor the Celestial Kitty."

"Follow me. I will take care of you if you will help me."

"What's in it for us?" Harry asked, stepping forward. He hissed and showed his sharp fangs.

Patrick stepped back. He looked at the angry cat and tried to smile. "I will get you away from that creep."

"We have to leave!" Belle said to Harry. "We don't know if Dad will ever return. You saw how he fell. What if he died?"

"What do you want us to do?" Harry asked.

"No time for talk," Patrick said. "Just follow me to the Grande Hotel."

Patrick watched as the cats formed a pyramid next to the door. Belle climbed to the top and grabbed the knob with her paws. She turned it and the door opened.

"I'm calling you *good paws* from now on," Patrick said.

Harry pulled the door open and they were free.

"If you can do that, why stay?" Patrick asked.

"Our dad," Belle replied.

"Yes, we honor him," Harry added as the cats ran out the door.

Patrick took a step to follow the others when his world fell dark.

"Who are you?" Tino laughed and wrapped Patrick inside a tarp. "How dare you release my uncle's rats? Uncle Fab will not be happy about this. I promised I'd take care of them."

Tino threw Patrick into the crate and slammed the door shut. "You're not getting out anytime soon, my friend." Tino grabbed the water gun and hit Patrick on the side. Patrick's muddy fur wilted, and his bright brands slowly appeared. Tino's smirk turned into a huge grin. "My, my, what do we have here?"

With D'oreo in the lead, the thirteen cats arrived at the garden courtyard of the Grande Hotel. Sitting silently on a stone wall, they waited for the scrappy black cat to arrive. As they waited, their tails shifted in unison just like a clock.

"Blimey, they're reproducing like rabbits out there!" A voice yelled from one of the rooms.

"Trevor, are you crazy? Where are you going with all my shoes?"

"Lovey, the super moon woke me, and I tell you … there are cats all over the place. I just want to shoo them away."

"Not with *my* shoes!"

"The resort is infested with cats!"

As the couple argued, D'oreo jumped off the wall. The others followed. They crouched and hid inside the bushes.

"And pray tell, what cats are you talking about, dear?" The woman stood on the small balcony and frowned.

"The dozen or so on that wall. Don't you see —" The man glanced around the yard. "They were just there. A blitz of them, I tell you."

"Put my shoes back and go to bed, Trevor. We have a busy day tomorrow." The woman walked away.

The man peered over the railing. "Where did they go?"

Hiding near the boy's window, the cats nestled together.

"Where is that black cat?" D'oreo asked.

"He was a big talker," Harry said.

"I'll find him," D'oreo replied.

Tino blinked several times. Staring into the crate, the golden sun, star, and moon glowed brightly against the black fur. Laughing, he tossed the water gun aside.

"Looks like that tale about you is true after all. Tonight, you turn into a man. When you do, I will release you." Tino winked at Patrick. "After you grant my wish of course."

Tino stepped back and laughed.

"What do I want most in this world? Let me think." Tino tapped his chin. "Ahaaa … I want far away from my uncle and his stupid rats. But where?"

Tino knelt and glared at Celestial KittyCat through the slats. The cat huddled in a corner and growled.

"Fine, I'll sleep on it and tell you in the morning. You're not going anywhere. It was I, Tino, who caught the most famous of all cats in Italy."

Tino puffed out his chest. Picking up the key, he stuffed it into his back pocket.

"In the morning, I'll find you all crumpled up as a man."

Tino laughed as he danced his way into his bedroom.

D'oreo peeked through the window. Celestial KittyCat was licking his fur inside the locked crate.

"Mew," D'oreo said.

Patrick stood. He meowed out long and hard and pointed in the direction of Tino's bedroom.

D'oreo nodded. He ran to the broken pane and entered. Avoiding Tino who was sprawled out on his stomach, D'oreo inched his way to the bed.

"Now, where is that key?"

D'oreo looked on the nightstand. No key. He searched the floor. No key. Jumping onto the bed, he checked Tino's hands. No key. Then he saw something glimmering inside Tino's back pocket. Slowly and quietly, D'oreo pulled out the key.

Tino snored and rolled over.

D'oreo startled and dropped the key between the bed and the wall. "Darn," D'oreo said, creeping across the covers.

Tino snored, and this time, he rolled over onto D'oreo.

D'oreo froze. When Tino snored again, D'oreo sighed with relief. Slowly, he squeezed out from under Tino's leg and fished for the shiny metal. Using his paws and fangs, he grabbed the key. Pushing on the partly opened door, he stepped into the other room.

Patrick jumped up.

"I'm here to rescue you," D'oreo said.

"That's the word. Rescue. I was going to rescue you," Patrick replied.

"You didn't do a very good job." D'oreo laughed.

Patrick nodded and shook his head.

D'oreo fumbled with the key as Patrick hollered out instructions.

Just as the lock clicked, two hands swooped down and grabbed D'oreo.

"You didn't leave. Why not?" Tino picked up the lock and laughed as he threw the cat into the crate.

D'oreo hissed.

Tino frowned. "Key must have fallen out of my pocket."

D'oreo sighed with a soft, "Mew," and watched as the bedroom door slammed shut.

Chapter Eleven

It is said, "May you receive what you wish." This is not about wishing but desperation ...

After a full night of deep sleep, Megan was prepared to tackle the new day. *Call him Robert? Don't think so. That man is going to be trouble!* Megan smirked as she accepted the food tray from a hotel staff. The young man smiled at her and she nodded.

"Thanks," Megan said.

Megan stepped into Tyler's room and maneuvered around his opened books. She placed the food on his nightstand. Tyler was sleeping soundly. Megan reached over and gingerly placed the back of her hand against his forehead. Still hot.

"Great," she whispered.

"Oh, hi, Aunt Meg."

"Sorry, Ty. You're still running a fever. You need to take your meds before I leave. I need you feeling better."

Tyler nodded.

"How are you feeling? Did you get any sleep? I left pancakes on your nightstand. Hungry?"

Tyler's eyes widened with all the questions. Running his hand through his disheveled hair, he swallowed. "My throat hurts ... a lot." He reached for his glasses from the nightstand.

"Let's get those meds in you and a couple bites of food. I wish I could stay but —"

"Don't worry ..." Tyler yawned, "... I'll feel better soon. I promise." He crossed his heart.

"That's why I worry." Megan handed him his pills and grabbed a glass from behind the lamp. She walked toward the bathroom.

"I have water here." Tyler reached over to the other nightstand.

"Okay." Megan lifted the cover off the breakfast. The aroma made her stomach growl.

"I am a little hungry," Tyler said.

Megan watched him take a couple of bites. "Try to take a shower today. Warm water might make you feel better. And don't forget to take your meds later."

"I won't." Tyler nodded.

Megan kissed him on the forehead before heading for the door. She glanced back. "I won't call 'cuz I don't want to wake you. Doctor said you need sleep. Vincenzo knows how to reach me."

Tyler nodded again.

Twelve pairs of Cheshire-like eyes watched from the bushes across from Tyler's balcony. The gray-haired man stood next to his railing and peered to the left and then to the right. He leaned over and laughed.

"Good! No sign of those nasty cats. Ah, there are my shoes!"

"Trevor?" A female human voice yelled from inside. "What are you doing?"

"Looking for my shoes, Lovey," the man replied.

"We need to leave, or we'll miss our tour. You're still not looking for those cats are you?"

"Of course not. Just checking the weather." The man peered over the railing again.

"Good. Let's go. Lock that door."

"Here kitty, kitty," the man whispered.

"Trevor!" screamed the female voice.

The door opened on the boy's balcony and food flew into the courtyard. Belle and Harry ran toward the sweet aroma. Belle scanned the yard before motioning the others to join. Sharing what little there was, they ate. After climbing a tree, one-by-one they jumped onto the railing before landing on the boy's balcony. They licked their paws as they waited for D'oreo and the black straggly cat that had freed them.

The boy set the dirty dishes next to the TV. He shoved two sticks of gum into his mouth. He sighed. After stepping into the bathroom, he placed his glasses on the sink and tossed his gum into the wastebasket. As he brushed his teeth, he reached down and scratched his leg.

It was her chance, and she reached out just as the boy stepped away. The tiny greenish hand slowly disappeared back into the toile.

Tossing his pj's on the floor, the boy stepped into the shower.

A greenish leg reached out and hooked onto the waste basket. The basket inched toward the toile. The green hand grabbed the chewed gum and used it to attach the bottom of the wallpaper more securely. The small hand reached out again and grabbed Tyler's glasses from the sink. After a few quiet moments, a curly head of long, light brownish-greenish hair struggled as a youthful face appeared with deep blue-green eyes, a flawless complexion, and ruby red lips. She continued to struggle but her body remained embedded deeply inside the toile. After a few exhausting moments, her right shoulder and arm waved through the air.

Tyler's hand reached out from behind the curtain and searched for a towel.

"Where is it?" he asked.

The little green hand grabbed the towel and handed it to Tyler's flailing arm. She giggled before disappearing back into the wallpaper.

Tyler wrapped the towel around his waist and yanked the curtain aside. Stepping out, he reached for his glasses.

"I put them right here!"

Tyler stepped toward the door and the little green hands darted back out from the paper. With the boy so close, the pull to keep the girl bound into the paper felt somehow weaker. Now, with both hands free, the little arms stretched out to grab the boy. However, Tyler knelt for his pj's from off the floor, and the hands touched nothing but air.

Aunt Meg was right. I do feel better.

Tyler dressed in jeans before pulling out a light blue t-shirt with a large shark on the front from inside his duffle bag. The little stuffed Celestial KittyCat was still in the pocket. It jarred his memory of Vincenzo's story …

'A man turned into a cat and then back into a man, legend of a love story gone wrong, something big is definitely going to happen in Italy after the celestial alignment …'

"Sure." Tyler laughed.

He pushed the toy in deeper and searched for his glasses. On his nightstand, Tyler found only his headband. After placing it into his pocket, he grabbed the bomb papers. He folded and tucked them into his back pocket.

"They must have fallen on the bathroom floor," Tyler said.

Tyler knelt and rummaged through the empty waste basket. He frowned. No glasses and no gum.

"Wait a minute …"

He walked up to the hanging toile and stared at it.

What's going on? This looks like Aunt Meg's wallpaper …

Tyler stepped closer. He rubbed his hand over the paper and nothing happened. As he tried to pull the paper from the wall, two small greenish hands grabbed Tyler's leg and pulled.

Tyler screamed. He felt light, which reminded him of a balloon floating through the air. His throat ached and his world grew hazy around him. Tyler kicked and flailed his arms. He reached for the sink's pedestal but his arms were too short. He grabbed the waste basket and held onto the rim. He tried to scream but his throat hurt too much. His grip was slipping. He couldn't …

"Waaaaaa …"

The little greenish hands pulled Tyler deeper into the toile. He could feel his body shrinking and stretching. As he struggled to see, his world changed from full color to a world tinted in a light bluish green.

Tyler stood motionless under a large tree. His throat no longer hurt. In the distance, he could see a farmhouse. Tyler shook his head and blinked several times.

"I must be hallucinating from the fever," he said.

"No, you are not," a young voice replied.

After hearing the boy scream, the cats formed their pyramid in front of the glass door. Belle turned the handle while Harry and the others pushed the door open. They scrambled in and searched the room and small bathroom and shower. Bombarded with the boy's scent, the cats continued to search. He had to be somewhere. A knock on the door startled the animals. Belle ran to the door and sniffed.

"Food," she whispered. "Must be for the boy."

"We must find that boy," Harry said. "If the human enters, they will find us. Quickly, everyone, show time!"

One-by-one, the cats crawled under the bed sheet and maneuvered between the opened books.

"Just as in The Catman's act," Curry said, trying not to snicker.

"Hush!" Belle scolded.

Two moved upward, two downward, two to the right, and three to the left. Belle and Harry crouched in the middle. Allie crawled to the pillow and poked out her back and head. With her ears lowered, only her straggling black hair could be seen.

Patrick glanced at the clock.

Still Celestial KittyCat.

With twelve hours until midnight and the celestial alignment, he needed to hurry. He had to get to CallaLyly soon. Only problem was that he was stuck in a crate with D'oreo.

D'oreo mewed and rubbed against Patrick. He walked around and purred as if he was Patrick's best friend.

Stretching and yawning, Patrick stared at Tino's bedroom door.

"Has to be a way out," D'oreo said, sitting next to Patrick.

"Then we wake him up."

"How?"

"You are a cat, yell!"

The screeching and meowing started out low.

"Pretend you are fighting with me," Patrick whispered.

D'oreo nodded. D'oreo ran and hit the side of the crate. He clawed and hissed and screamed as loud as he could.

"Remind me never to piss you off!" Patrick said as he ran and hit the side of the crate.

They darted and hissed and screamed and both froze as cold water splattered through the crate. When they were drenched like sewer rats, Tino laughed.

"That should shut you up for a while." Tino knelt and stared into the crate. "Why are you not a man yet? Huh …? I want my wish. If you are not a man by the time I return from visiting Uncle Fab, get ready to take a deep dip in the River Arno. I have a suitcase all ready for you both." Again, Tino laughed. He tugged on the lock several times before tossing the key into the bedroom.

"That didn't go as planned," Patrick said, licking the water off his paws.

D'oreo sighed and frowned.

Vincenzo knocked three times. He had promised Signorina Brandt he'd personally take Tyler his lunch. He was checking on her nephew's condition throughout the day. With no answer, Vincenzo slowly opened the door. The boy was asleep. He carefully placed the lunch tray on the desk. He listened and could hear the boy snoring.

Best to let him sleep as the doctore suggested.

Vincenzo picked up the dirty dishes and adjusted the glass door for better air flow. Before leaving, he leaned over and saw Tyler's hair.

Poor boy. In Italy, sick in bed, having no fun. Just studying.

Vincenzo locked the door behind him. He would return later with dinner.

Chapter Twelve

It is said, "Don't believe what your eyes are telling you. All they see are the limitations." This is not about seeing limitations but experiencing what our eyes must deal with ...

After dragging the boy through the lantern, CallaLyly dodged his kicking feet and grabbing hands. Several times, he caught her good on the side of the head. She pushed him away, and he finally stopped wrestling.

"I must be hallucinating from the fever," he said.

"No, you are not," CallaLyly replied.

"Who are you? I was just in my bathroom. Now, I'm out here under a ..." Tyler glanced around, "... tree. What did you do to me?"

"I did nothing to you."

Taking a step closer, the boy charged. As a dark head of hair aimed straight for her gut, CallaLyly stepped aside. The boy fell and remained motionless.

"Have you hurt yourself?" she asked.

No reply.

CallaLyly stepped over and knelt next to the boy. "Are you alive?" CallaLyly lowered her head to see if the boy was still breathing.

The boy rolled and grabbed her. He held her down. She screamed as she stared into the eyes of the boy who was breathing directly into her face.

"Would you please remove yourself?" CallaLyly asked.

"Not until you tell me what's going on!" the boy demanded. "Who are you?"

"Please pardon my rude acquaintance. I am CallaLyly of the House of Montevelli of Siena. You may refer to me as Lyly of the House of Montevelli. And you? What house are you from?"

"I'm from the house of *kicking your ass* if you don't tell me what's going on."

"You speak English, I assume?"

"I speak whatever language I want. How did I get here?"

CallaLyly held her hand to his lips. The boy slapped it away.

"You must kiss my hand. It is customary," CallaLyly said.

"Customary, mushomary!" the boy replied.

"Please remove yourself from me," CallaLyly said, pushing against the boy.

"Only if you promise to tell me what's going on."

"Yes, I will."

The boy stood and stepped away. CallaLyly brushed out her dress. She tried to adjust her hair. Picking out a blade of grass, she sighed.

"Ahh, your spectacles." She pulled the rimless glasses from her dress pocket.

"You stole my glasses?"

"I watched you through the lanterns. You are now in the wallcovering with me."

"Impossible. Where are we?"

"You are in the wallcovering," CallaLyly repeated. "I pulled you in."

"Why?"

"May I ask your name, signore."

"Tyler ... Tyler Charles."

"Nice to meet you, Tyler Charles."

"Now, talk or else." Tyler bunched up his fists.

"Perhaps we should sit."

"I don't want to sit. I want to go back to my room." The boy glanced around. "Why does everything look so weird?"

"This is a two-dimensional world."

"Two-dimensional ... impossible."

"No, it is not," CallaLyly replied. "Come, let us sit and talk." CallaLyly walked over to the large tree and sat on the grass. She patted the ground next to her.

"Place looks like a cartoon," Tyler said.

"What house are you from, Tyler Charles?"

"Um, House of ... of Charles?"

"It is my pleasure to make your acquaintance, Tyler from the House of Charles. I assume you being a Charles, your House is from the Country of England, just as Patrick. How wonderful."

"No. I'm from Massachusetts. That's in America. Who's Patrick?"

"America? That's part of the New World. England territory."

"Not since the revolution." Tyler smirked.

CallaLyly frowned. "You and I have quite a bit to discuss, Tyler of the House of Charles of Massachusetts. Judging from the manner of your dress and speech, we are without a doubt, worlds apart. May I ask what is the year I acquired you from, Tyler of the House of Charles of Massachusetts?"

Tyler laughed. "You talk funny. It's the early two thousands."

"Is this what we are to become? Disheveled boys as yourself? I dare comprehend our vast uncultured future."

Sitting up straighter, Tyler brushed his dark hair into place. He adjusted his bent glasses and straightened his t-shirt. "Nothing wrong with how I'm dressed. My friends dress this way."

"That is better I suppose. With the two thousands, I am over two centuries old, and I do not feel a day over seventeen." CallaLyly's eyes teared.

"You don't look that old." Tyler nodded. "I mean you look seventeen." He bit his lip.

"It feels as yesterday, Tyler of the House of Charles, that I was seventeen but only a slight while now that I have any comprehension of my being. I seem to have been in a dream."

"Can you call me Tyler and not the house thing. Sounds stupid. We don't talk like that anymore."

"Stupid … vernacular I am not familiar with." CallaLyly frowned. "If you mean silly, then I understand. I shall no longer refer to your House. It is a title. Who we are. Who I am. Where we are from."

Tyler sighed. "Who cares where you're from? I come from … you come from … good or bad. We have a first and last name, sometimes a middle. I'm Tyler Daniel Charles." He smiled and reached out his hand.

"I see."

"We shake hands." Tyler grabbed hers and shook it. "I won't kiss your hand and you don't kiss mine … unsanitary. Where are we? Why is everything so yellow and green?"

"We are in a wallcovering."

"You mean that toile that was in the bathroom? Aunt Meg must have put it up for some reason."

"What is a … toile?"

"My aunt collects old wallpaper. So, how did you get in this thing?"

"Depicting my home of Siena tells a story, an unfortunate turn of events. My ill-fated life."

"Who's Patrick?"

"Patrick was my friend. He was trying to help my family with our trade. Unfortunately, he was turned into a black cat by a mystic from the Far East. That same mystic put me in here." CallaLyly waved her arms through the air.

Tyler shook his head and laughed. "That stupid story is true then. Of that Celestial KittyCat."

"I know nothing of a Celestial KittyCat, however, Patrick was turned into a black cat." CallaLyly placed her hand over her heart.

"Your Patrick is famous. He's known as the Celestial KittyCat, and if anyone captures him, he has to grant them a wish at midnight. I have a stuffed version of him in my bag … back in my room … that I'm not *in* anymore!"

"Stuffed?" Lyly gasped. "Someone stuffed my Patrick?"

"No, not *your* Patrick." Tyler snickered. "It's a toy."

"Oh." Lyly sighed. "That is a relief. Then, will you help us?"

Tyler nodded, "I guess."

"There is hope then."

"Vincenzo said the alignment was something big and would happen tonight."

"Who is Vincenzo?"

"He runs the hotel."

"Hotel?"

"That bathroom was in the hotel."

"Oh." Lyly stared at Tyler. "Then you will help me, Tyler Daniel Charles?"

Tyler climbed onto a lower branch and pointed to a small lantern. "What is this?"

"This is how I pulled you through," Lyly said. "I fastened the wallcovering … I mean toile with adhesive that I found in your waste container."

"My throat gum?" Tyler stuck his head up to the lantern. "Hey, that's my bathroom. This is not cool. Were you spying on me when I was in the shower?" Tyler frowned.

"I would never …! I assure you."

"Yeah right. This must be some kind of a portal. Wish my dad could see it."

"This portal as you call it," said Lyly, "comes and goes. It expands and appears randomly." The lantern fell black. "Just as I said, the portal is now closed."

"Can I call you Lyly and not the House thing, and you call me just Tyler?"

"I suppose, Tyler," she sighed. "It is, however, most unrefined."

Tyler frowned again.

Chapter Thirteen

It is said, "You are never given a dream without the power for it to come true." This is not about the dream but the power of a truth...

Tyler no longer felt ill or hungry. Once his eyes fully adjusted to the bright background, his nerves settled a little.

"This place is cool," Tyler whispered.

Tyler's mind ran through all the possibilities. He nodded to Lyly then took off. He ran through the two-dimensional forests and several vineyards. He took time to pet a farm animal that was standing next to a fence. As he darted into one of the farmhouses, he yelled out, "Hi, Lyly," to a two-dimensional duplicate before he darted into another forest. Everything was nothing more than ink and paper, and life around him remained somewhat frozen.

"*Hi* sheep, *Hi* cows, *Hi* chickens," Tyler yelled out. "This is weird."

Tyler reached for a farmhouse door and his fingers slapped against the solid backdrop. He laughed.

"How is this possible?"

Tyler ran through his everyday physics theories and formulas that he could remember. He understood that his body was made of matter and moved through space and time. In this world, however, everything was flat with only a few colors.

94

"Impossible!"

If only his father were here to experience it with him. Many times Tyler wanted to share things with his father but that man was always just too busy to take the time. Tyler stopped and glanced out at the continuing pattern. He sat and rested on his knees.

"This place must go on forever."

Tyler circled back to the living Lyly. She sat on a swing and cried.

"You, okay?" he asked. "Want a push?"

"Gattino Celestiale Gatto." Lyly repeated her words. "Gattino Celestiale Gatto."

"I know what that means," Tyler said. "Vincenzo told us about that story. It's about that Celestial KittyCat. You're the girl in the love story."

"My poor family. They must have assumed I ran away. I would never hurt them in that manner, and they will never know the truth."

Tyler froze. "Aunt Meg! When she comes home tonight, she'll think I was kidnapped or something. I have to go back." Tyler sat on the ground next to the swing. Lyly was the prettiest girl he'd ever seen, and he didn't want to leave her alone. Not when she was so upset. "The answer always lies in physics."

"Physics?" Lyly asked.

"Something my dad always says." Tyler studied her. "Tell me about your dream, Lyly?"

Lyly wiped away a tear. "There was a dark-haired boy. I do not know his name. Patrick was in it too. And the celestial alignment."

Tyler nodded. "Tonight at midnight."

Lyly brushed away another tear.

"The celestial alignment must trigger something," Tyler said. "We just have to figure out what that something is. Then we can fix your problem. Is Patrick here?"

"No, I am alone and I understand, Tyler. We must fix my problem." She smiled.

Tyler smiled back. "You'll have to spill the beans."

"I have no legumes."

Tyler laughed. "Not beans or legumes, Lyly. You have to tell me the whole story. And don't leave anything out. What you leave out may be important and hold the key."

"I have no key, either."

"Oh, man." He shook his head.

"What man?"

"Just as my Aunt Meg says, 'Lost in translation.' Okay, talk."

Lyly glanced into the distance and frowned. "It was just before first light. I was enjoying a very delightful dream, although I cannot remember it all now. My family was to host a gala that evening. We were filled with such anticipation. I remember how the letters on the invitation felt. They were gold and burgundy and I could close my eyes and read the words just by touch."

"Raised?"

Lyly stared at him.

"You know, the letters felt higher than the rest of the paper?"

"Yes, Tyler, raised." Lyly closed her eyes and read the invitation with her fingers.

THE HOUSE of MONTEVELLI of SIENA
CORDIALLY INVITES YOU TO THE
ANNUAL COMMONER'S BANK GALA
Saturday, June 13TH
Contrada Pantera, Via Saverania 31
6 o'clock in the evening

She sighed. "I had heard a commotion coming from my father's study."

"Commotion?"

"My parents were arguing," she said. "My parents never argued. I was quiet and sat on the landing to hear better."

"Oh? Snooping on your parents?"

"It was not proper, yes, but my parents never argued. Not like that."

"Domenico, how could you!" her mother screamed out. "She is our *daughter*. You would not do this to our son."

"He is an infant," her father said. His voice was stern and low. "I would not consider this if I had another choice."

"Choice? What do you mean? Tonight we host the event of the season. Everyone will attend."

"An illusion, my dear. Just an illusion. The union of Houses will help our finances. Our merchants are not selling. Many have stopped producing. They cannot pay their loans. When my merchants do not pay, *we* have no funds."

Delfina cried.

"Our farmers are paying with their crops. Times are hard for them. I can no longer rely on just eggs and legumes. We are running out of time."

Delfina wiped her eyes with her handkerchief.

"Tonight, our daughter will meet her future husband," Domenico said. "Within four nights and when the moon is at its fullest during the celestial alignment, we will announce their pending nuptial. It will become a magical night in many ways."

Delfina glared at her husband. "How could you promise our daughter to a family we despise? Agost of the House of de'Leon of Florence is a total buffoon. There, I said it and without manners." Delfina stepped toward the door. "And that father … he is mean-spirited! There, I said it again."

"He may be a buffoon but he is a buffoon with deep pockets. We need his finances to grow ours and help our people. And manners can be learned, Delfina," Domenico said, shaking his head. "It is done. Prepare your daughter for her future commitment."

Delfina stepped into the foyer and slammed the door. She stepped up to a lantern that was sitting on the landing. She picked it up and glanced up to the second floor. She frowned. Holding the lantern in front of her, she opened the study door. "Your daughter already knows."

"You must go after her," Domenico said, pulling a pipe from his pocket.

"She needs time," Delfina replied. "When she returns, I will talk with her."

CallaLyly ran down the dark path aiming for the stables.

"How can my parents negotiate me as if I were a horse?"

Her tears fell and she didn't bother to wipe them away. Pulling her cape tighter around her shoulders, CallaLyly ran into the murky streets. The shadows covering the stables sent chills all through her. Crying, she darted into the darkness and almost knocked over a worker.

"Oh, my deepest apologies," CallaLyly said. "I did not see you."

"I am sorry, my lady," the boy said.

"I know you. You are Dante of the House of Merle, yes?"

Bowing, Dante replied, "Yes, my lady. We met previously. Something wrong?"

Dante's dark hair and complexion almost matched his work attire. His long hair was pulled and tied behind his head. He was slim and petite.

"I am fine. Honest." She crossed her heart. "I just needed to clear my head. May I borrow a horse? Any will do."

"For you, my lady, not just any horse but my favorite, Tomassino. I am training him for the Palio. He is swift and accommodating."

Dante fitted the horse with the proper saddle and reins. CallaLyly watched as he worked.

"Here you are, my lady," Dante said.

CallaLyly hoisted herself up and settled in. "Thank you, and I wish you well with your training."

Dante nodded.

"I promise that I will return shortly."

Dante waved. "Take all the time you need."

No longer in sight of the stables and with just the early light peeking over the horizon, CallaLyly struggled to guide the horse through the trees.

"This way, you silly creature," she lectured.

The horse refused to obey and aimed in the opposite direction. CallaLyly resisted the urge to pull on the reins. When the horse stopped at a pond, she sighed.

"I give up, Tomassino," CallaLyly said, sliding down.

The horse snorted before dunking his head underwater.

"You make me laugh."

The horse raised his head and snorted before dunking under again.

"You stay put. I need a little walk."

CallaLyly glanced around the open meadow and sighed. A large rock, larger than a house, looked out of place. She walked over and rested her hands on the cold stone. CallaLyly shivered. The cold would soon be her future after the arranged marriage. She wiped away another tear.

"I arise today through the strength of heaven …" a deep voice said.

CallaLyly saw no one.

"… light of the sun, radiance of the moon, splendor of the fire …" the voice continued.

CallaLyly took a step and the voice stopped.

After a few moments of silence, the voice continued. "Speed of the lightning, swiftness of the wind, depth of the sea …"

CallaLyly stood silently and breathed in the words as the man recited them.

"… Christ in the mouth of everyone who speaks of me, Christ in every eye that sees me, Christ in every ear that hears me. Amen." The voice fell silent.

With her curiosity taking over, CallaLyly stepped slowly around the boulder. A tall man stood next to a pure black horse. He fastened a belt around his waist and turned. He smiled at her.

CallaLyly ran back to her horse. She stood by the water and sighed.

"Why are you in the pond, you strange creature?" CallaLyly asked the horse. "Now, what will I do? I cannot ride you like this?"

"Hello?" the deep voice said from behind her. "I must apologize. You caught me at my weakest time."

With her heart pounding, CallaLyly turned around. The man was lean with a kind smile. His blonde hair framed his deep blue eyes.

Bowing, the man chuckled. "I mean you no harm, my lady. I am merely passing through your beautiful land. I am enjoying the olive trees. They are full this time of year." His English accent amused her.

CallaLyly studied how he was dressed. He was not from nobility, more of a commoner. *Harmless enough,* CallaLyly thought before saying, "I did not mean to interfere with your prayer time …"

The horse stepped out of the water and shook. As the sprinkles hit them, CallaLyly and the man laughed.

"You heard my Breastplate?" he asked.

"Breastplate?"

"It is a guarding prayer attributed to my Irish mother. Her favorite saint was Saint Patrick. I was named after him. I pray every morning just before dawn."

"It is quite lovely." CallaLyly reached out her hand. "I am CallaLyly of the House of Montevelli of Siena. I prefer Lyly."

"Beautiful name," he said, lowering his eyes and kissing the back of her hand. "Calla is derived from the Greek. It means a beautiful Lily, Lyly of the House of Montevelli of Siena."

"I suppose that means I was named after my mother's favorite flower."

They laughed again and again he bowed. "May I introduce myself?"

CallaLyly nodded.

"I am Patrick of the House of Barrett of Hampshire. My father is English."

"You have come far, Patrick of the House of Barrett of Hampshire."

"An adventure, my lady. My mother tossed me to the door and said, *'Patrick follow your star.'* And here I am, traveling the land with my steed, Squire."

"I see." CallaLyly glanced around.

"I was a bit of a mischievous child. No saint am I."

"I wish you well as you follow your star. I hope you find your way."

"Thank you, my lady." His smile lit his face.

"He seemed very nice," Lyly said to Tyler. "We talked for a long time. He made me forget about my troubles. I invited him to our gala that evening. He graciously accepted. I knew I would have a fine and pleasant evening because of Patrick. Remember, I was to be betrothed to a buffoon. It was a thought that nauseated me. Therefore, I planned accordingly…"

Tyler sighed and shook his head.

"Good Saturday eve, Sir Montevelli and my lady," Patrick said, kissing the mother's hand. "I see where CalaLyly inherits her beauty."

Giggling, CallaLyly stepped forward. "Mother … Father … may I introduce Patrick of the House of Barrett of Hampshire. We met this morn, and as a traveling guest of our town, I knew you would want me to welcome him accordingly to our home and gala. He leaves on the morrow."

Both of their brows rose.

"Welcome?" Domenico cleared his throat. "Uh, of course, of course. Please … partake of the evening's festivities."

Her mother glared at her. "Met this morn?"

Wanting to avoid her mother's in-depth questions, CallaLyly took Patrick by the arm. "Since we completed our greetings, I shall show Patrick our gardens." Before her parents could object, CallaLyly added, "As his time is so limited here."

However, as Domenico tried to speak, CallaLyly hurried Patrick through the lobby and into the garden courtyard.

"Fortunately, for myself and with Patrick in tow, the garden courtyard was filled with loud merriment and many nobles and townsfolk. They were discussing the upcoming horse race, which was good for us, or so I thought."

Chapter Fourteen

It is said, "Two souls never find each other by chance."
This is not about finding as they have already been found . . .

Giovanni of the House of de'Leon of Florence was a self-proclaimed man known as *All Eyes*. He could stand perfectly still yet sense three-hundred-sixty degrees without moving. Yellowish, snowy hair, tugged into a bun, clashed against his extra-large spectacles that barely clung to his long-fat nose. Giovanni rendered himself as a keen banker and one of the sharpest dressed noblemen in town. His navy-blue coat acquired during his last trip to France was complemented by a white ruffled shirt. Adorned with cropped pants worn above the knees and white silk stockings, he would have made his wife proud had she still been alive.

"I never lose, Assistant," Giovanni said to his chubby manservant.

The dark-haired man nodded and replied, "Yesss ... *All Eyes*." Leonardo frowned as he always did and looked away.

"Assistant, do you believe this absurd gala that is before our eyes?" He scowled and squinted. "Our genteel nobles associating with the riff-raff of these ghastly townspeople!"

"Yesss ... *All Eyes*."

"Assistant, *we* must now stand in line *behind* these buffoons. All so they can pay with a few hens and eggs. Insult!"

"Yesss ... *Old Eyes*."

"What did you say?" Giovanni turned and glared at his assistant. The man had worked for him for years and he never even took the time to learn his name.

"Uh, yesss … *All Eyes.*"

"Assistant, Agost believes that he is a part of this riff-raff and as entertainment no less." Giovanni refused to turn as the voices roared with laughter behind him. Why embarrass himself even more? How could his own buffoon of a son make such a spectacle of himself? Sighing, he turned slightly and watched as Agost tossed several balls into the air. He huffed once before gluing his gaze back onto the fiery blaze.

Beyond marrying age, Agost had to be unioned soon. The combining of the two Houses was a flawless idea, especially since no other fair maiden would have his awkward son.

"I thought Agost was invited as the future groom. Not to entertain." Leonardo, his assistant, sighed. "Do not allow your son's behavior to upset you so. He is still so young in mind and heart."

"It's more of a pending business dealing." Giovanni laughed and tugged at his pants.

"Business? A future groom is all about *love*, not business."

Giovanni laughed again. "Agost does not wish to meet the bride any more than the bride wishes to meet him. Better that he remains preoccupied with his toys."

Leonardo sighed.

"Assistant?" Giovanni frowned. "Something bothering you?"

Leonardo grinned before shaking his head.

"Oh, Assistant, when will this end? I am most happy the nobles from Florence are not here to witness Agost as a Court Jester."

"The nobles from Siena are here," Leonardo said, nodding.

"Unfortunate, that is true." Giovanni shook his head. "Unfortunate."

Giovanni glanced over his shoulder and shuddered. Agost, dressed in striped pants of various colors, looked ridiculous. A huge yellow bow clung to his neck. His long, curly, red hair made him look even more clownish. He stood in the middle of a crowd of onlookers and tossed his bright red balls into the air.

"He has the crowd eating out of his hands," Leonardo said as Giovanni sighed. "I've never seen Agost happier."

Giovanni cringed. "Well, it is time, Assistant, for him to have his crude awakening for he will soon meet his future bride."

"Yesss … *All Eyes.*"

"Once our Houses are one …" Giovanni grinned, "… I will squelch Domenico's fire once and for all. His absurdity of allowing the commoners to purchase the nobles' land is ridiculous and unacceptable. No, once the Houses are one, The Commoner's Bank of Siena will no longer provide funding to these peasants."

"Yesss … *All Eyes.*"

"The feudal system will return to its full glory. Place the farmland back into the hands where it belongs under the domain of the nobility. These peasants are here merely to tend to our needs and our lands." Giovanni gazed into the sky allowing his chin to guide him.

"Yesss … *All Eyes.*"

"I will —" Giovanni watched as CallaLyly escorted a young man by the arm through the crowd. "What?"

"Signore?" Leonardo asked.

"How dare she!" Giovanni's eyes widened and his anger soared.

CallaLyly now stood next to an Asian man, smiling and laughing. The man's gray mustache draped down his chest and almost touched his waist. The man wore a large multicolored hat that sat crookedly on his head. His long, red robe almost sparkled against the flames of the large fire.

"Assistant! With whom is the daughter of Domenico and Delfina standing next to? She is laughing and partaking too happily with the merriment." Giovanni frowned.

"The other entertainment?"

"No, not the Asian man ... the other one! The blonde. Who is that man?" Giovanni asked, glaring across the courtyard.

Leonardo took a step closer and shook his head. "You mean the intelligent and handsome looking young one? I believe she is holding his hand."

"Oh, Tyler," Lyly said, wiping her eyes. "I felt so happy in that moment. There is no way I could grasp what was to come. I sensed that Patrick felt as I. With such a crowd, I calmed myself about running into the de'Leons of Florence. I did not wish to talk to Giovanni or his son. The air felt heavenly, and the food and drink was divine. Patrick and I were having such fun talking friendly with Master Joroku."

"Who was Master Joroku?" Tyler asked.

"I told Master Joroku that he was amazing," Lyly said, rolling her eyes. "He was the most popular Asian entertainer in the world. He created silhouettes with just a touch of his fingers. I watched him do it. He used black and white paper. His spit was his glue."

"How did he cut paper with just a finger?" Tyler asked.

Lyly giggled. "His fingernails were long and made from gold. They were as sharp as knives. He had me stand next to Patrick and we held hands. Oh, how I felt holding Patrick's hand. My stomach twisted and I felt warm all over."

"Oh?"

"Yes, it felt like I had swallowed a hundred butterflies. When I had to let go of Patrick's hand, I was left empty inside. I remember that Patrick said I was pretty. He actually said I was pretty."

Tyler nodded.

Giovanni watched as the Asian man created a silhouette for the happy couple. His anger roared from somewhere deep within. *How dare she embarrass my family in this manner!* "I am paying for this night," he whispered to Leonardo.

"Excuse me?" Leonardo leaned over to hear better.

With his bony index finger pointing toward the happy couple, Giovanni screamed, "Assistant! Retrieve CallaLyly's parents at once!"

Leonardo rubbed his ear and shook his head. He nodded before darting through the laughing crowd.

Giovanni harshly pushed his way toward his son. He stood in front of Agost and watched as he juggle several items. As the cups and bowls of various sizes flew through the air, Giovanni sighed and grunted.

Giovanni stepped forward and boldly stated, "I forgot to tell you, Agost. Tonight you will be introduced to your future bride." Giovanni narrowed his eyes. "This is *not* an option." He stood back and crossed his arms.

Agost dropped his clay cups and bowls. As they crashed around him, the townspeople stood back in awe. They sighed and mumbled to each other, and Agost stood speechless just staring at his father.

"Discard that silly yellow bow that's around your neck!" Giovanni ordered.

Tattleman, an older though smaller in stature Asian man with a flowing black goatee, walked over to Master Joroku. He adjusted his long blue robe and tilted his head. His highly-pulled ponytail flung forward swiping across his wrinkled face.

"What have you learned, Tattleman?" Master Joroku asked as he rearranged his supplies.

"I have seen and heard much," Tattleman replied.

"Tell me."

"The two Houses of Montevelli of Siena and de'Leon of Florence have ... situations."

Master Joroku glanced over at the juggler and smiled. "Situations? Ah good. We have found the potential flies for my web. Two are always better than one."

Tattleman nodded.

Laughing and walking ahead of Lyly, Patrick watched as the fire-eater gained the attention of the townsfolk. The nobles stood to the side and conversed amongst themselves. Patrick chuckled.

He turned and said, "Lyly, the Fire-Eater should breathe a little nobility onto the ..."

Lyly was gone.

He searched the crowd but there was no sign of her. *When did she leave?* Maybe her parents would know where she was. As he searched, Patrick thought about how beautiful she was when he noticed her in the receiving line. A few guests had stepped aside and that was when he saw her. She was smiling and her eyes sparkled as she talked to the guests. Her long, plum-colored dress, delicately pinched above her thin waist, was adorned with a lavender silk tie. Her long, light brown curls flowed freely past her shoulders, which gave her a seductive lure.

As his memory kept his thoughts busy, Patrick searched for Lyly. He stepped closer to the house, and the sounds of someone crying grabbed his attention. He walked through the grass and into the secluded garden. Sitting alone on a bench, Lyly cried into her hands. Every so often, she'd push her hair from her face. He watched as her tears fell onto the chiseled paper of their silhouette. Taking a step closer, Lyly released the profile allowing it to fall to the grass. Patrick sat down beside her.

"Lyly, what could possibly be wrong?" Patrick reached for her hand but she pulled away. "Did I offend you or your parents in some manner? Is that why you are crying? If yes, then I beg for your forgiveness and will immediately seek theirs."

Lyly wiped her face and stared at him. Her swollen eyes touched his heart and he frowned. "This is not of your making." Lyly sniffled. "Patrick, I may no longer speak with you, and I must ask that you depart our home at once. If you refuse, my parents will be forced to have you physically removed." She picked up the silhouette and smiled. "I will walk you to your horse and bid you farewell. I can do, at least, that much. That is all. I ask that you honor my parents' wish."

Patrick stared into her eyes. "Is this *your* wish too, Lyly? If yes, then I will leave. However, I request to know the reason behind such an action. Is there something you are not telling me?"

Gently, Lyly rubbed the silhouette between her fingers. She sighed and nodded. "What you see here tonight is only an illusion. An illusion that is crumbling. The union of my House with another will allow our community to survive. The towns people rely heavily upon my family for their financial security. I was told only this morn that my parents are penniless. All they have left is this house …"

"I see," Patrick said. "I presume that you are what will bind the two Houses?"

"Yes." Lyly wiped a tear that was threatening to fall. "I am betrothed to Agost. My father just introduced us a few minutes ago and the young man was so shocked that he ran away."

"He ran away?"

Lyly nodded. "I was in shock too. I just stood there and stared at my father. He said there was no choice on my part. That *he* will announce our engagement in four nights hence."

As her tears fell, Patrick wiped each one with the back of his hand. "From what I can surmise, the other House is the sole winner." Patrick took in a deep breath. "Perhaps, I can be of some help to your family."

"Do not jest at such a difficult time."

"I do not jest, Lyly. Your family requires funding and I may be able to supply an investor …"

"But … you do not look as if …"

Lyly gazed at his tattered jacket and he chuckled.

"I do not look like what … a noble?" Patrick laughed. "My mother has a saying … *'Do not judge a book by its cover.'* I travel as a peasant to avoid thieves and beggars." Patrick smiled and added, "I have an allotted inheritance due me. I will simply request it a little sooner."

Lyly shook her head. "How would you know of the amount that is required?"

"Please, pray tell, Lyly. How much?"

Lyly leaned over and whispered into his ear.

"Done," he said.

Furrowing her brows, Lyly frowned. "It must be proven in four night's time. They will not believe you unless it is in hand."

"I have a way to show proof of my funding," Patrick said, smiling. "However, I must send a note to my mother."

Lyly nodded and stood. She took Patrick's hand and together they hid in the shadows as they aimed for her father's study.

"Here is my father's quill," Lyly said. "You may borrow a piece of my father's parchment."

"No need," Patrick replied, taking the silhouette from Lyly's hand. Patrick pulled the black paper from off the white. He stared at it before handing the backing to Lyly. On the white silhouette, Patrick wrote out his instructions for his mother. Then he smiled and said, "I must speak to Dante."

"How do you know Dante?"

"I met him out front just tonight," Patrick replied.

Lyly giggled. "Follow me, I will take you to Dante and your horse."

"Dante, my boy," Patrick said. "I offer a bag of gold coins for your service."

Dante nodded. "And what is this service, signore?"

"Please, travel to England and hand this silhouette to my mother. Wait for her to answer. Then return with her reply. You must hurry, for you must return by the fourth night."

"England, signore?"

"Consider it as training for the Palio. Dante, may you travel as quickly as a wildfire spreads ... quickly and enduringly ..."

Dante stared at the pouch. As he tossed it gently in his hands, he searched for his father amidst the commoners.

"Papa, I have good news." Dante handed the pouch to his father and grinned.

"Dante, who did you steal this from?"

"Papa, it is not stolen," Dante replied. "I swear and there is more. I was hired to travel faraway. I will share my pay with you. Take half of these coins and tell no one of my absence. If asked, I am in training for the Palio. I shall return in four nights."

Dante's father stood in awe and held tightly to the bag of gold. Dante jumped onto Tomassino and waved once before darting into the mist.

Agost sulked against a tree. He glared at his father and the Assistant.

"I have no patience for your lack of maturity," Giovanni said to his youngest son. As he spoke, Giovanni watched a short Asian man amble toward them. "It is settled, Agost. Accept what I offer or your genteel way of life will change … dramatically. Mark my words."

"I will never love her," Agost whispered. "She is a stranger to me. Place whatever requirements you feel are necessary." Agost sighed and walked across the yard. He looked out at the crowd before crouching behind a large bush.

"Will this dreadful night never end, Assistant?" Giovanni asked, shaking his head.

"I don't know … *All Eyes*," the Assistant replied.

The Asian man bowed before speaking softly, "Master Joroku may be of assistance. Help him to help you." The Asian man pointed at the large bush where Agost was now hiding.

"Who is this Master Joroku you speak of." Giovanni lifted his chin and took in a deep breath.

Bowing again, the Asian replied, "I am Tattleman, aide to Master Joroku. He has the answer to your dilemma. He can help with your son. If you will follow me."

Giovanni laughed and tugged on his pants. "What do I have to lose?"

They walked as a small group toward a man standing by a large copper cauldron. Several guests surrounded the man, laughing and talking. The Asian man walked up to Joroku and whispered something to him. Joroku nodded and hurried the guests away.

Standing alone, the man nodded and Giovanni stepped forward. "You can help me?"

"I have the answer to your dilemma." Joroku smiled and pulled a golden vial from his sleeve. "Master Joroku always has the solutions."

Lifting his nose into the air again, Giovanni huffed. "Nonsense. You are no better than the common peddler!"

"Tattleman has told me of your troubles. You need your son to fall in love with the daughter of the House of Montevelli, yes? I sell you this love potion and you give it to your son. Just a small price to pay to solve your problems. I guarantee its viability."

"And what about the girl? She would need it as well?"

"The girl has no choice in the matter. Just pay what I am owned and you will see the attitude change within your son."

"How quickly does it work?"

"Immediate," Master Joroku replied, shaking the vial gently.

"How much does he need?"

"Just a small drop."

Giovanni handed a bag of gold to the man. "Do not leave town, Master Joroku. I will add this potion to Agost's breakfast in the morn of the fourth night. If it does not work, I shall return."

Master Joroku bowed and smiled.

"I never lose," Giovanni whispered to Assistant.

"Yesss … *All Eyes.*"

In a sleep deprived state, Dante clung onto Tomassino's reins. "I am fire, call me Fuoco. I am fire, call me Fuoco …" Exhausted and hungry, Dante sighed. He had arrived at the shore of the English Channel. He stared at the ship that would soon depart for England. Dante counted out the exact amount he would need for the fare.

"Five will do for both," the captain said. "Your horse will have the best possible accommodations and sustenance with a guaranteed return."

After filling his belly, Dante fell asleep and arrived in England well rested. To Dante's excitement, the palatial House of Barrett was only a short distance from the docks. Dante was greeted warmly by an aging Lady Barrett.

"You bring news of my son, Patrick?"

Her lively, Irish brogue accent and bright red hair amused Dante. He bowed and smiled. "Yes, my … uh … Lady Barrett. I am Dante. I arrive with news of your son, Patrick." Dante stepped forward and handed her the white silhouette.

She read Patrick's note and smiled. "I see," she said. "So … my son has followed his star. I shall return with my answer shortly. Please wait here."

Looking about the plush English home, Dante knew that Patrick was a nobleman as he so declared. After several moments, Lady Barrett returned and handed him a sealed scroll with their family crest. She also returned the folded silhouette.

"I wish you Godspeed. I send with you my infinitus love to my son, Patrick."

Dante nodded. After slipping the silhouette into the open end of the scroll, Dante jumped onto Tomassino and flew like fire to the docks. In a few hours, he would rush through the back country, and again, spreading like wildfire … quickly and enduringly.

It was the morning of the fourth. Giovanni stared at the golden vial and nodded.

"Assistant, we must add this liquid to Agost's morning beverage." Giovanni rocked on the heels of his feet. "Agost will not know what hit him. He will soon be lovey-dovey over CallaLyly of the House of Montevelli of Siena."

"Yesss … *All Eyes.*"

Giovanni gazed into the shadows. "I cannot take any chances, Assistant."

After allowing several drops to fall into his drink, Giovanni sprinkled the remaining liquid over the eggs, and the bacon, and the buttered pancakes. The golden love potion oozed down the sides of the food as if mimicking a rich syrup.

"As I said, Assistant, now *all* his bites are covered."

After dropping the empty vial into his pocket, Giovanni watched as the kitchen marm entered.

"I will take this right up to Agost," the marm said. "Don't you worry none, signore."

Giovanni grabbed the tray from the woman and frowned. "Thank you. However, for this morn, I wish to have a quiet moment with my son."

With her eyes widening, she frowned. "There is always a first."

"Do come in, signora," Agost said. "I am famished."

"Then you will make your dishes clean of all their deliciousness, my son." Giovanni entered carrying the breakfast tray. He was smiling.

"Father?" Agost's eyes widened and his brows raised. "I am most puzzled. You have never greeted me in such a manner before. Nor do I believe you have ever stepped foot into my bedroom."

Giovanni placed the tray on the bed and nodded. "I believe that to be untrue."

"It is unfortunately very true," Agost replied.

Giovanni lifted the silver lids and allowed the aroma to fill the room. "Enjoy and prepare yourself, for we leave shortly for Siena and the marriage announcement." Giovanni hovered over his son taking in a deep whiff. "Try the pancakes. They were exceptional this morning, even if I do say so myself."

"If I take a bite," Agost shook his head, "will you leave?"

"Yes, of course."

Agost sliced into the syrupy pancakes. With a fork full, Agost slipped the sliver utensil into his mouth.

"Don't take forever," Giovanni ordered. "However, do eat. For your good health."

Agost watched as his father closed the door behind him. He then spit the food into a cloth napkin. He rinsed his mouth with water and retched into a jar.

"He must be trying to knock me out with an elixir or something. I'll wake up in the hands of that young woman and her family. Not here, Father, not today."

Agost walked in circles around his room. He had to think. His father had never greeted him in such a manner before nor delivered his meal. Suspicious, just too suspicious. Agost tossed his breakfast out the window. He laughed as it splattered across the greenery below.

He packed his clothes and grabbed a few pouches of gold that he had stolen from his father's study just last night. After writing a brief note, Agost arranged the empty tray on his bed. In the middle, was a note ...

> I am following my own star
> not yours. Farwell my
> father, Agost

Chapter Fifteen

It is said, "Don't believe what your eyes are telling you for all they show are limitations." This is not about limitations but our imaginary boundaries ...

Giovanni screamed and threw his son's note on the floor. "Assistant!" Giovanni paced across Agost's bedroom. "Assistant!"

"Yes, signore?"

"That fool is nothing but a fraud. Master Joroku will pay for this!"

Assistant read over the note and sighed. "Oh, no. What will we do without Agost to marry the girl?"

Giovanni paced. "Let me think ... let me think." He glared at his Assistant. "Ah-ha ... since I am paying for tonight's events anyway, we will still arrive on time. And the announcement will be declared as planned."

"But ... we do not have the groom, Agost." The Assistant frowned.

"Your point, Assistant?" Giovanni laughed. "We pretend."

"Pretend? That is most dishonest, *All Eyes.*"

"Shut up, you idiot. I will not be made a laughingstock by my buffoon of a son."

"Yesss ... *All Eyes.*" Assistant frowned and sighed.

"With or without my son, I will acquire that bank. One way or another. And ... Master Joroku will make it happen. I have already instructed him to appear during the announcement. He should have more than just potions up that draping sleeve of his. Besides, he still has *my* bag of gold and his potion came with a guarantee."

Assistant cringed.

"I never lose," Giovanni said. "Request my coach. We are leaving for Siena."

"Yess … *All Eyes.*"

The kitchen marm watched as the carriage left the grounds.

"Good riddance," she said. "What in the … quick come see!"

The kitchen staff ran to the window. They laughed as they watched a fox, a dog, a rabbit, and a frog frolic in the garden as if they were the best of friends.

"If I had not seen this with my own eyes, I would not have believed it," the kitchen marm said, laughing. "Wonder what has gotten into them today?"

Giovanni and Assistant found Tattleman in town selling the tiny vials of love.

"Tattleman is practically giving that stuff away! That Master Joroku pilfered me of my gold. I will make him pay, mark my words." Giovanni felt his blood pressure rising. "Assistant, grab that swindler by the collar and toss him into my coach. We're going to make a little visit to Joroku. I will wait for you in the carriage."

The door to Giovanni's coach flew open and Tattleman rolled onto the floor. Tattleman, keeping his gaze lowered, raised his head before bowing.

"Take me to your master!" Giovanni demanded.

As the carriage rocked the short distance to Joroku's tent, Giovanni glared at Tattleman who cowered on the floor. The coach stopped and the door opened. Assistant stepped over Tattleman and jumped to the ground. Grabbing the frightened man by the neck, Assistant soon threw Tattleman at his master's feet.

"And what is this?" Joroku asked, helping Tattleman to stand.

"My gold back, if you please ... with interest!" Giovanni yelled. "Your potion is phooey."

"Your son obviously did not digest the liquid," Master Joroku replied.

"I watched him take a bite. The potion was in his food. I placed it there myself."

"True, one bite is all it takes." Joroku paused as if in thought. "However, not possible," Joroku yelled. "The boy must have spit it out. My potion is foolproof. Quite powerful."

"My Assistant will pummel both of you. Give me my gold!"

"Yesss ... *All Eyes*." Assistant clenched his fists.

Tattleman fell to the floor and covered his head. He moaned and scooted closer to Joroku.

Master Joroku raised his hands and his five-inch golden nails shimmered like a full moon. He flicked his fingers and Tattleman floated into the air. He hovered above their heads.

Giovanni's and Assistant's eyes widened.

Joroku lowered his hands and Tattleman slowly landed at Giovanni's feet. Without a sound, Joroku raised his hands again and waved them over the floor. Giovanni and Assistant fell to their knees. Neither could move.

Tattleman inched his way over to Joroku and whispered.

Joroku laughed. "I have news that will cost you more bags of gold." Joroku removed his hands from the frozen men. "Stand."

Giovanni and Assistant stood but could not remove their eyes from the strange man, Joroku.

"The night of the gala … Tattleman was sitting in a tree and overheard a young man named Patrick. He was talking with the girl, CallaLyly."

Giovanni's eyes widened. "Go on."

"Patrick is no peasant. Very rich nobleman. Large inheritance. He will invest in the Commoner's Bank of Siena. That will allow the bank to continue. Maybe expand in the future."

"I cannot allow that to happen." Giovanni glanced at Assistant then back at Joroku. "You must have more than just a pesky love potion for me?"

"Will cost you more gold, much more gold."

Giovanni's mind twirled through the possibilities. "Get rid of Patrick and CallaLyly and we have a deal." Giovanni snarled.

"Four bags of gold," Joroku said.

"Done." Giovanni retrieved the pouches from his jacket and laughed as he handed them over.

Joroku pulled out a duplicate of Lyly's and Patrick's silhouette from his copper pot and Giovanni grinned.

As a veil of sadness flooded through her, Lyly's tears fell. Slowly, she tied a purple ribbon around her waist. She studied herself in the mirror. The blue silk dress fitted tightly. It was her mother's choice for the evening. An evening that would start a lifetime of heartache. If Patrick did not appear with Dante and some good news, her life would soon be over. She was sure her parents felt just as disappointed about the arranged marriage. A contract set into motion by her father and sealed with the witnessing of the union between their bank and the Banca de'Leon. Nothing could be undone if the proof did not arrive on time.

Lyly was to remain in her father's study until her mother came for her. Glancing at the clock, she sighed. It was almost time for the announcement. Stepping to the lanterns, she blew out a few candles to allow the shadows to consume the corners and mimic the deep sorrow that now slept in the recesses of her soul.

As her mother's footsteps echoed down the hall, Lyly sank into the closest chair.

"I told Domenico earlier. No peasants allowed … nor townsfolk … nor farmers … nor merchants … nor entrepreneurs."

Assistant nodded.

"The last thing I want are those hens and eggs and legumes." Giovanni puffed out his chest and sighed. "Unless they are presented as part of the feast."

The carriage pulled to a stop in front of the House of Montevelli. The horses, decorated with red blankets and golden trim, glittered in the lamp light. Giovanni waited as the horseman opened the carriage door. He stepped out and tugged on his deep navy-blue pants. After adjusting his velvet jacket, he waved and smiled at CallaLyly's parents waited for him on the stoop.

After nodding to several nobles, he glanced into the coach and frowned, "Agost, please stay until Assistant comes for you. Better this way."

"Patrick!" Lyly said, running to him. "I thought you were Mother."

"With all the nobles arriving, I had no difficulty entering the house."

Lyly giggled. "You're dressed just like the valets." She smiled as she admired his knee length pants and flowing white shirt.

"Dante is almost here," Patrick said. "We shall have our proof."

Lyly twirled across the room. "I will hug you!"

Lyly ran to Patrick as the study door flew open. Master Joroku stepped inside.

Swinging back and forth, Lyly peered at Tyler. "My life was to be not as I had imagined or planned."

Tyler shook his head. "Where I come from, people choose who they marry. Not forced into it with someone they hate. That is crazy."

"If crazy means out of the ordinary, then here it is ordinary. Family loyalty requires me to respect my arranged marriage."

"Still nuts," Tyler replied. "I want to marry someone I love, not someone that my parents pick out. And especially not for money."

"I believe that I like that part of your world."

Tyler sat up straighter and smiled.

Dante rode past the stables and straight to the entrance. He passed several nobles as they arrived in their carriages. He needed to find Patrick. After asking several valets, one motioned Dante in the direction of the lobby. Instead, Dante walked the horse to the holding pen.

"Well hello, my friend," a valet said. "You have returned from your training, I see."

"How did you find out about my training?" Dante asked. He hoped that the gold was still a secret.

"We Panteras are tired of being called Nonna (*Grandma*) since we haven't won a Palio in almost fifty years. I heard your name spoken with others as a possible jockey since the other was taken with injury."

"Really?" Dante asked. His heart leaped to hear such wonderful news. Maybe he had a chance after all. "Tell me more when I return later, my friend."

After tying Tomassino to a ring, Dante searched for a place to hide the scroll. He remembered a loose stone in the garden wall. Carefully he pulled out the rock. He glanced around before pushing the paper into the hole. Dante replaced the stone and ran to find Patrick. He would retrieve the scroll later. Better to be safe than sorry. If anyone should steal the papers away from him, all would be lost.

Dante slipped through the shadows and aimed for the study. He opened the door and stepped into darkness.

"Patrick?" Dante whispered.

No answer.

Dante froze as dark shadows swirled through the room. A wind as strong as a summer tornado spun yet moved nothing. Dante hid in the darkness, allowing his eyes to adjust. The winds raged and rang through his ears. He inched his way to the massive windows and heavy drapery. The dark cloth provided the perfect hiding space. His heart raced. Peeking around the curtain, Dante gasped as shards of light flashed. Dante fought against the confusion that threatened his reality when a lightning bolt shattered across the middle of the room.

Patrick held Lyly in his arms. It was as if their feet were somehow locked together. Dante wanted to help the two, but how? He watched as Master Joroku glared wickedly at the young couple. The man's multi-colored hat and long red robe seemed to glow with each wave of his arms. Master Joroku tossed several sheets of paper onto the floor. Each piece came alive and crawled toward the couple as if vines growing on a trellis.

Sounds of gibberish filled Dante's ears. Ghost-like buildings floated quietly through the air as if only whisps of smoke. A medieval scene flashed before Dante's eyes. The curtains vibrated from his trembling hands. Several Siena buildings floated in next. A ghost of an olive tree flashed past.

Farmhouses and vineyards? Are those sheep?

Dante tried to inch closer but his feet refused to move. He was trapped behind the drapery. As the ghostly objects disappeared into the sheets of paper, he shuddered as they formed a miniature print. Each arranged itself according to the directions of Master Joroku. It was as if the man was painting a scene through his symphonic hands.

When the tornado dwindled, a bolt of lightning streamed from Master Joroku's sleeve. It wrapped around Patrick as if a noose. A flash and Patrick was yanked from Lyly's arms. Patrick faded into the darkness then reappeared as a black mist. No wait … a cat! A black cat with glowing copper eyes.

Joroku swiped his hand along the floor and Lyly's feet jerked out from under her. She hovered delicately for only a moment over the paper. As Joroku moved his hands, Lyly spun as freely as a spinning wheel. Several times she twirled. As if with no friction, Lyly spun faster and faster. Joroku pounded his hand into the air and Lyly was sucked into the cloth paper. *Lyly was gone.*

Master Joroku's fingers moved effortless as though playing a piano. He grabbed the growling cat and petted him a few times. Then with his long golden index finger, Joroku emblazed a sun, a star, and a moon onto the side of Patrick's fur. The golden emblems shined as if just falling from the heavens.

The study door flew open and the cat hissed. Master Joroku dropped the cat and watched as Patrick ran into the lobby and then into the courtyard. Several women screamed as the cat scurried through the waiting noblemen. The cloth paper twirled into rolls and, as if they had legs, flew into the anteroom. Master Joroku slammed the door as he walked out.

Breathing heavily, Dante fell to the floor. He struggled to hold his weight. "Where can I hide from such evil?"

Giovanni presented himself as the life of the party. His *All Eyes* were in top form, giving him a complete circular view. Loud and excited voices filled the courtyard. Giovanni glanced over at the darkened study windows and smiled.

All should be over with soon.

Giovanni watched as Delfina and Domenico stood solemnly near the tables. Their faces, morose and sullen, gave Giovanni a chuckle. Master Joroku entered the courtyard and walked slowly with his head held high. He nodded as the guests greeted him.

Giovanni grabbed the cue and stepped forward. With a puffed-out chest, he spoke loudly. "Lady Montevelli, those of importance have arrived. May we begin? Agost is waiting patiently to join Lady CallaLyly. He is as joyful as I. We will soon union our Houses, and I will guarantee their success." Giovanni rocked on his heels and gleamed.

Domenico nodded to his wife and sighed before stepping over to Giovanni. Delfina headed for the study to find her daughter.

"We are excited for this union." Domenico smiled and raised his hands into the air.

"Assistant, please bring Agost to us." Giovanni rubbed his nose and looked around the courtyard. He hummed a short tune.

Running as if fleeing a fight, Delfina raced to her husband. She grabbed his arm and shook with such force that Domenico almost lost his balance. As they whispered back and forth, his hands jerked through the air.

Giovanni watched as Assistant hurried across the lawn. Holding back a laugh, he leaned forward allowing Assistant to now whisper into his ear.

"Oh, dear," Giovanni yelled out, his voice flat and unemotional. "Nobles and noblewomen ... oh, the most dreadful of dread!" Giovanni bent over and grabbed his stomach. "Oh, woe is me!" He stood and wiped his forehead with the back of his hand. "My son ... oh, the shame ... Agost is so traumatized and embarrassed he does not even possess the strength to leave our carriage." Giovanni moaned. "Oh, may the lord help us!"

The courtyard grew silent. Only mumbled whispers could be heard.

Giovanni cleared his throat and glared over at Delfina and Domenico. "You!" he yelled. "It is *your* daughter who has shamed our families!"

The crowd gasped.

Giovanni glanced around and sneered. "Assistant informs me that *your* daughter, CallaLyly of the House of Montevelli, has left town with a blonde peasant!" Giovanni moaned and grabbed his stomach again. "And ... on the back of a black horse no less!"

"How dreadful for Agost!" a man's voice yelled out.

"Yes, yes, poor Agost," a female voice said.

"Oh, the shame!" another voice yelled from somewhere within the anxious crowd.

"Yes, oh, yes," Giovanni said, leaning against Assistant. "My son now requires my personal attention of the highest order."

"Dreadful!" a guest yelled.

"What delightful gossip," a woman said who was standing near Giovanni.

Giovanni turned to her and bowed.

Delfina burst into tears. She ran into the house and disappeared inside the darkness. Domenico stood alone in the courtyard. He gazed into the heavens and shook his head. His bank would be worth only pennies tomorrow.

"Twenty-four hours," Giovanni whispered to Domenico. "Plenty of time to vacate."

Tattleman cringed as he splattered the glue on the wall. He sighed as the smelly sludge changed from a shiny cream to dull white. Then he carefully placed a roll of paper onto the wall of the windowless anteroom. With each stroke of the brush, Tattleman knowingly imprisoned CallaLyly for an eternity.

Each covering was of a different scene and a different color. It was important to allow Master Joroku's prisoner to have the ability to enjoy the different avenues of life now that she would forever be tied to a reality of a two-dimensional world. With each roll pasted to the wall, Tattleman read off Joroku's incantation to seal in the magic.

With the last of the paper covering the door, Tattleman sealed the room from the rest of the world. He had already carefully blocked and covered the door from the outside so that no one would remember the small room that was hidden behind the old study. When the last toile was firmly in place, Tattleman closed his eyes and sent a message to Joroku. Joroku blinked twice and Tattleman faded into a mist and seeped effortlessly through the wall. He reappeared next to Joroku holding a large brush in one hand and a bucket of glue in the other.

"Thank you," Tattleman said, gasping for fresh air.

"All done?" Joroku asked.

Tattleman nodded before walking away.

Giovanni laughed. "That room shall never be missed." He grabbed his belt and rocked back and forth on his heels. "Thank you, Master Joroku. No one will ever know." He chuckled and picked up the torn piece of the seafaring paper. "The young nobleman in there as well?"

Master Joroku shook his head. "No … something better." He gave Giovanni a crooked smile. "He is now an immortal feline."

Giovanni laughed louder until his stomach ached. "Delicious, indeed!"

"Yesss … *All Eyes*," Assistant replied, nodding.

Giovanni turned to Assistant and laughed again. "Assistant! Call in my loans. I wish to be paid in full. Bankrupt these commoners, and I shall sell off their homes and their lands. I will finally be rid of those vermin forever."

"Yesss … *All Eyes*."

"I never lose!"

Lyly cried as she listened through the wallpapered door. Her life, or what was left of it, was forever sealed within a two-dimensional world.

Chapter Sixteen

It is said, "A prisoner can only be imprisoned if their mind allows it." This is not about being imprisoned but rather of using one's mind to escape ...

Lyly yawned and stretched her arms out over her head. Feeling a tingling in her toes, she shook her legs to alleviate the discomfort. Her eyes felt swollen so she allowed them to linger shut just a little longer.

Not too much more, or my day shall be wasted. I need to rise.

The nightmare seemed so real, and Lyly bolted up and forced her eyes open. A bright yellow glow surrounded her. She squinted and gazed out at the horizon ... if that was a horizon. A blue green forest now filled her view. A Tuscany farmland ... no a sprinkle of farmhouses and sheep.

"Everything's so strange looking." She glanced up and sighed. *I slept under a blue green tree with lanterns and a swing?*

Lyly glanced around. "Where am I?" She stood and the world twirled around her. She leaned against the tree and rubbed her head. The tree felt somewhat normal to use as a support. However, as her hand ran along the large trunk, the bark felt smooth and not rough as a tree should.

"This is not wood ... it's ..."

She touched the lantern and it too felt flimsy and not firm.

"Paper?"

She took a few steps toward the house and stopped.

"Everything looks ... flat."

Her heart pounded as her thoughts surrounded her. She felt challenged as if her reality had been washed clean from a tsunami. Lyly glanced down at her blue silk dress and brown leather slippers.

"I wore this for the announcement ... I waited in father's study ..." A bright light had blinded her and now she remembered. "Patrick!" Lyly screamed. "Patrick, where are you?"

Lyly sat and rocked back and forth. Her tears fell and her body shook. Her memory replayed over and over through her mind. Several times, she wiped her eyes dry. Lyly screamed. She screamed again and again but the sound didn't echo. Her voice was flat and lifeless. Lyly touched her feet, then her legs, and then her stomach. Everything seemed to be intact but she had been sucked into a dark void. How could she have survived? Lyly stood. The world no longer seemed real. She screamed and reached out to touch anything.

"I must be dreaming," she said as she ran down the hill. "I'm inside a nightmare. I just need to wake up."

Lyly pinched her arm. Nothing happened. She pinched it harder until it hurt. Nothing happened.

"I'm still here." Lyly frowned.

She slapped her face several times and again nothing happened. The horizon looked flat. The tree was taller than her but in a different way. The hill was a hill but didn't rise toward the heavens as the hills that surrounded her home. Nothing moved, then again, everything moved. Lyly walked up to a cow and it raised its eyes and stared at her. She touched the cow and it felt smooth and cold. She pushed on the cow and the animal would not move. It remained in the same spot and chewed on its cud without moving its mouth. Only the cow's eyes moved.

"This is all wrong!" Lyly touched the fence and sighed. "Why am I here?"

Lyly's eyes slowly adjusted to the bright yellow with a blue-green hue background. She blinked several times. Within the Tuscany landscape, the vineyards, cows, chickens, and other animals stood rigid and silent. Nothing moved, not even the wind.

"Hello, anyone here?" Lyly ran through the field and the tall grass didn't brush up against her legs. Nothing touched her legs or feet not even the ground.

Lyly ran up to a sheep and stared at it. She tried to walk around the animal, however, she could not. She could walk up to it, in front of it, and stand on the other side of it, however, she could not step behind it. It was as if the animal was part of the horizon.

The ground felt firm, and then again, it felt as if it was nothing. She reached down to grab a hand full of grass and her fingers touched only a smooth and cold surface.

"Oh, my," Lyly said.

Near the horizon, a young girl sat on a swing. Lyly glanced around and looked for anyone else. Lyly ran toward the young girl. At the bottom of the hill, Lyly's feet slipped out from under her and she fell against the hard ground. Something white and sticky covered her hands. Placing her hands to her face, she took in a deep breath. Lyly licked her fingers ... "Paste?"

The girl sat on a swing and did not move. Her back was toward Lyly and she could only see her hair that waved down to her waist. Lyly wiped the slimy white substance against her hips. Shaking her head, she approached the girl on the swing.

"Please accept my apology as I slid on something," Lyly said as she stepped closer. "Not a ladylike entrance I must say."

The girl remained silent and stiff.

"Good day to you. I am CallaLyly of the House of Montevelli of Siena. Please call me Lyly." Lyly stared at the silent girl. "Please excuse my rudeness but why is it that your hair and hands are outlined a blue green? Is that the color of your native country or land?"

Again, no response.

Lyly stepped closer and reached out to touch the girl's shoulder. Instead of a warm rounded back, Lyly touched a cold and smooth surface. She yanked her hand away and screamed. Again, Lyly could not step in front of the girl to see her face. She could only step to the sides or behind.

"You are nothing more than paper!"

The more Lyly glared at the girl, the more Lyly's heart pounded.

"Oh, no!" Lyly whispered.

The back of the dress, although now a blue green, matched the back of Lyly's dress. The slippers matched her slippers. Lyly ran down the hill and up the next. Another girl, with her back toward Lyly sat motionless wearing the same outfit.

Lyly screamed and fell to the ground. She cried and covered her eyes.

"All the girls are me!"

Patrick crouched between the bushes and stared at the torches. He couldn't see much from where he sat. He ran to a tree and studied it.

"If I'm really a cat, I should be able to make that."

Patrick stepped back and ran. His hind legs stretched and propelled him high into the air. He spread out his arms and legs and his stomach slapped against the branch. Patrick coughed once as he landed on his side back on the ground.

"That didn't work," he hissed.

Again, Patrick stepped back and ran. He jumped and this time aimed his claws at the branch. He landed, as any cat would, onto the limb. He meowed once and sat.

"Ah-ha! I did it."

He jumped across to the next higher branch. Taking his time, he eventually made it up high enough to see what he needed to see. Patrick glanced out over the Montevelli estate. He frowned as he looked at his furry paws.

From where he sat, the aroma of cooked meat filled the air. His stomach growled and the urge to eat felt overwhelming. Patrick jumped from branch to branch before landing back on the ground.

"Not bad," he said.

Patrick ran toward the tables. Large men's shoes and ladies' heels were everywhere. He tore through the courtyard and darted between the legs. Several women screamed. Men jumped aside as a black furry mess darted past. Patrick couldn't seem to overcome a powerful urge to eat. As he knocked over the dishes and bowls, he screeched, "Meow!" Darting from table to table, he grabbed a piece of meat before scurrying toward the bushes.

"Scat you cat!" a staff member yelled out, snapping a damp cloth.

"Get this creature away from me!" A lady stomped her heels, and a man swung his foot at him.

Patrick sat between the thick leaves and twigs and panted. His mind was intact but what happened to his body? Something kept swatting him from behind. He turned around in circles chasing a long black cord until he realized that the long black cord was a part of him.

I have a tail!

He sighed and ate the small portion of stolen meat. He peeked through the leaves and stared at the man who had tried to kick him. *Scat you cat,* was what that man had said. Patrick glanced over at the study window and a bright light flashed across his memory. *A lightning bolt had hit me!*

Patrick remembered trying to protect Lyly from the mystic, Joroku. He closed his eyes and allowed his mind to wander. Joroku had pulled them apart. Then ghost-like objects floated across the room. She had disappeared into a paper roll and a thick mist had devoured him. The pain he felt filled him with dread and he hissed. Patrick's heart pounded as he scooted deeper into the bushes. He glanced down at his side and stared at the golden brands. Patrick licked his paws and cleaned his whiskers. Some of the food that he had stepped on still clung to his fur and tasted good.

How long shall I stay a cat?

Lyly ran. Maybe there was an end to this madness and a way home.

"Mother … Father!" Lyly's heart pounded. "Mother! Father! I am here. I don't know where I am. Please answer me!"

No response.

Lyly ran and the brightness of the yellow background slowly faded and a white line filled her vision. Past the line, the glow of buildings outlined in black filled her view. Lyly reached out and the white light felt a little sticky. She took several steps back and ran. When she reached the white slimy stuff, she jumped and landed hard. She rolled twice before standing. Glancing down at her dress, she gasped. Instead of the blue green hue, she was now as creamy as a glass of fresh milk.

Lyly frowned. "That's the circular amphitheater of the Piazza del Campo," she said, studying her surroundings.

Lyly walked toward the white buildings that were outlined in black and sighed. No horses … no people … yet everything looked … flat. She stepped up to the Mangia Tower. She reached for the door and her hand slapped against the hard surface. Touching a window provided the same result. Her fingers simply slipped across the smooth paper. Lyly walked across the square and stood in front of the storefronts. Peering into a window, she sighed — the room was bare. Memories of shopping with her mother flooded her thoughts.

"Mother!" she cried out. "Mother, please find me!"

The fountain sprayed the water into the creamy air. Lyly touched her throat. No feeling of thirst. Lyly touched her stomach. No feeling of hunger.

Am I to eat and drink paper?

Lyly ran to the fountain and reached into the water. It didn't feel wet. She sighed. The flowing sprays were nothing more than vertical lines. She sat on the edge of the fountain and frowned.

"Everything is made of paper. This whole world is fake." She spread out her fingers and wiggled them. She closed her eyes. She opened her mouth. "Everything seems to be working. I am still alive. I am not paper."

Off in the distance, the Duomo, made of white with a black outline, rose upward toward the clouds. She thought about the real cathedral in Siena and smiled. It was constructed from black and white marble stripes. Lyly spent many hours in worship there with her parents and friends. Her baby brother was even baptized in its massive inner sanctum.

"An answer?" she whispered.

Lyly screamed as she touched the windows and doors of the massive building. Nothing worked. Everything felt smooth and cold to the touch. Lyly walked up to the doors and kicked. Her foot bounced off the massive oak.

I shall keep venturing forward.

As she walked, identical replicas of her Siena town filled her view. She sat next to the third recreation of her town's fountain and screamed. Lyly picked on the white substance that had now dried on her skin.

"I guess I'll use my spit to clean myself."

Rubbing her legs, Lyly remembered Master Joroku spitting on the silhouette. His spit was more of a glue than saliva. Her heart warmed as she thought about Patrick and holding his hand. Lyly stared into the cream-colored clouds and tears filled her eyes.

"I had found happiness and comfort gazing into your eyes, Patrick." Lyly wiped away another tear. "I wonder where you are now. Were you the black cat that lay on the floor? It had to be you for you are not here with me now. Are you suffering and as confused as I?"

She thought about the evening and the joy she had felt with Patrick. Those few precious moments allowed her to forget about the future and the arranged marriage to Agost. Did the arranged marriage have anything to do with that mystic? And how was it that Master Joroku's powers were so strong? Did Agost's father orchestrate all of this?

Dawn crested across the pink and green marbled Duomo of Florence. Throughout the darkness, Patrick had hidden inside the back of a stagecoach. He now jumped to the dirt and stared at the Florencian estate. He had found a secluded garden and walked into the morning sunlight. After he recited his prayer of the Breastplate, which was a protective prayer, he sighed. *I need this now more than ever.*

He arched his back and stretched out his front paws, which forced his tail into the air. His stomach growled as his hunger grew. A mouse scurried across the grass. Without thinking, Patrick pounced and grabbed the struggling creature between his sharp teeth. His new body seemed to have a mind of its own. In a way, it felt as if he was watching himself do things. Necessary things. Nasty things. Patrick cracked the creature's neck and tore into the fresh meat. The last few morsels, he ate in a gentleman's fashion. After licking his paws clean, Patrick sat back and again stared into the morning sun.

My initiation into this life has begun.

The urge to drink pulled Patrick from his private thoughts. A small pond sent an aroma of wetness across the yard. He gazed at his reflection and nodded.

"I'm a rather handsome cat."

His large ears and dark brows adorned his bright copper eyes. The rising sun sprayed him with warmth. He glanced at his side and sighed. Vertical golden brands of a sun, star, and moon reflected brightly from his dark fur. He thought for a moment before shrugging and sipping on the water. With his tummy full, Patrick jumped onto a brick wall and rested in the warm sunlight. He thought about Lyly and he still fancied her. He had been powerless to protect her from that madman. Now, he wondered what had happened to her. Was she really inside a roll of wallpaper? And if yes, how would she survive?

Dante would have returned with joyous news from Patrick's mum by now. However, Patrick would not be there to save Lyly's family from bankruptcy. And Lyly's parents would be distraught over their daughter's sudden disappearance. He licked his fur and yawned. The warmth felt wonderful and he closed his eyes. As sleep engulfed his world, Patrick's last thought was of finding another mouse.

Lyly's mind wandered as she watched a red glow appear and then disappear.

"Now what could that be?"

She stopped at the edge of the cream-colored world and stared out over the wide, white stripe. Stepping back, Lyly ran and jumped over the wet slime. She landed on her hands and feet. Glancing up, she gasped.

"A recreation of my bedroom?" Lyly stood and looked around.

Sitting on her bed was another her. Only this time, her face was visible. Lyly walked over to the girl and stared into her eyes. They were dull and empty and gave Lyly the chills. In this room, her bed was not as flat and smooth. She could touch the mattress and move the blankets. She yawned and her eyes felt heavy. Lyly sat on the bed and stared at herself that was just sitting there. She shrugged once before resting against the pillow and falling asleep.

Lyly woke and sat up. She stared at the girl and sighed. *Still inside my nightmare.* She glanced at her duplicate and said, "Good morn, my lady."

Lyly wasn't sure if it was morning or evening. The sun did not seem to rise or fall. She stood and stretched out her arms and brushed her fingers through her hair. Her mirror still stood in the corner. She stepped forward and sighed. No reflection greeted her. She touched it and frowned.

"Paper."

Lyly touched her stomach. She still did not feel hungry or thirsty. She wiped her eyes and they were no longer swollen. Lyly left her small room and walked back into her nightmare. Instead of a countryside to explore, more bedrooms lay ahead and all were the same.

"Mother? Father?" Lyly yelled out, however, all remained eerily silent.

Lyly avoided the paper duplicates of herself that were sitting on each bed. She continued to walk and search for a way home. In the far distance, puffy white and blue clouds loomed. She hurried her pace and stopped at the solid white line. Again she ran and jumped across, and this time, landed near a red pagoda. The lush, green gardens and a small, white bridge that crossed over a clear stream was beautiful.

"This looks to be something I studied of the orient once."

Lyly ran to the bridge and gazed over the railing. She frowned.

"Just as I thought. Lines that resemble flowing water and flat fish."

Lyly walked and passed many pagodas with lush gardens. She touched each one hopeful that something would open. Their beautiful red coloring was just paint on paper. Garden after garden remained empty of people. Lyly yawned several times. She fought to stay awake.

Fighting the desire to sleep, Lyly jumped into the most colorful of worlds. Holding up her hands, she shielded her eyes from the bright light.

"Oh, my … a deck of cards?"

Lyly ran up to a golden fence that encircled a palace and royal courtyard. A black and white chess set was laid out and ready to be played.

Lyly giggled. "No people, just chess pieces."

Lyly walked up to the queen that towered over her. She placed her hands on the queen's skirt and pushed. Only a smooth and cold surface pushed back. The set was not real and was blended into the background.

Lyly yawned. Her eyes felt heavy. *Why am I so tired?* Lyly ran until she could run no more. As she sat on the smooth and cold surface, her eyes closed and sleep surrounded her.

An easy supply of food came from scraps and leftovers at the outdoor cafes. Patrick watched from a distance and waited. When the humans stood to leave, Patrick jumped. He grabbed the leftover chunks and ran into the nearest bushes to eat. Long tablecloths were the best hiding areas. Sitting under a table and licking his paws, a sense of being watched crawled up Patrick's back. He hissed and turned.

"I've been watching you." A Siamese cat with only one eye hunched down and hissed.

Patrick arched his spine and could feel his fur rising off his back. "I have no qualms with you, my cat friend." Patrick replied. "I'll share my bounty if it pleases you."

"You are no cat!" the Siamese cat hissed. "What are you?"

"On the contrary, I'm the finest of all cats and I desire no trouble."

The two circled each other dancing a sideways dance.

"Where I come from," the Siamese snarled, "it is wicked magic that makes you like us. Your brands display your curse. None of us will honor you." The one-eyed cat jumped onto Patrick's back and dug in his claws. Patrick twisted and lunged and grabbed hold of his new friend's neck. He bit down hard and his friend hissed.

Patrick freed himself and backed out from under the table. He darted across the street and down a dark alley. A bright light flashed and the ground rumbled. Droplets fell and puddled surrounded him. He ran through the streets and into the forest. Mud had formed from where the horses had passed. He rolled through the sludge and it clung easily to his fur. He stood and stepped aside. Glancing back, he smiled.

No one shall ever see my brands again.

The stray cat that had rolled around with him earlier reminded Patrick of his brothers and when they would rough house together. Being the middle son, Patrick often felt jealous of his older brother. And his younger brother always blamed Patrick for everything that went wrong. It was one of the reasons his parents sent him on his quest to *find his star.*

Patrick sat under a tree that sheltered him from the rain. He licked his wounds and thought of his family. It hurt to believe that he may never see them again.

Lyly stopped running when her world changed into an endless blue sea filled with green boats and seafaring vessels. They appeared to be moving against an opal-colored sky, milky white, with shades of various pastels.

Lyly stared out at the endless sea and said, "Red sky at night, sailors take delight. Red sky in morning, sailors take warning."

What she was looking at was not real. Lyly stepped onto the ocean and shook her head. As she walked, she touched the boats that she passed. All were smooth and cold. She searched for a comfortable place to rest. Everything was flat and rigid. No place to sleep. No place to rest. The last boat was pushed up against a blue green line that raised high into the heavens and far below her feet. Her eyes fought to remain open. Her legs felt heavy and her back ached. She stood at another wide, white line and stared out at the yellow horizon. She ran and jumped and cried. Lyly had landed back where she had started. She stood and walked over to the only empty swing. She sat and allowed her legs to rest.

"So sleepy," Lyly whispered.

Before closing her eyes, she stared at the lanterns. A light twinkled from somewhere deep behind the glass. Lyly knelt by the bottom lantern and stared into the light. From somewhere inside, she could see Tattleman. He was holding a bucket and a brush. As the man walked away, Lyly screamed out.

"Help me!"

Tattleman stopped and turned. He stared into the lantern from the other side. "I'm sorry." Tattleman stepped back and faded into a light mist. The room darkened and the world around her threw her back into the shadows.

Lyly rested her head under the large tree. She closed her eyes and allowed the powers of her dreams to shimmer. She thought of Patrick and wondered what he was experiencing. Was he thinking of her?

"I'm sorry, Patrick," Lyly whispered. "I caused your grief. You were just trying to help me and my family. Please forgive me. I long to be with you once again." Remembering a line from Patrick's morning prayer, Lyly whispered. "And please send me the help I need to return to my life and family and Patrick ... amen."

Chapter Seventeen

It is said, "Many are called to the feast but few are chosen to eat." This is not about the food but the selection ...

"Our world as we knew it had ended," Lyly said. "I had watched as Patrick was turned into a cat and disappeared and did nothing. I cannot comprehend the life my parents and baby brother led after Giovanni de'Leon bankrupted them. It makes me want to wail as my family never learned the truth about me and my imprisonment. I must stay positive. There must be a reason I awoke in this toile some two-hundred years later. Here I am and here you are. Tyler, what is your plan to rescue me?"

Tyler's heart reached out to Lyly. He sat quietly wondering how he could fix everything. "Uh ... I don't know. I mean, you living on a wall is cool and all, but ..."

Tyler allowed his mind to roll. This place was a two-dimensional world and, therefore, the transformation had to involve physics. Could the real-world actually reverse and turn inside out? And the celestial alignment at midnight ... would that reverse everything again?

"I think ..."

"I am tired of living in the toiles, Tyler. That strange word you keep repeating. *Cool*, what does cool mean?" Lyly tilted her head and frowned. "Does cool have anything to do with an immediate plan to solve the repeating unreality that surrounds me?"

Tyler shook his head. He glanced around and sighed. "Cool just means that it's awesome."

"Awesome? I do not know that word either."

Oh, boy, here we go again. Stepping away from the tree and Lyly, Tyler stared into the never dimming sky. Then it hit him as if an apple had just fallen from a tree. "Did you say, same repeating … unreality?"

"Yes. Why?"

Tyler smiled. Blinking several times, he replied, "If there was a way in … then there *is* a way out. Everything mirrors from inside a universe."

"Awesome," Lyly said, laughing. "Where do we find these mirrors?"

Tyler shook his head. "I need to find these portals or holes you've talked about. There has to be a sequence, something we can decipher."

"Follow me, Tyler Charles." Tyler followed Lyly down the path. When they reached the edge of the toile, they stopped and she whispered, "There is a problem."

"What problem?" Tyler stood and stared into the nothingness. "Where are we going? Lyly, there is nothing here."

"There was," Lyly replied. "But we are no longer in the toile room."

"What do you mean by *toile room*?"

"The portals, as you call them, are on another toile. And the toiles are in the anteroom."

"You mean you must be next to the other paper to travel across?"

"Yes," Lyly said, crying. "Oh, what shall we ever do, Tyler? We are now forever locked inside this one panel inside your bathroom!"

"Wait," Tyler yelled out. "You follow me now."

Tyler led Lyly to the top of the panel. Stepping near the corner, he pointed. "Is this what you are looking for?"

"I don't understand."

"You are locked inside a mini-universe. May not be one that we are used to, but a universe all the same. This panel was ripped. Therefore, a small piece must still remain attached inside that room."

"Yes, yes," Lyly cried out. "Yes, I can see it, we can go now."

The two stepped into the mist and the light dimmed. "Must be dark in this room," Tyler said.

"Yes, it is," Lyly replied. "However, I know my way around."

Tyler glanced up and the sky lit only along the horizon. He laughed as he followed Lyly.

"What is funny?" Lyly asked.

"We are definitely inside the other room." He stopped and pointed to the horizon. "That must be my aunt's work light."

Again, the two stood by the edge. Tyler turned and glanced over his shoulder. Behind, the world was a light greenish yellow. Straight ahead, the world was a long brightly lit highway. Beyond the thin white strip was a horizon of indigo blues and bright reds.

"What is this?" he asked, reaching out and touching the white strip.

"Oh, that is nothing," Lyly replied. "It is just where the two papers meet."

"Can it hurt us?"

"Of course not, we remain inside the panels." Lyly laughed. "Not in the glue. Follow me."

Lyly ran across the white strip and stopped. She signaled for Tyler to follow. He took a step and paused. With one foot on the white strip, he tried to grab onto the edge of the toile for support. However, his fingers refused to touch anything and fell into nothingness. His heart pounded and his hands shook. He glanced over at Lyly and frowned.

Lyly huffed and walked back to Tyler. "What are you doing?"

Tyler shook his head.

Lyly sighed and grabbed his hand. She yanked him across the white line. "Are you good now, Tyler Charles?"

Tyler glanced back at the white line and nodded.

The two walked toward a large structure that towered above the other wooden buildings. Various shops lined the vacant streets.

"Where are all the people?" Tyler asked.

"No other people," Lyly replied. "I was placed in here alone."

"How long have you been stuck in these toiles?"

"Over two-hundred and fifty years from my calculations."

Tyler sighed again as he followed her down the streets.

"We must pass another town square and …"

"And what?" Tyler asked.

"A half of one."

"Half?"

"You'll see."

Tyler walked slightly behind Lyly and studied the landscape. Every so often he'd glance at the horizon and wonder what his aunt was doing. Then he'd laugh as he envisioned her face if he suddenly stuck his head out of one of the papers.

The two entered the third town and stopped. Lyly pointed to the fountain. "Look, Tyler, half a fountain."

"Now, *that* is too cool!" Tyler ran to the strange structure and watched as half of the water fell back into the small pool. The other half simply disappeared into nothingness. He walked to the edge and tried to glance over. All that was there was another white line. "This is just nuts. The water is cut in half."

Lyly stood near a house and giggled. "Tyler, this is a depiction of the rooms of my home. Master Joroku pulled all of this from my memory. This is the only room that feels real."

"Oh?"

Lyly nodded. "I can actually sleep between the blankets."

Tyler chuckled. "Probably a good thing your house wasn't on the edge of town, otherwise it would have been cut into two just like that fountain out there."

Lyly laughed. "This whole place is a replica of our town square. Its name is Piazza del Campo. We hold our festivals here and the Palio … our horse race."

"Pizza del Campo." Tyler mimicked her accent.

Lyly giggled. "Not pizza … piazza."

"Piazza," Tyler repeated.

Lyly pointed up. "That is our bell tower, the Mangia Tower that's housed in the Siena town hall."

Looking up, Tyler replied, "That man-gee tower is tall." Glancing to his right, he pointed at a black and white façade. "What's that?"

"That is the Siena Duomo."

"Doo-mo?"

"Our cathedral," Lyly replied.

"Great, why don't we start there and end up back here? If you see anything that moves it might be a portal, so try opening it."

Searching amidst the half town, they studied everything that might open. Door handles, knobs, and windows proved futile. Nothing moved nor allowed to be grasped.

Lyly sighed. "Maybe the piazza will have something."

Wanting to cheer her up, Tyler thought before replying, "I'll race you."

Tyler arrived in the half square and watched as Lyly dragged her feet. She stared at the ground as she walked. Tyler lifted his leg as if he was mounting a horse.

"Lyly, watch ..." As if a jockey preparing to ride, Tyler skipped around the half square.

Lyly stood in front of a shop and grinned. "Maybe we'll have some luck in here."

"What is this horse race you call the Palio?" Tyler yelled out as he continued to skip in circles.

Lyly glanced through the window. "It's a celebration of our history with Florence and our faith. The jockey's come from our thirteen contradas."

Tyler galloped toward Lyly. "You mean like a neighborhood?"

"It's the divided areas we live in. Each contrada has a jockey. They dress in their neighborhood ... or as you call it ... colors. It's a lot of fun."

"What's your neighborhood's name?"

"Pantera."

Tyler galloped and stopped in front of Lyly. He raised his arms and yelled, "I win in the name of Pantera Contrada."

Lyly giggled. "It would be our first win in almost fifty years."

Tyler smiled.

"We are referred to as Nonnas."

"What's that?"

"Grandmothers. It's an insult." Peeking through another storefront, Lyly raised her voice. "Tyler, it's a woman with a mask! I can see her. She's standing next to a ladder."

Tyler ran to Lyly and watched as his aunt rolled up a strip of wallpaper before carefully inserting it into a cardboard tube. She removed her mask and said, "It's taking me longer today. Seems harder to dislodge compared to yesterday. I'm being careful to not tear anything."

"Oh, no," Tyler said.

"What's wrong?" Lyly asked.

"That's no woman. That's my Aunt Meg!"

Together the two watched as Aunt Meg and a man worked.

"This is amazing!" Tyler said. "This is more than just a portal. I can see everything. It's as though this window is a window into the other universe connecting them … somehow."

The man pointed to the rolls on the floor. "I agree. However, too late for me." He held up a small strip of torn toile.

"You're obviously not being careful …" Megan continued to talk to the man.

"Who is that nobleman with your aunt?" Lyly asked.

Tyler laughed. "He's no nobleman. Aunt Meg said there was some mix-up and she had to share the toile with somebody named Robert or Roberto … whatever. She's not happy about it."

"This Robert or Roberto of the House of Whatever, he fancies your aunt," Lyly said.

Tyler laughed again. "No, not Robert or Roberto whatever. I just said that because I don't know his last name." Tyler glanced back into the room. Then he paused. "And what do you mean by fancy my Aunt Meg?"

"His heart is fond to her," Lyly replied.

"What?" He stared at Lyly. "What do you mean by that?"

"As you say, he likes her."

"How do you know?"

She giggled. "Just look at the way he steals a peek at her now and then."

"Aunt Meg doesn't like him at all 'cause he's taking half of her toiles. She said so. She calls him the *enemy*."

"I beg to differ. I believe she fancies him as well."

"I don't think so."

Tyler tried to get a better look. If his aunt was … Tyler felt a pull, and as he yelled out, his head and shoulders were sucked through the window and into the room where his aunt was working. He froze as he stared at them. *What if they see me?*

"I need to finish," Megan said, returning to the other side of the room.

As quickly as he was pulled into the room, he felt his body being jerked backwards. Lyly grabbed onto Tyler as they fell to the ground.

Landing on top of her, Tyler blushed. "Sorry." Standing, he reached down and helped Lyly up. "That's so way cool." Turning around, Tyler sighed. "The portal has closed."

"Tyler, I am concerned. We are running out of time."

"Maybe it's reversing. Let's get back to your bedroom."

Climbing the ladder, Megan's stomach growled. Working without a lunch break probably wasn't such a good idea. Blinking, she took a long, hard look as the girl in the toile paper ran and a boy who looked just like Tyler was right behind her! He was wearing what looked like blue jeans and a t-shirt with a shark on it. Shaking her head, Megan turned away feeling guilty.

Now, I'm seeing things. First Tyler's head and now ... I obviously have Tyler on the brain. I wish I could be with him. Hopefully, Vincenzo's checking in on him throughout the day.

After taking in a deep breath, she felt a little better. If there were any problems, Vincenzo would certainly call. Glancing back at the toile, everything looked normal. "Just guilt," she said.

"I agree. Let's eat." Robert stood and counted his rolls. "Perfect timing ... lunch ... together?"

"That's fine." Megan listened to her stomach growl. "Wait till you see what I have for pickin's today. It'll put your stuff to shame." She giggled.

"I doubt it, Megan. Just wait to see what I have to offer." Robert smiled.

The female attendant arrived with Tyler's noonday meal. She switched the trays and walked back into the hallway. As the door clicked shut behind her, the cats crawled out from under the covers. They filled their bellies with the meatball lasagna.

"Help me open the door," Belle said to the others.

Together, the cats opened the glass door and Belle ran out. She was running back to The Catman's house.

"Tsk, Tsk." Tino frowned at the crate. "Still not a man yet?"

Angry copper and green eyes stared back at him. Patrick and D'oreo huddled together and hissed.

"I promised Uncle Fab I'd take care of you rats," Tino laughed. "Now, I need to find your friends." Tino walked around the room. "You are more trouble than you are worth. If you are not a man by midnight … I will toss both of you into the river."

Megan walked exhausted up to the hotel desk and smiled. "Hi, I'm Megan Brandt. Is Vincenzo still here or did he leave me a note?" She scratched her neck and sighed. It was time for a hot shower and a meal.

"Ah, si … Signorina Brandt. I am Angelina."

"That's right, Vincenzo covered for you last night. Feeling better?"

"Si … much better." Angelina replied. "Vincenzo said that Tyler ate all his meals and took his medication." She smiled.

"Thank you. Makes me feel better."

"Si, no worry. We are here to help. Your dinner was just taken up to your room."

"Along with my breakfast order," Megan said, "could I also order a lunch to go with my AM pickup? Working late and all."

"But of course." Angelina nodded as she wrote on a notepad. "What would you like? I can leave the order with the staff."

"Two chef's meals to go. Anything will do."

Earlier that day, Robert or Roberto, had offered a hot Italian entrée of veal scallopini over linguini, which put her small meal to shame. Megan had simply stood there and grinned.

"You're still my enemy," Megan said as she waited for the elevator.

Patrick glanced at the clock. One hour before midnight and the celestial alignment, and his only chance to save Lyly. He looked at D'oreo and sighed. D'oreo leaned against Patrick and purred. Patrick inched himself away. Tino's snores echoed through the room.

"Now, what?" Patrick asked, sitting back on his legs. "How can I get out of here ... Belle?"

Belle stood next to the crate and winked. She dropped the key and stepped back.

Megan leaned her cardboard tubes against the wall. Opening Tyler's door, she peered inside. It looked like he was sleeping soundly. She walked to the opened balcony doors and sighed. After closing and locking them, she stood by Tyler's bed. While contemplating on whether to check for a fever, Megan decided it would be best to not wake him. After locking his door behind her, Megan picked up her tubes and headed for her room.

Belle unlocked the crate and led the way to the small glassless windowpane. D'oreo ran through first with Patrick closely behind.

Farewell, Tino, Patrick said to himself.

"Damn you, Celestial KittyCat!" Tino grabbed onto Belle's hind leg. He yanked her back and rolled her into the bed sheet. Tossing the sheet and cat into the crate, he shook his head. "You weren't going to turn into a man anyway. Just a stupid legend. You are all nothing but stupid rats!"

He tugged on the lock several times.

Belle peeked out of the sheets and meowed.

"Shut-up, you," Tino said. "Where are your friends?"

Tyler and Lyly stood in the only semi-real bedroom and stared at the large paned window.

"Tyler …" Lyly pushed her nose up against the paper glass. "For a split second, this window showed a garden but it never fully appeared. Just a glimpse."

"Answer is here somewhere." Tyler looked through the window and saw nothing. "Inside our universe, everything has a mirrored self. Maybe the portals are reversing or manifesting. We're close to the alignment time."

"That is the *awesome* part?" she asked.

Tyler glanced around. A flickering grabbed his attention. "Over here!" Tyler ran to a mirror and stared at it. Inside were people walking around a courtyard.

"My parents!" Lyly yelled. "That is *my* courtyard."

Tyler's eyes widened.

"It is the day of the announcement. There is Giovanni of the House of de'Leon of Florence and Master Joroku. He's cutting out silhouettes liked he did of me and Patrick." Lyly placed her hands on the mirror. "Maybe it's a way back."

The mirror clouded over and their reflection stared back for only a moment before turning, once again, to paper.

"It is gone," Lyly said, wiping away a tear.

"Must be a reflection of what's to come. Remember? Everything's in reverse."

"The window!" Lyly said, darting back across the room. "I'm afraid to touch it."

"It's the way back," Tyler said. "Let's touch it together."

Lyly grabbed Tyler's hand and frowned. "Without Patrick, nothing can be reversed."

"Or maybe …" Tyler smiled. "This may be our only chance."

Lyly took in a deep breath and grabbed Tyler's hand. They touched the windowpanes and the portal opened. A foggy presence surrounded them. A clock chimed once as they, together, merged into the nothingness.

Patrick couldn't believe his bad luck. The glass door was locked. However, Good Paws, Belle's nickname, should be here soon and she would open it.

D'oreo jumped onto the balcony, alone, and scratched on the glass.

"Where is Good Paws?" Patrick asked.

"You mean Belle? Tino grabbed her."

"Then how do we get in?"

Again, D'oreo scratched on the glass. Inside Tyler's room, eleven cats formed a pyramid. Harry, the gray tabby, climbed on top and turned the knob.

"You are all Good Paws," Patrick said, running inside. Patrick entered the bathroom and stared at the toile. He jumped onto the sink and stared into the mirror. It was odd, but his reflection seemed reversed somehow. He could definitely see Lyly with the boy and they were fading into a misty shadow. Patrick knew it was now or never. He nudged on the mirror and nothing happened. With the first chime of midnight, he watched as his reversed reflection clouded into a thick mist before surrounding him.

"Blimey," Trevor, the British man, whispered. "That's where they are. I knew it. They are still here inside this hotel. Somebody in *that* room is hoarding cats. Probably part of that cat show. Plenty of 'em, a whole bloody clowder!" He turned to his wife who now wore bright, red cheeks.

"See anything good?" His wife snickered.

"I've seen just about enough, Lovey." *Enough to speak to the Hotel Management.*

Chapter Eighteen

It is said, "Perseverance leads to success while procrastination leads to failure." This is not about failure but about payback...

Sunlight peeked through the hotel curtains. Megan pulled the covers over her head and moaned. *Fifteen more minutes, I swear.* However, she needed to check on Tyler before leaving.

She stepped into Tyler's room. The TV was playing an Italian dog show. Again, the balcony doors were open.

Poor kid, must've stayed up all night and just fell asleep.

Walking toward the TV, Megan avoided the opened books that were scattered across the floor. She stopped and stared at something black poking from out under the blankets. Taking a double take, she laughed. Just a sock that now rested on the rug. Turning off the TV, she sighed.

"Ty," Megan whispered. "Breakfast'll be here shortly. I need to talk to you. Don't want to worry about you all day." Megan picked up the sock and tossed it onto the dirty clothes pile. "Darn ... I need to get my phone. I'll be right back."

"That tail of yours is going to get you into trouble one day," Harry scolded. "It's *your* tail, control it!"

"Sorry," D'oreo replied. "It's a habit."

It was D'oreo who pushed the sock out when the woman walked by, and he was the first to jump out from under the covers. All eleven cats sat at the end of the bed, and Harry marched back and forth in front of them.

"Okay, team," Harry said. "We have a problem. We must protect Celestial KittyCat. He needs time to fix everything. When that woman returns, we need her to believe that the boy is still here.

"How do we do that?" Trixie asked. "We only speak cat!"

"I can't pronounce their words," Cherie whined. "Hurts my mouth."

"Humans must bathe in water," Harry said.

"Water?" Gigi repeated. "I have to get wet?"

"I'm not allowing my precious fur to wilt," Allie said. "No way."

"We are not bathing," Harry explained. "But that woman must believe that the boy is." Harry shook his head. "Just follow me."

The cats made a beeline for the bathroom. Harry pushed the door shut. Forming another pyramid, Harry reached up and turned the lock. Allie was in charge of the toilet. Cherie and Gigi and Minnie and Trixie were in charge of the shower. Harry stood at the ready and listened through the door.

"Grazie!" Megan said. "Was hoping to get something in him."

"Prego," a man replied.

Harry's stomach growled as he heard the dishes rattle.

Megan knocked on the bathroom door. "Ty? I brought your breakfast in. I was hoping we could have a few minutes before I leave."

Harry nodded to Allie who flushed the toilet.

"Ty? You okay? Stomach bothering you? Is there anything I can do?"

Harry sat on the toilet and balanced precariously across the large opening. If he fell in now, it was all over.

Plop ... plop ... plop ... and then a long ... pa rump!

"Ew ... guess not. Just take your time, and when you're ready, eat something."

Harry glanced over at the girls and winked. The shower ran full force almost knocking Cherie over. Harry held back a laugh.

"I'm leaving now," Megan yelled. "I'll have Vincenzo keep an eye on you."

Curry peeked under the bathroom door and watched as the woman stepped into the hallway and closed the door. "Clear!"

The bathroom door opened and the cats ran out. For the next hour, they feasted on pancakes, sausage, eggs, and bacon. D'oreo drank the milk as Cherie dried her fur.

With a full tummy, Harry turned on the dog channel and leaned against a pillow. "Perhaps in my next life, I'll come back as a human."

They clung to each other as the fog dissipated. The portal closed and the darkness faded behind them.

"This is cool," Tyler said. "We just traveled through space and time." He shook out his hair. "Unbelievable!"

Lyly glared at him.

"Wanted to make sure that everything came through." Tyler laughed and wiped his hands on his pants.

"Maybe we were stuck in this space and time and are now back in my reality." Lyly smiled and ran to the window. She glanced out and sighed. "We are in my father's study. I was expecting my mother but Patrick entered the room." Lyly's eyes lowered. "I do pray that Patrick is here. Do you think he will be a man or a black cat?"

Tyler shrugged.

"What do we do if he is still a cat?"

The doorknob rattled and Lyly held back a scream. "Is it Patrick? Lyly whispered. "Oh, no, it may be Master Joroku. He came in right after Patrick. Then he made us disappear."

"I'll hide and jump him." Tyler stationed himself behind the thick drapery.

The door slowly opened and an elegant lady with dark hair entered. "Lyly, here you are. I most expected you would still be in your bedroom sulking."

"Mother?" Lyly raced and grabbed her mother in a strong embrace. "Is it truly you? Oh, how I have missed you! I love you mother." Lyly cried in her mother's arms.

"I love you too, my darling daughter. Now, now." Pulling away, she wiped her daughter's tears with a handkerchief. "There … there … just like when you were a little girl. I must speak with your father before the announcement. It is of utmost importance. Please wait here until I return."

Tyler stepped out and sighed. "I just saw that Master Joroku in the garden. He's in a line with people waiting for their silhouettes. He looks busy."

Lyly stared out the window and wiped away a tear. "Yes, that is he. He does not look like he is leaving any time soon." Lyly turned to Tyler and smiled. "I have a plan."

"What?" Tyler glared at her.

"Roll up the bottoms of your pants to your knees and I'll find a white shirt. You, Tyler, will be a valet."

"A what? Why?"

"A valet. You can move about freely and no one shall question you." She glanced at his feet and sighed. "What are those things?"

Tyler glanced down and laughed. "Converse sneakers." He shrugged.

"Our worlds are vastly different, Tyler Charles." Lyly frowned.

Patrick jumped to the ground and the portal disappeared. He recognized where he was. *I'm back.* He glanced around. "Squire!" Patrick ran toward him. "I missed you."

Squire kicked and Patrick rolled across the dirt.

"Finicky, horse!"

Squire peered at him and snorted.

"Squire …. it's me, Patrick. I'm back. Did you miss —"

Patrick sailed through the air and landed on all fours.

"Sorry to bother you, boy," Patrick said. "I'm just an annoying cat to you right now. No wonder you don't recognize me. I meow and you neigh."

Squire snorted again before turning away.

D'oreo walked into the bathroom for the umpteenth time. Celestial KittyCat had just disappeared into the fog and he was still stuck here in the future. D'oreo jumped onto the sink and rammed his head into the mirror. The glass shook and D'oreo ran back into the bedroom fearing the glass might shatter. He sat back and glanced at the TV and sighed. Shaking his head, he again entered the bathroom.

"There must be a way back!" D'oreo whispered.

He jumped onto the toilet and looked at the water. *No way!* The green and yellow wallpaper grabbed his attention. He dropped to the floor and sat back. Glancing into the bedroom, he sighed. The other cats were still mesmerized with the TV show about dogs. He stared at the toile and concentrated. Just before his eyes crossed, D'oreo ran as fast as he could. His head crashed against the paper and he rolled twice before landing in front of the toilet.

"This is nuts!"

"D'oreo," Harry yelled out. "What are you doing?"

"Trying to fix a problem." With his head pounding, D'oreo jumped onto the sink and turned on the water. He slurped the cool liquid and waited. As the water heated, the steam rose and the reflection of the toile grabbed his attention.

"Will you look at that!"

Placing a paw on the misty mirror, D'oreo felt the pull as the portal opened.

Patrick didn't understand why he wasn't human yet. Something was not right. Was Lyly still a prisoner in the paper? Patrick ran toward the study and jumped right into another cat. He fell back and rolled several times. He stood and shook himself off.

"D'oreo?" Patrick shook his head. "My friend, what are you doing here?"

D'oreo nodded and took a step. The world whirled around them. Now standing on two feet, Patrick glanced down. They were both dressed as valets.

"D'oreo, my sincere friend." Patrick hugged him. "It was you. You were the missing piece. If I had known, I would have brought you with me."

"You had no idea I was Dante?" D'oreo asked.

"No, but it is so good to see you." Patrick laughed.

"I knew who you were. I watched as you were changed into a cat."

"Explains you being so cozy with me." Patrick sighed. "The last time I saw Lyly, I was paralyzed and the Asian man had flung her into a scroll!"

"I hid behind the drapery." Dante's eyes teared. "I ran. I was mad with fear and bumped into the cook delivering a tray of food. She dropped everything. I helped her to pick it up. She was really mad and kept yelling at me."

Patrick laughed.

"I tried to tell her what I saw happen to you and CallaLyly. I wanted to tell her how you were branded."

"Thus, the legend of Celestial KittyCat," Patrick replied. "But how were *you* changed?"

"Well … I wanted to get away from the madness. I ran to find Tomassino but instead I ran into Tattleman. He was right behind me. Must have heard what I told the cook."

Patrick shook his head.

"And behind that lunatic was Master Joroku. That's all I remember until I was licking my paws."

"How did you get into the portal?" Patrick asked.

"Same as you," D'oreo said.

Patrick sighed. "I lived a long life as a scrappy old black cat. Always hiding and sneaking around."

"I lived a cushy life as a kitten. I never grew any older. I was always loved and cared for. I am cute …" Dante smiled. "Still am!"

"Did you return with —?"

"Yes," D'oreo rocked back on his heels. "Your mother was quite pleased and sends her most infinitus love. I hid the document.

Patrick's heart pounded. "I returned to my mother's home once."

"What happened?" D'oreo asked. "Did she throw a shoe at you?"

"No, never got that close." Patrick wiped his eyes. "I watched her as she worked her gardens. She looked sad. Their Great Danes barked and I had no choice but to leave."

D'oreo laughed.

"Where is my package, my friend?" asked Patrick.

Tyler and Lyly hid in the shrubbery and watched as the horse drawn carriages arrived.

"Let's make a plan," Lyly said. "You look good as a valet."

"Thank you, my lady." Tyler bowed.

"Coachman! Why have we stopped?" Giovanni yelled out.

"Signore, there is a line," the driver replied.

"Go, Tyler, go!" Lyly pushed Tyler onto the lawn. "Go! Be a valet. Open his door and lower the steps. And … do not forget to say, 'My hand, signore.'"

So much for plans! Tyler stepped forward and opened the door. He held out his hand. "Signore, my hand."

"Your head will do, valet." Giovanni replied.

"My what?"

Giovanni squeezed Tyler's head to help balance as he stepped from the carriage.

"Uhhhh." Tyler cringed.

"Come, Assistant," Giovanni said. "Agost, wait until Assistant comes for you."

Tyler sighed as Giovanni let go. Assistant jumped from the coach and followed the man.

"Coachman," Giovanni said. "Leave the carriage. My son will remain here until I request his presence."

"Yes, signore." The coachman handed Tyler the reins. "When you get a chance, valet, do park it as I will be partaking of hot toddies."

Tyler nodded motioning the other coaches to pass.

Lyly grabbed the reins and twisted them into the spokes of the wheels. "We need to contain Agost before his father sends that Assistant," she whispered.

"I have an idea." Tyler pulled the small lock and two keys from his pocket. "I have a lock."

"Good idea," she said. "What else do you have?"

Next, Tyler pulled the eyeglass band from his pocket. "And this!"

"What about those things on your converse sneakers?"

"My laces? No, I need those."

"Go into the coach and show Agost a trick." Lyly pointed to the door. "He likes tricks. Then tie his hands with that band and your laces. Use the lock to keep Agost in the carriage. Because you are the valet, you will move the carriage somewhere past the horse stall where no one will hear Agost screaming."

"Fine, but I want my shoelaces back!" Tyler untied his shoes and huffed. "If I trip, it's all your fault."

"Shh," she said. "Just go!"

Tyler opened the carriage door and peered inside. It was too dark to see much. He climbed in and closed the door. "Agost, I have a trick to share with yah. You'll like it."

No reply. The man didn't move.

Tyler sighed. "Signore? I have a magic trick to share with you."

Again the man did not move.

Tyler scooted closer and reached out. His hand squeezed the man's shoulder. The material deflated with his touch. Tyler jumped back and the man's head rolled onto the floor. Tyler froze.

"Uh, Lyly!" Tyler yelled out. "Can you come here for a moment?"

Dante walked with Patrick to the garden wall. Squire snorted and pushed on Patrick's sleeve.

"Who likes me now?" Patrick asked, rubbing his bruised ribs.

"It's here somewhere." Dante searched the wall. "A loose stone is here. I pried it out and hid the scroll inside."

"And you don't remember which one?"

"It *has* been a little over two-hundred and fifty years! Oh, here it is." Dante maneuvered the small stone from the wall and reached in. Pulling out the scroll, he smiled.

"Thank you, D'oreo … Dante. I must find Lyly. She should be in her father's study. Come with me?"

"Dante!" a voice called out.

"Go," Dante whispered. "I will be there, shortly." He turned to the caller. "Happy to see, you," Dante said.

"Look who was trying to sneak away," the valet replied, handing the reins to Dante. "Your little horse is a wanderer."

"Thank you, my friend."

"Great news for you, Dante. I just overheard two men discussing the Palio. They speak of you as their top candidate for our Pantera Contrada."

"Thank you, my friend." Dante sighed. *So good to be home and as my old self!*

Tyler peeked out of the coach. "Lyly, where are you?" He whispered. "There is a problem here! Lyly?" After jumping down the last step, Tyler ran around the carriage and bumped into Giovanni's assistant. "I'm sorry. Have you seen Lyly?"

The man grabbed onto the coach and frowned. "Who?"

"Lyly?" Tyler said. "Of the House of Montevelli?"

The man dusted off his trousers and shook his head.

"Have you seen —"

The man pointed toward the courtyard. "Tell, *Old Eyes* that Leonardo resigns!" The man ran down the road and disappeared into the darkness.

"Who?"

Staying low, Lyly wandered through the crowd from one end of the courtyard to the other. Her insides squealed *home*, however, her long journey had only brought her full circle to the very problem she had left centuries ago. *I must change it.* Lyly had to find Patrick. Had time released him as a young man or as a black cat?

Lyly watched as Master Joroku finished with a young couple and Giovanni approached. She glanced through the crowd but there was no sign of either assistants.

Spotting her parents, Lyly's heart soared. Just resting her eyes on them gave her courage a boost. Quickening her pace, she bravely strolled past her enemies. *Go ahead, grab me. I'll scream like a wild animal!* She pushed through the crowd and her stomach churned.

Giovanni glanced at Lyly and shouted out, "Why are you still here?" Giovanni turned to Master Joroku and spoke between clinched teeth. "Rid them from my sight! Assistant is positioned with the sad news of their fleeing. They cannot be seen!" He laughed nervously. "I never lose."

Slipping in next to her mother, Lyly sighed with a sense of relief as Giovanni yelled at Master Joroku. The master stood silent and lowered his head.

"I was just about to retrieve you. Your father must make the announcement," Delfina said.

"Mother, it is urgent I speak with you first. I will not —"

"Hush child, your father is about to speak."

"But Mother —"

"No but's, CallaLyly of the House of Montevelli, show some respect for your father."

"Fine." Lyly smirked and crossed her arms. "Some things never change."

"May I have everyone's attention?" Domenico yelled out to the crowd. The crowd hushed in small waves. "You're attention please …" He clapped his hands.

Giovanni flailed his arms wildly at Master Joroku and pointed directly at her. "Do something you fool! She's standing right there."

The crowd hushed and turned toward the arguing men. Tattleman walked up to Master Joroku.

"We leave," Master Joroku stated, handing Giovanni four bags of gold coins. Tattleman picked up the copper pot and grinned. Walking away, the two left Giovanni standing alone in the middle of the garden. All eyes were planted directly on him.

"Where are you going?' Giovani shouted. "We have a contractual deal. Mark my words, Assistant will find and trash you!" He huffed out his chest. Murmurs ran through the crowd.

"We are pleased that you have joined us this evening …" Domenico yelled out, raising his arms.

"Quiet yourselves, now!" Delfina said as loud as she could.

"Mother? What about respect?" Lyly asked.

Delfina glanced at her daughter and smiled before turning to the crowd. She stepped boldly forward and said, "We only have one daughter, CallaLyly, whom we love dearly …"

Lyly frowned. *The marriage announcement.*

"We will NOT allow our daughter to enter into a loveless marriage," her mother said. "There … I said it."

Applause and shouts filled the air.

Lyly glared at her mother and gasped. She ran to her and hugged her in close. "I love you, Mother."

"You can thank your father later," Delfina said.

"Thank you, Delfina," Domenico whispered, giving his wife a kiss on the cheek. "I'll take it from here."

A few men from the crowd roared with laughter.

"I've said what I wanted to say and what I should have said from the start," Delfina whispered to her daughter.

Lyly slipped her hand into her mother's.

Giovanni de'Leon sauntered forward. "Well … well … seems you have forgotten, Domenico. We have an agreement. Your daughter's hand to my son, and in exchange, I protect you from bankruptcy."

The crowd exploded in whispers.

"Forfeiting your home and land …" Giovanni said, "… will help pay for tonight's gala that I have so handsomely sponsored. Poor Agost. He waits patiently for the announcement. He will be quite disappointed."

The whispers grew louder.

"Noblemen and noblewomen," Domenico yelled out. "Yes, it is true, my family is bankrupt. We are the only institution in Siena that lends to those in need or with a vision. We are now in need ourselves for a noble family or families to invest in our Commoner's Bank of Siena to allow us to continue the good cause."

A hand pushed through the crowd and waved a paper in the air. The crowd parted as Patrick and Dante walked forward.

"I am that nobleman." Patrick stated. "I will invest in your bank."

Lyly's heart leaped. "Patrick. You're here!"

"As are you." Patrick bowed. "It is wonderful to see you again, CallaLyly of the House of Montevelli of Siena."

"As I of you, Patrick of the House of Barrett of Hampshire."

Patrick handed Domenico the scroll and bowed to Lyly's mother. "My lady." He gazed into Lyly's eyes and gently placed their silhouette into her hand.

Lyly held the silhouette up and smiled. She placed her hand over her heart as she read:

> Mother and Father,
>   I have found my star. Her name is CallaLyly of the House of Montevelli of Siena. I wish to use my inheritance in a business proposition with the family regarding their banking institution. I sincerely thank you for showing me the way out of the castle door.
>   Your loving son, Patrick.

Tyler stepped up to Lyly and whispered, "You can't judge a book by its cover."

Lyly looked at him and frowned.

"Something my mother always said. She *is* a wise woman." Tyler whispered to Lyly who nodded and turned to her mother. As she whispered to her mother, Delfina wiped her eyes and smiled.

"I am Patrick of the House of Barrett of Hampshire from the country of England. With my inheritance, I shall be a silent investor in the Commoner's Bank of Siena."

"Fraud!" Giovanni yelled. "He is merely a valet. Nothing but a commoner. A deceiving jokester. Throw him out along with the

Montevellis! If you know what is good for all of you." Giovanni glared at the citizens.

Domenico broke the seal and sighed. "Oh, my!" He passed the scroll to several noblemen who were standing near.

"I know very well of Patrick as the mischievous middle son of the Noble House of Katherine and William Barrett of England," a man stated. "It was rumored that when the House of Barrett was presented before the King of England, Patrick's horseplaying knocked King George on his bum."

"All true, I am afraid." Patrick chuckled. "The King was not at all amused."

Delfina laughed and pointed her finger at Giovanni. "Giovanni of the House of de'Leon of Florence. You are the fraud. Mean spirited too. Where is your son, Agost? The *pumpkin* head? Agost is a no show. Inside your coach sits a dressed-up pumpkin with an overcoat. It is you who have breached our contract!"

Loud gasps echoed from the crowd.

"A lie! Agost is with Assistant," Giovanni yelled.

"I believe you have a problem," Delfina said.

"Problem?" Giovanni asked.

"Leonardo resigned," Delfina added with a nod.

"Who?" Giovanni asked.

"Your assistant!" Domenico yelled out, laughing. "You know not the name of your *own* personal assistant?"

Giovanni stared at the glaring eyes of the angry crowd. He bowed and slowly backed his way out of the courtyard. Standing near the entrance, he yelled, "Assistant! Where are you? Assistant ... I shall have your head!"

"Tyler," Lyly said, holding his hand. "My family will forever be in your debt, Tyler of the House of Charles of Massachusetts."

"Cool," Tyler said, laughing.

Chapter Nineteen

It is said, " A man who lives forever never really lives."
This is not about living but rather about surviving ...

Then and Now

After leaving the House of Montevelli, Joroku settled into the curve of the velvet seat of his horse drawn coach. He watched as Tattleman placed his copper pot onto the floor. Tattleman sat and smiled.

"Tattleman," Joroku said. "In Florence, our love potions sell faster. Then we will travel."

"Yes." Tattleman nodded.

Joroku stared at the copper pot and smiled. It was a dear friend and traveled with him throughout the lands never leaving his side. He made quite a taking in Domenico's courtyard tonight, then again, he also lost quite a bit. All for an announcement that was never to be. He held up a silhouette and laughed. He thought of the noble couples and remembered their delight as he delicately swirled and sliced the paper into the darkened forms. With each slice, a small piece of their spirit landed directly inside his copper pot. He could feel the surge as their spirits merged within the magic filling him with energy. He still had a small piece of Lyly's and Patrick's spirit in there too.

Each time a person's essence was captured, the copper pot glowed. Not once did the happy couples notice the pot as Joroku's golden nails carved the intricate design. Just like when he cut the silhouette for Lyly and her friend, Patrick. They were too much in love to feel their souls bleed.

"Four bags of gold!" Joroku glared at Tattleman. "I will destroy him."

The copper pot glowed at his feet.

Joroku laughed. "Do not haunt me, Mother." Joroku gently nudged the pot with his foot.

He gazed at the house and shook his head. Lyly and Patrick would have been an easy curse — an easy four bags of gold. The pot glowed again and a dense mist slowly rose into the air.

"No!" Joroku pulled away from the pot and shivered.

"Master!" Tattleman screamed. "It is happening again."

"No!" Joroku yelled. "Not again. No more ... I have no time for this!"

"*Time shall wait.*" A soft voice from the mist replied. "*You must remember ...*"

The mist swirled around Joroku. Tattleman sat back and hugged his knees to his chest and closed his eyes. Joroku felt his body dissolve into the vapors. Through the haze he glared at Tattleman who sat frozen with fear. Joroku held his breath as he was sucked into the copper pot.

Tattleman opened an eye and stared at the copper pot. No mist. The carriage rocked back and forth through the forest as if nothing had happened. But something had just happened, and it had happened before.

The warm winds of June filled the air with a sweet aroma from the deep plum blossoms. Kukiko stood next to her father and took in a deep breath. She wiped away a tear as she remembered her mother.

"Still crying?" her father asked.

Kukiko glanced at him and nodded. "No, I am fine."

"You must learn to accept death along with life. We will die one day too."

"But Mother was still young and beautiful." Kukiko wiped away another tear.

"We have no power over illnesses, child." He huffed. "Learn from this."

Kukiko took in another deep breath and stared up at the large brick structure that loomed darkly against the rising mountains. The vines and moss that covered the outer walls sent chills up her spine. Guards from the top watched down on their every move.

"This is how a general lives?" Kukiko asked, rolling her eyes.

"No, this is the emperor's palace, and you will act with dignity and not shame our homeland of Japan."

"Then you should have left me at home." Kukiko sighed.

"You are promised to another. He is a wealthy king of his country. I want nothing to interfere with that. Your life and our dignity rests in that union. Therefore, you remain with me until the marriage."

"You mean married to my new grandfather!"

"He is not related to you." Her father stared at her and frowned.

"Does it matter? He is older than you are. And he smells."

"We will not discuss this now."

"Mother didn't want me marrying him," Kukiko said. "I heard her tell you such."

"You will be taken care of. Never want for anything."

"Maybe freedom," she whispered.

"Excuse me?"

"Nothing."

A guard walked up and bowed. "Sir, this way. General Huang is expecting you."

Ambassador Harada nodded.

Kukiko walked beside her father refusing to make eye contact with the guards. She lowered her gaze as they entered through the large double doors. A musty aroma of aged wood and moldy bricks surrounded her. She held her hand to her face and frowned.

"This way, sir," the guard said, opening another door.

As they entered the lavish room, the guards bowed. Kukiko glanced cautiously around the room making sure she did not look anyone directly in the eyes. The bright red room with intricate golden carvings made her uncomfortable. Although Japan was China's neighbor, how they decorated was quite different.

"Ambassador Harada," General Huang stepped forward and bowed. "It is nice to meet you. We have much to discuss."

"May I introduce my daughter, Kukiko." The general waved his hand.

Kukiko stepped forward and bowed.

"A beautiful flower from the east." General Haung rubbed Kukiko's cheek. "Delicate and lovely. I see why you brought her with you. If I owned such a treasure, I too would keep her close."

Ambassador Harada nodded.

Kukiko sat on a thin cushion and rested her arms on the bedroom windowsill. She watched as birds flew through the small garden. They seemed to be enjoying the fresh blooms. A small pond filled with colorful fish decorated one side.

"Miss," a young lady said, bringing in a tray of food. "Your dinner."

"What a lovely garden," Kukiko said. "How do I get down there?"

"Oh, miss, that would be forbidden."

"Oh, please … just the garden. I've seen other girls out there today."

"Let me ask the mother," the girl replied.

Kukiko stared out the window as her tears fell. "If only I could be a sparrow and fly free."

"Flying free is not always freedom," an older woman said from the door. "Birds are eaten by animals. Would you want to be eaten?"

"Better to be dead than to marry an old man."

The woman laughed. "Child, marrying an old man may be a blessing." She bowed and then winked.

Kukiko giggled.

"You wish to walk the garden?" the old woman asked.

Kukiko nodded.

"Eat first, then walk," she said, smiling. "I will allow it. However, no farther than the one garden."

"Yes," Kukiko replied.

Kukiko stood under the blooming trees and twirled. She allowed her arms to fly freely through the air. "Freedom! I am a bird and I can fly."

"Freedom is a choice," a deep voice said.

Kukiko froze. She glanced around and spotted a young man sitting on the brick wall. He stared at her as he bit into a bright red apple. "Those birds never leave this yard. Clipped wings." He chuckled. "Some freedom."

Kukiko squinted at him. "Who are you?"

"These apples are my favorite," he replied. "Out of all our trees, I come here to pick one every day." He jumped and landed effortlessly on the grass. "I'm Jong, the general's son."

She stared at him.

"I do not bite," he said. "You may talk to me."

Kukiko glanced around. If that old woman saw her talking to this boy, she would never be allowed to enjoy the garden again.

"I said, I am the general's son. No one is allowed out here when I am here."

"Then I shall leave."

He grabbed her arm. "Don't leave. I didn't mean you. I meant the other women who live here. They are not allowed near me. Do you have a name?"

"Kukiko, I am the daughter of the ambassador."

"Yes," Jong said. "Japan. I was in Japan once. Nice place."

Kukiko giggled.

"Your mother passed recently. I am sorry. I met your father. Interesting man. Most disagreeable."

"I must return to my room. Father would not allow me to speak with you." Kukiko turned and walked toward the wooden door to the palace.

"Is your life so unpleasant that surrounded by this beauty does not lift you up?"

"My circumstances are none of your concern."

"I come here every evening," Jong said. "Perhaps we can speak again tomorrow."

"Perhaps," Kukiko replied.

As the sun lowered behind the palace towers, the garden fell dark. Kukiko ran down the stairs constantly glancing over her shoulder for one of the maidens or the old woman. Over the next five evenings, she met Jong beneath the stars inside that small garden. She rested her head on his shoulder as he told her stories about a sun, a star, and a moon.

"That's the planet Venus," Jong said. "The brightest star in the sky."

"I wonder why?"

"It is the star of love," Jong replied.

"Love?" Kukiko sat up and stared at him.

Jong nodded. "It only shows itself to couples in love."

Kukiko giggled.

Jong leaned over and kissed her.

"Oh, my," she whispered.

"Kukiko … marry me," Jong pleaded. "I will love you forever."

"It is written in the stars," she whispered.

"The stars?"

"Yes, my mother was ill and before she died she told me she would have it written in the stars, and I would marry someone who would love me forever."

"I promise to love you forever. We will marry."

"My father will never agree."

"Then we leave together … in the darkness. I know of a place in the mountains where we can go. No one will ever find us."

Under the celestial alignment of the sun, Venus, and a full moon, the happy couple named their son, Joroku. They had combined the first two letters of their names, and in the middle, they added *ro*, two letters from her mother's name.

Over a year prior, the old woman had watched as they climbed the brick wall together. She nodded and smiled. The next morning, she reported the girl missing to the guards.

"Go and find them!" The emperor screamed at General Huang. "Your son was promised to my eldest daughter!"

"We will find them," the guards replied.

"You! Old woman … leave this place, now!"

The forest breeze sent chills up the old woman's spine. She glanced into the trees and noticed a crow and owl sitting on an upper branch.

"Not a good sign," she said. "Nothing good ever happens when you two sit together."

She hurried her pace to her cave. Near the entrance sat her copper pot. She searched the shadows for a guard but all remained quiet. She stepped closer and peered inside. A baby, wrapped in a blanket, slept soundly. Written in black ink on a small white cloth were the letters … Joroku.

"I have seen enough." Joroku squealed as his spirit swirled out of the copper pot. After falling back into the seat, he shook out his arms. "I hate it when that happens."

"Go back to your clippings," the mystic voice whispered.

"It relaxes me," Joroku replied.

"Remember the meaning. Kukiko is snow and Jong is glory. It snows gloriously on the mountain when you were taken and your parents killed. Your true mother lived a lifetime in just one year."

"Are you okay?" Tattleman asked.

"I am fine!" Joroku sat up and adjusted his robe. "Are we almost there?"

"Yes," Tattleman replied. "You were gone a long time this time."

Joroku bowed.

"I am proud of you, my son." The mother sorceress' voice had whispered out from the copper pot.

Joroku looked over at Tattleman who was sleeping again. The sorceress appeared only to him and would remain cloaked within a white veil. He had watched as the trees passed by outside and tried to ignore her. The sorceress had told him that he was stolen from his parents when he was just a baby. He understood that much. But why?

It was on a cold winter morning when Joroku watched his adoptive mother die. "Mother, you grow weaker by the day." The young Joroku ran to her.

She struggled to breathe. "My dear child. My life has come full circle. As I leave this plane of existence, I must tell you everything."

Expelled from the royal palace, she had fought the emperor's rules on black magic. Her desire was to secure love with the use of her love potions.

"It is only now that I am ready to share this with you, Joroku. I have always loved you as my true son. However —"

"Mother, I am your son." Joroku shook his head. "I know that the guards brought me to you, but it is you I love."

Joroku listened as the sorceress revealed the full story of his birth. As she spoke, his anger grew.

"Now, you must know about the curse, my child."

"Curse?"

"Yes. The emperor ordered me, the evil sorceress, to place a curse on you. You will live forever, my son. My heart breaks for you, Joroku. Your parents fell in love because of my love potions. But they were both promised to another. The emperor's eldest daughter was promised to your father. She was an ugly woman both inside and out, and twice his age. And your mother was promised to an elderly king of a faraway land. Because of their union, you are cursed to forever walk upon this world." She held his hand. "It is time for me to go, Joroku. I will love you forever. Stand close, for I am passing all my powers to you. I will be with you in spirit."

The young Joroku watched as a bright light passed from her hand and into his. The warmth radiated up his arm and into his chest. As it encased his heart, he screamed. "Mother!" Joroku hugged the sorceress' lifeless body and cried. "I will avenge you and my parents!"

Joroku stared out at the carriage. He wiped away a tear as he remembered the first time the sorceress appeared to him from inside the copper pot. He was sitting inside their dark cave after he had spread her ashes in the forest. He had saved a small amount for the copper pot. Tossing the ashes in, a swirling mist blocked his view.

"Joroku, I am here as promised," the sorceress' head cloaked in white appeared within the mist.

He sat back and stared at his fading mother and his tears fell. The following day, Joroku trekked back to the palace where his real parents had met. He hid between the apple trees in the garden. When the sun lowered behind the towers, he stepped into the tall grass and laid a parchment under the moonlight. Exceeding the sorceress' strengths by a thousand folds, Joroku transferred his body into the parchment that was addressed as:

Special Delivery — Emperor's Eyes Only

Within the privacy of his living quarters, the emperor had unrolled the gift and laughed as a young man climbed out.

"What? How?" The emperor laughed again. "What a wonderful and amusing gift. Who sent you? I must thank them and use you in my festivities."

"Jong and Kukiko's child. I am Master Joroku. Raised by the sorceress from the cave. The cave you banished her to so many years ago."

The emperor froze.

With a wave of his hand, Master Joroku lifted the emperor into the air and twirled him about. As the wind spun the man in place, Joroku swiped his arm across the floor and the emperor was sucked into the parchment. He then placed the parchment inside a frame and hung it on the palace wall above the emperor's bed.

The sorceress repeated her words. "I am very proud of you, my son."

"I heard you, Mother."

"Why did you not answer?" she asked. "Were you ignoring me?"

"Just deep in thought."

"How wonderful of you to free that girl and release the young man. But why?"

Joroku chuckled. "In memory of my parents."

"There is still one thing you need to resolve," she said. "And the time has come."

Joroku had fought against that issue for centuries. Especially, since it involved his beloved parents. "I'm in a jovial mood right now. I shall think about it later."

The glow faded into the shadows, and the pot became quiet once again. Tattleman snored and Joroku glanced at the elderly man. *Soon, I will have to find a new assistant.* Over the centuries, Joroku had hired many aides and each lasted about fifty years or so.

"Cursed to an endless life." Joroku laughed.

Tattleman stirred and yawned.

"Florence is the love capital and my potions will sell fast. Soon, Tattleman, we travel to Shanghai."

Joroku thought back to when he had first met Domenico. He and Tattleman were finishing up at the piazza for the night. Joroku had laughed and waved his arms over the little vials. He looked at his assistant and said, "I chisel silhouettes and you capture the buyers. Only a few of my famous love potions remain."

"Brings me great pleasure to spy upon others for you." Tattleman nodded as he rocked against his heels.

"Who is that?" Joroku asked.

"I do not know. He has been watching you for some time now."

Joroku frowned as the heavyset man approached. "Is there anything I can help you with, my kind signore?" Joroku waved his arms over the little vials.

The man nodded and walked cautiously forward. He held his head high and said, "I am Domenico of the House of Montevelli of Siena." Domenico bowed. "My daughter is to wed the son of Giovanni of the House of de'Leon of Florence. I would like you to work at my gala." Domenico smiled. "I will provide a good sum for your talents."

"Oh?" Joroku glanced at Tattleman and nodded. "I will add fireworks to the offer."

Domenico smiled. "Should be profitable."

"Tell the details to my assistant, Tattleman." Joroku turned and smiled at a young couple.

Chapter Twenty

It is said, "You can't take it with you." This is not about what you can't take but rather what you can …

Megan stood back and stared at the walls. *After these panels with the girl in the medieval house, I'll only have a half panel left for tomorrow.* Megan smiled and rested her hands on her hips. "Right on schedule in spite of everything and everyone."

"Did you say something?" Robert asked.

"Sorry, talking to myself. I do that sometimes." Giggling, she glanced at Roberto … or call me Robert … and watched as he removed a seafaring panel that once covered the inside doorway. "I think I can leave a little earlier today. Maybe have dinner with Ty."

"That would be nice." Roberto stood back and studied the panel.

"He's been sick and I believe my stomach is telling me it's time for lunch."

"Then we eat!" Roberto said, stretching out his back. He walked out of the room and shuffled through his packages. He mumbled and huffed.

"Is something wrong?"

"I believe I left all my goodies behind." He looked at her and laughed. "I will need to visit a market."

"Robert …" Megan sighed for even when she wins she usually loses. "I have enough for the both of us."

"You brought wine?"

Megan rolled her eyes.

"I know, I know," Robert sighed. "I should never drink wine when I work." Robert now rolled his eyes.

Megan shook her head and laughed.

"You obviously have no Italian blood in you."

Megan tossed a water bottle at him. "I have an award-winning meal instead. From a famous hotel chef!"

Robert gulped the water. "I love your American clear wine!"

"Let the festivities begin!" Domenico yelled and raised his arms. "Along with the celestial alignment tonight, we celebrate a new vision."

Tyler glanced around the courtyard and sighed. The music played and he watched as the guests mingled. He walked over to the musicians. He had seen musicians on the TV once, but since it wasn't his type of music, he had flipped the channel. Now, he was standing in front of real Italian musicians. As their arms gently swayed across the strings, he closed his eyes and felt a cool breeze caress his face.

A strong grip yanked him from his thoughts and the world twirled around him. He opened his eyes and stared into Lyly's smiling face. Lyly ran around Tyler pulling him with her. The musicians and torch lighting blurred as he whirled.

"Come dance with me, Tyler!"

"I can't dance," he replied.

Patrick grabbed Tyler's other hand. They ran in a circle and Lyly squealed. Tyler prayed his feet would cooperate, otherwise, he would end up on the ground. Dante jumped in and the four danced together holding hands. Tyler's heart pounded and the touch of Lyly's soft skin made his mind soar. He had never felt this way about any girl. Girls always hated him for being a geek.

"I'm hungry," Lyly yelled.

Still holding onto Tyler, Lyly pulled him toward a table filled with food.

"Try this, Tyler!" Lyly shoved a piece of meat into his mouth.

Tyler gagged and coughed. "What is it?"

"Roast pig. You will relish it."

Tyler picked up another piece and nibbled on it slowly.

"Such a baby, Tyler. Take a big bite."

Tyler shrugged and pushed a larger piece of pork into his mouth. "Yummy."

"Knew you would enjoy it." She laughed. "I want you to meet my baby brother. His nanny will bring him out later."

Patrick panted and stepped up to the table. He grabbed a piece of pork and took a big bite. "Tyler, I want you to meet my friend, Fuoco."

Tyler frowned. "No ... that's Dante."

"Not anymore," Patrick replied. "Hear ye, hear ye ... from this day forward ... Dante shall be known as Fuoco. Dante is on fire! You are fire, my friend." Patrick patted Dante on the back. "Maybe your contrada will have a chance to win with you as their fuoco."

"My father will back you," Lyly said.

"Did I hear *Father?*" Domenico stepped up and hugged Lyly. "Something about the Palio di Siena?" Domenico raised his brows.

"Yes, Father. And ... Father ..."

"Yes, child."

"Thank you. I should have trusted you. I should have known you would not allow such a farce to continue. No matter the consequence."

"Your mother made me realize that you have a mind of your own. You have a destiny to fulfill. Your mother is very persistent, kept filling my head with her recurring dreams."

"Really, Father?" Lyly winked at Tyler. "Tell us about them."

"In her dreams, you disappeared ... poof." He waved his hand through the air. "We lost everything and Giovanni tossed us to the street. We became beggars. We had to work for a feudal lord."

"Sounds more of a nightmare and not a dream." Lyly giggled.

"She dreamt that she ran errands for her mistress to the Merle Shoppe for extra funds. A place she now avoids."

"And why was that Father?"

Tyler stepped closer.

"In her dream, we had lent to everyone through our Commoner's Bank and everyone went bankrupt after Giovanni called in his loans. Everyone except for Dante's father. He did quite well for himself."

"Dante is one of our valets." Lyly glanced at Tyler and smiled.

Domenico looked up at the sky. "Merle had told your mother that it was strange."

"Strange?" Lyly repeated.

"Seemed that Dante had also disappeared about the same time you did."

"Then what happened, Father?"

"Your mother told Merle that it was painful for her and she would never stop searching for you. She also said she would have done things differently if she had known. He thanked her for her kindness and told her he was given an inheritance of gold. It saved him from the likes of Giovanni de'Leon."

"Known what, Father?"

"She never said," he replied.

"What about you, Father? Do you have strange dreams?" Lyly glanced at Tyler.

Domenico nodded. "I have this strange urge to prepare and clean a nobleman's formal wear."

"A cleaner for clothes? What an odd sensation." She kissed him on the cheek. "Thank you, Father. These strange urges should diminish." She waved her hand at Tyler. "I wish for you to meet my dearest friend, Tyler of the House of Charles of Massachusetts. He is a dear, dear friend and I will explain it to you someday."

Domenico tilted his head and frowned.

Tyler held out his hand. "Nice to meet you, signore."

"Another new valet?" Domenico looked Tyler over. As his eyes fell to the boy's shoes. He frowned. "What are those things?"

Tyler laughed. "Converse."

"Strange boy," Domenico replied. "Very strange." Domenico turned to Dante and wrapped his arm around his shoulders.

Patrick bowed in front of Lyly. "Lyly, may I have this dance?"

She curtsied. "Yes, you may, Sir Patrick."

Patrick twirled Lyly until she fell into his arms. They laughed and looked intently into each other's eyes. Tyler's stomach tightened and he felt his face flush. It bothered him. He stared at his sneakers.

Lyly had said that Robert fancied my Aunt Meg. Lyly fancied Patrick. She would never fancy Tyler. With his heart pounding, he glanced back at the musicians and sighed. He didn't belong here. He had to get back to his hotel room.

"Tyler," Lyly yelled out. "Are you enjoying the festivities?"

"I have to leave, Lyly."

Lyly stopped dancing and stared at Tyler. "What do you mean?"

"I have to get back to my time. I don't know how, but my Aunt Meg probably has the polizia searching for me."

"Fuoco and I have been working on this," Patrick said, waving for Dante.

"What do you mean?" Tyler asked.

"We covered for you," Patrick replied.

"How?"

"Dante, explain." Patrick smiled.

"My cat partners are in your hotel room," Dante said.

"Are you serious?" Tyler took a step back.

"Yes, I am quite serious," Dante replied. "They are quite ingenious as they are show cats."

"Show cats cannot impersonate me. What about the food and my books and …" Tyler laughed and then frowned. "I have to get back. But I don't know how."

"We will figure it out …" Lyly glared at Patrick and Dante. "All of us … together we will fix it."

Patrick and Dante nodded.

The answer was just within Tyler's reach, somewhere. However, he didn't have much time. Portals did not remain open forever. If he didn't find one soon, he would be stuck here forever.

Tyler glanced around the courtyard. No double from anyone about their sudden appearance. Therefore, they had to have slipped back to the exact point when they were pulled away, which meant that it never happened. But it did, which meant that Tyler had to re-write the timeline and not create a new one. He had to re-establish a past point-in-time, and it had to happen before midnight. The celestial alignment was the key.

He glanced around and frowned. Even Master Joroku was playing a new part, a new action. The man was no longer here; he should be, but he wasn't. The fireworks ... the fireworks had something to do with it. But what?

What would his dad say or do? Tyler walked around the courtyard and tapped on his head. He had to think like his father. *Think, Tyler, think.* As he walked, he thought about the hotel, the plane ride, his home, and ... Kevin Smitters.

"Patrick, how would you handle a bully?"

"What is a ... bully?"

"A person that picks on you," Tyler replied. "Someone who always wants to fight."

"Oh, a nemesis." Patrick laughed. "Why ... I would make him my friend."

"Seriously?" Tyler frowned.

"Yes." Patrick laughed. "A true friend cannot be an enemy at the same time. First, I would take them down and then I would extend my hand."

"Does it always work?"

"Sometimes it ends in my favor and sometimes not. Does not work with animals though. However, I've made many friends of previous enemies. If they're not to be, they never come back." Patrick pulled Tyler to the ground. Patrick then stood and held out a hand. "See how easy it is, my friend?"

Tyler stood and brushed off his pants. He picked up the paper that had fallen from his back pocket. He opened it and read:

WHAT ACTUALLY OCCURS
WHEN A BOMB EXPLODES
by Dr. Daniel Charles, MIT

"What is written on the parchment?" Patrick asked.

"How I will return," Tyler replied.

Chapter Twenty-One

It is said, "A friend is someone who holds the lock that fits the key and a key that fits the lock." This is not about the lock or key but about the friendship ...

Megan watched as Robert devoured the last of his lunch. "Don't like it, huh?"

Smacking his lips, Robert dunked his crusty bread into the remaining sauce. "Calamari and chicken piccata are my favorites. How did you know?"

"Lucky guess?" Megan sighed and rubbed her forehead. She stood and paced across the room. *He's always trying to placate me.* Staring into the small room with the toiles, her heart pounded. "You trying to win me over? Robert ... or Roberto ... or whatever you go by at the moment?"

Robert glanced up at her and frowned. "Are you mad that I ate your food? Have I offended you?"

"No ... and ... yes ..." Megan eyes widened. "You took my toiles and there's nothing I can do about it."

"Still mad about the toiles?"

"Damn right I am. I don't know how you did it but those toiles were supposed to be mine." Megan stepped near the window and peered out. "My company had exclusive rights. I was going to start a whole new division and now that's gone."

Raising his hands, Robert sighed. "You're still upset and I understand."

Megan stomped her foot. "There you go again!"

He smiled and lowered his voice. "I understand, Megan. I apologize but I did nothing wrong. I used my savings for my new business. When I was contacted about the toiles, I had to borrow money from my parents to pay for them."

"New business?"

"Yes, in Milan."

"By yourself?" she asked.

"Yes."

"Who contacted you?"

"A third party."

"Third party?

He nodded. "I completed my undergraduate at Columbia and it's been nice hearing your slang. In the states they called me Robert. You call me Robert. I had missed that."

Megan looked away and sighed. "You put everything on the line?"

"There's that slang. I love it. I would toast you if only we had some wine."

She smiled. "Whoo boy ... I could use some wine about now."

The joyous sounds of the festivities echoed from off the house. Tyler, Lyly, Patrick, and Dante stood together to talk. Tyler shared his father's paper on molecular distribution, and the three passed the paper around. Each scratched their heads as they read.

"If I can somehow disrupt the air molecules, a portal should appear." Tyler shrugged.

"How can we do that?" Lyly asked, shaking her head.

Patrick looked at the paper again and sighed. "Would banging on a drum work?"

Tyler nodded. "Something loud just might work."

"Right now, everything is nothing but smoke and mirrors," Lyly replied.

Tyler took a step back and nodded again. "What did you say?"

Lyly sighed. "I said … everything is smoke and mirrors."

"Go on," Tyler replied, raising his brows.

"Illusion, but a *reality* illusion." Now, Lyly shrugged.

Slapping his hands on his head, Tyler gasped. "That's it! Mirrors and smoke and noise. Where can we get a big mirror … and some smoke … and we'll need to bang on some pans or something. That just might disrupt the molecules. Yes, yes." Tyler's eyes widened. "It just might work. We need to open a portal."

"I have a mirror in my room," Lyly said. "Tyler, come with me. It is too heavy for me to lift."

Patrick laughed. "I shall gather branches to start a fire."

"I should find a copper plate in the kitchen," Dante added.

"We need to hurry," Tyler said, running after Lyly. "We do not have a lot of time. It's almost midnight."

They darted up the marble stairs. As their footsteps echoed through the high ceilings, a matronly woman holding a baby raised her index finger. Lyly nodded before tiptoeing to her room.

"That is my baby brother, Alberto," Lyly whispered.

"I figured that one out," Tyler replied, panting.

They each grabbed an end of her large mirror. They struggled down the stairs and into the courtyard.

"This thing is heavy," she whined.

"Yes, it is," he replied, trying to catch his breath.

Stepping into the side yard, the two struggled to lean the large mirror against a tree.

"Phew, that was close." Tyler pulled out his dad's paper and read through it again.

"Yes, it was." Lyly smiled as Patrick ran up with kindling.

Patrick sparked the branches into a small fire. He waved his hands and the smoke aimed for the mirror.

A loud bang echoed down the sidewalk as Dante ran into the courtyard. "Will this work?" Dante asked.

Tyler nodded. "Stand near the mirror and bang on the copper plate. Did you bring something to use?"

Dante held up a large metal spoon and smiled.

"That'll work and ... don't stop," Tyler said.

Surrounded by smoke and the banging from the metal tin, Tyler stared into the mirror. The reflections from his three friends filled his view. He rubbed his eyes as the smoke intensified.

Lyly yelled out, "Do you see anything, Tyler?"

Tyler shook his head. "Stop! It's not working."

"My hands feel like they'll fall off from all this banging," Dante said.

Tyler read through his father's paper again. For the first time, he knew he was feeling as Lyly had felt when she first disappeared. His aunt was probably worried sick. He just disappeared, just like Lyly did. If he couldn't get back, how would his parents feel? And ... Aunt Meg would be devastated since she agreed to bring him with her. She would carry the guilt with her for the rest of her life.

I can't let that happen. Think, Tyler, think.

There had to be a way back. The answers were hiding somewhere within the laws of physics. It was just a matter of him figuring it out.

"A bomb?" Lyly said, reading over Tyler's shoulder.

"Not a big bomb. Just something that is lit by a fuse." Tyler shrugged.

"How about fireworks?" Dante pointed to the center of the courtyard.

Tyler glanced over at the men setting up Master Joroku's firesticks.

"Do you think they would work?" Dante asked. "I mean, they might disturb these molecule-things that you speak of."

"They just might." Tyler raised his hand to high-five Dante. But Dante just stared at him. "Fireworks are made from gunpowder. They just might aggravate the molecules enough to entice a portal to open." *But would the portal be visible?*

"Let us borrow those fireworks." Patrick waved for the others to follow.

The small group walked up to the workers and stood solemnly quiet with large smiles. "May we assist in setting up?"

The men nodded and gave out orders. The men piled the sticks onto Patrick's outstretched arms. Each time they turned to grab more, Lyly pulled several away. Dante grabbed the sticks and ran back to the tree and mirror.

Dante and Tyler pushed the firesticks into the ground. As the two worked, Patrick pulled Lyly aside. "I think our friend is sad about leaving you. He fancies you, Lyly." Patrick grinned.

"We owe him much. I do want him to understand that I will never forget him."

"As will I, always in gratitude," Patrick whispered. "Perhaps you should speak with him in private."

Lyly nodded and walked over to Tyler. "Tyler, you will forever be locked within my heart."

Tyler glanced up at her and smiled. "I've never had so much fun."

"May I keep your lock and key?"

Tyler stood. "I will keep one key and give you the other." He handed Lyly the lock and one key. He held the other and stared at it.

"I always knew it was you who would help us." Lyly leaned in and kissed him on his cheek.

Tyler felt his face flush.

"We are ready," Dante said, breaking their spell. "Patrick will light the fireworks when Domenico lights his. That way no one will hear."

Tyler nodded as he stared at Lyly. "Goodbye, my friends," Tyler said. "You're the best friends I've ever had. I'll never forget you."

"As you are ours," Patrick replied, patting Tyler on the shoulder.

Tyler demonstrated a *high-five*.

Patrick smiled and added, "Should you run into our cat friends with The Catman of Florence, please tell them we are most grateful as the mission was a success."

Dante laughed. "Yes, tell them that D'oreo enjoyed his time."

The fireworks across the yard exploded and lit the sky. Patrick lit their batch and they stood back. Patrick waved and blew on his small fire and the smoke filled the mirror. Tyler pulled off his glasses and shoved them into his pocket. His heart pounded. The fireworks blew up around him and, for the first time in weeks, he felt confident. Tyler took in a deep breath and charged at the mirror.

"This is crazy!" Tyler yelled. "I see the portal!"

His dad's paper on the movement of molecules with an explosive force was proving correct. He couldn't wait to tell him himself.

"Tyler of the House of Charles of Massachusetts, wait!" Lyly screamed and ran to him. "Tyler, I can't let you go until I tell you."

"Tell me what?"

"You're the coolest boy I ever met. I will never forget you."

"I'll remember you too but I gotta go."

"I dreamt of a boy with two different colored brown eyes, and that boy showed me the way home. It was written in the stars, Tyler. I will remember you forever."

Tyler smiled.

"Goodbye, Tyler." Lyly leaned in and kissed him on the lips.

"Lyly?" Tyler opened his eyes and she was gone. He turned to the mirror and as the light faded, he jumped and landed in Lyly's indigo bedroom. He stared at his bluish hands and laughed. "It's working!" Tyler ran up to Lyly's two-dimensional double who was sitting on the bed. He leaned over and kissed her cheek. The girl did not move for Lyly had returned to her time. Tyler felt grateful. He glanced around and saw the next portal — a mirror that reflected the Campo Piazza. Tyler reached out and touched the cold glass and felt the pull. Taking in a deep breath, he stared at the half fountain where the water sprayed into nothingness. Now, his hands were a tinge of beige.

Tyler gazed into the water and tried to remember. The tree! He had to find the tree with the lamps. Tyler ran to the large window and could see his Aunt Meg working in the small room. He ran toward the solid white line. He closed his eyes and jumped. Now, his hands were a blueish green with a yellowish tint. He was back in the Tuscany toile. He raced past the sheep and the tree with the swing.

"The lantern … the last portal!"

The closer he ran to the light, the larger the bathroom sink and shower looked. He touched the lantern. Nothing happened. Tyler slapped the glass and waited. Nothing.

"Oh, no!"

Tyler sat on the swing and cried. "Aunt Meg must have removed the toile from my bathroom. I'm now doomed to be the green boy in the toile wallpaper … forever!"

"Godspeed, Tyler," Lyly whispered. She stared at the mirror and waved. Tyler had vanished. "May you find your way home as have I." Lyly spotted Patrick and Dante standing together. She could hear them talking.

"Do you remember that Tino chap and when Good Paws freed us?" Patrick chuckled.

"I shall miss my cat friends," Dante said with a hiss. "And The Catman. He always fed me extra sardines after each act." Dante shook his head. "Loved my tail, actually. Every time, I was right on cue." He chuckled. "I wonder if he'll remember me?"

"If Tyler's physics are correct," Patrick replied. "D'oreo nor Celestial KittyCat will ever have existed."

"Nor the girl in the toile wallpaper," Lyly said. "Tyler's on his journey home. I shall miss my friend."

"As shall we all. And forever grateful," Patrick said, patting Dante's shoulder. "However, tonight is a time for celebration. We shall watch the celestial alignment any minute now."

"Yes, it is almost midnight." Lyly said, taking Patrick by the arm. "We must all celebrate our good fortunes tonight."

"Thank you, signorina Lyly," Dante said, lowering his gaze. "However, I am hired by your father to be a valet from what I can remember of that day."

"Not tonight, Dante." Lyly smiled and grabbed Dante by the arm. "And forever my friend, it shall be Lyly, just Lyly." She thought about when she first met Tyler and smiled. *'I'm just Tyler. Not the house thing.'*

"Dante!" A valet ran up to Dante and leaned over to catch his breath. "I have been searching for you. Signor Marco from our Pantera Contrada is looking for you. He needs to speak with you. He needs a jockey replacement for the Palio."

Dante's eyes widened. "The *StarWriters* have answered my dreams." He clasped his hands together in prayer.

"Go Fuoco. Find your star," Patrick said, chuckling. "When you finish your conversation, we shall have much to celebrate."

Dante and the valet ran toward the stables. Patrick took Lyly's hand and kissed it gently. His warmth flooded through her and her heart pounded.

Patrick stared into Lyly's eyes and smiled. "I found my star."

Lyly nodded. For the first time in two plus centuries, the butterflies danced inside her stomach again. "Patrick, I worried about you during my confinement. What it must have been like living as a furry four-legged creature."

"Not that bad, the brand did itch though." He laughed and pulled her in close. "Then again, not much better than you as a prisoner in a wallcovering."

"Coverings," she corrected and smiled. "Tyler called them toiles. Something his aunt works with."

"I was of no help, please accept my —"

Lyly placed her fingers over his mouth. "Hush," she whispered. "It was because of me and my family that you suffered —"

Patrick's arms closed around her and she looked up and smiled. "There's something my heart has wanted to do since the first moment I met you."

"Oh?'

Patrick leaned down and placed his warm lips over hers. Her mind whirled and her heart pounded.

"Ah-ha!" Domenico yelled out from a distance. Delfina ran close behind waving her handkerchief. "I've been looking for you two!"

Lyly wiped her mouth and grinned.

Patrick took a step back but held onto Lyly's hand.

Lyly giggled. "Now, they find me. When I do not want to be found."

"Yoo-hoo!" Delfina yelled. "Lyly, I know you're celebrating, dear. But your father needs just a moment of Patrick's time. He's our new silent investor after all."

"Yes, Mother and Father," Lyly replied not wanting to release Patrick's hand.

"Thank you, Delfina," Domenico said. "I can take it from here." He wrapped his arm around Patrick's shoulders. "Just a moment of your time, Patrick. In my study. You can celebrate with your friends …" Domenico glanced around and frowned. "Now, where is Dante and your new friend, Tyler?"

"Dante's with Signor Marco," Patrick replied.

Domenico smiled. "Yes. Yes. Wonderful news. I whole heartedly endorsed him to represent the Pantera Contrada."

"Tyler had to return home," Lyly said, winking at Patrick.

"The boy with the strange footwear." Domenico laughed. "I shall always remember him. Where does a boy like that live?"

"Massachusetts," Lyly said. "It's in the new world."

"It's where?" Domenico asked and Delfina frowned.

Megan arrived at the hotel tired and hungry. Her pouch was filled with several cardboard tubes. She now looked forward to spending some quality time with Tyler. After the heated discussion earlier, most of her anger with Robert had faded. For the first time, Megan almost trusted him to lock up alone.

Tomorrow, our last day together … looking forward to it.

She attributed her pleasant thoughts to Robert's honesty. Starting a textile company in Milan could not be easy. As for her, she had the backing of her company.

Vincenzo was standing in his usual spot behind the front desk. As she approached, he motioned for her to stop. "Tyler has been resting for most of the day." Vincenzo smiled. "He ate all his meals. He enjoys the dog channel."

"Hmm … okay. Tyler usually enjoys his books more than TV," she replied.

"Perhaps a distraction since he is not feeling well." He smiled again. "I will have your dinner delivered shortly."

"Grazie, so much."

"Likewise, prego so much, Signorina Brandt."

Stepping out of the elevator, Megan sighed. She was tired and wanted nothing more than a nice evening with her nephew. Megan fussed with the lock. She opened the door and walked inside. Tyler was under the blankets. The Italian dog show was blasting from the TV. She turned it off and stood silently by his bed. Something from the bathroom grabbed her attention. She turned and took a step. A knock at the door announced their dinner. Opening the door, she stared at an older couple.

"Good evening," the man said with a heavy British accent.

Tyler stared at the three lanterns hanging at different heights. As he swung slightly, he glanced at his bluish green hands.

"Has to be the way back."

He cringed, remembering how Lyly had said that she spied on him while … he was in the bathroom and in the shower. She had pulled him into her world through the lowest lantern. He stared at it.

"Why isn't it opening?"

He kicked the lowest lantern and the sound echoed through the field. Even if Aunt Meg took the toile down, I still might have a chance. I would just re-enter into her bedroom … but then I'm stuck in a cardboard tube …

Hearing the key turn in the lock, Harry ushered the cats into the bathroom. If needed, they could pretend to be the boy again. The eleven cats stood near the toile and sniffed. It had fallen from the wall and was rolled up on the floor. A pounding echo filled the small room. The cat's ears flattened. As they turned to run, Harry yelled out.

"No, wait!" Harry said. "It may be Celestial KittyCat. He may need our help."

Allie, Gigi, and Minnie inched their way onto the paper. They spread the paper out and sniffed again. A slight mist rose from the bluish print and a shoe appeared.

"It smells of the boy," Harry said. "We need to help him out!"

Georgio and Fabio latched onto the sneaker and yanked. Their butts wiggled as they inched backward. A leg exited and then an arm.

Tyler felt the tug. Something was pulling him into the bottom lantern feet first. It reminded him of a balloon deflating. He felt himself shrinking and stretching. The bluish color was fading and turning back to normal. Tyler opened his eyes and stared at the tiny shower. His head was almost completely under the sink. He inched out and sat up.

The bell tower from the church across the street struck. Tyler counted and when he reached twelve, he sighed. "I'm back," he whispered. His heart pounded and he thought of Lyly. His insides warmed. "That was the coolest evv…er! Best summer vaca …"

He touched his lips and smiled. His first kiss. He rubbed his arms, and he was no longer cold. Tyler stood and removed the valet puffy-white shirt. He carefully rolled up the toile and walked into his room. Aunt Meg was talking to an older man at the door.

"There are no cats in here!" Megan's voice raised. "Must I call the front desk?"

"Trevor," the woman said. "Let's go. You're embarrassing me."

"Lovey, I know they're in here. I saw them walk through that glass door. There are over a dozen cats in this room!"

Tyler placed the rolled toile under his bed. "Hi, Aunt Meg." He waved at her.

Megan turned and smiled. "Ty, how're you feeling?"

"Great."

Megan reached out and hugged Tyler.

The British man barged into the room. "The cats are all in that bed!" He pointed at Tyler. "Ah-ha, you're hiding cats in here!" Trevor lifted the covers, revealing Tyler's books. His eyes widened and he frowned. "I could have sworn —"

"Are you satisfied?" Megan asked the man. "Leave or I'll call the front desk."

The man ran into the empty bathroom and frowned. He scratched his head. As he slowly walked back to his wife, he sighed.

The British woman pulled Trevor through the room and into the hallway. "I'm so sorry," she yelled back at Megan. "He will not bother you again." The woman pulled on the door. "He forgot to take his meds. You're going to that psychologist when we get home! Obsessed over some stray cats. What is wrong with you …" The woman's voice faded as the two ran down the hallway.

Tyler peeked out the balcony doors and watched as a gray tail disappeared over the brick fence.

They really were here.

He looked at his sneakers and chuckled.

Teeth marks!

"Was that crazy," Megan said, "or what?"

Tyler shrugged.

"I'm happy you're feeling better. I was worried about you. I'm sorry I had to work."

"That's okay."

"Can you believe that I thought I saw you in one of my toiles? Now, that's some heavy guilt."

Tyler raised his brows. "Really?"

Megan knelt and picked up the toile. "What's this doing under here?"

Tyler shrugged again.

"Seems to not like my tubes. Glad I found it. Would hate to leave the girl in the toile behind … now wouldn't I?"

Tyler smiled and thought about Lyly and their lingering kiss when a knock at the door startled them.

"Dinner," said the female staffer, placing the dinner trays on the desk. "Glad the boy is feeling better."

"Grazie," Tyler said.

"Prego," she replied.

Tyler hugged Aunt Meg. "Thank you for bringing me with you. I really had a great time."

"You didn't get a chance to go anywhere or see anything. Just watched that dog channel. I never knew you liked dogs."

"What?" Tyler laughed and smiled. "Something to listen to as I slept."

Eating their lasagna, Megan nodded. "Tomorrow afternoon we'll walk around Florence."

"I have a report I want to dissect," Tyler replied. "I'll be here waiting for you."

"I just need the morning to finish. The last strip is the girl in the medieval house."

"That's where —" Tyler thought about Lyly searching for portals in her bedroom.

"That's where what, Ty?"

"Nothing." He shook his head. "Good lasagna."

"I'm very glad you're feeling better. Good appetite. You must like Italian food."

Tyler chuckled. *The cats did.*

After dinner, Megan retired to her room. It felt good that things were finally looking up.

Chapter Twenty-Two

It is said, "Home is where the heart is." This is not about home but the heart ...

Megan had showered and was ready to finish up her morning's work. She approached the front desk and smiled at Vincenzo. He frowned.

"Something wrong?" Megan asked.

"My apologies, Signorina Brandt," Vincenzo said. "As you say, Paolo no show himself this morning. I have arranged a replacement, Mario."

Megan giggled. "You mean he's a *no show.*"

"Yes, that too," Vincenzo chuckled. "Someday, I will grasp your slang."

"I wanted to thank Paolo and give him this tip." She held up an envelope. "He's been wonderful. I'll just leave it with you."

"Glad to hear. I will personally hand it to him with your sincere thank you."

"I can always count on you, Vincenzo."

"Mario is waiting for you just outside."

Megan nodded and walked into the sunshine. A young man waved at her. She sat in the back of the car and opened her calendar. Mario drove past the fountain of the Pantera Contrada, and through the familiar winding and narrow streets. Mario soon pulled into an opening. Megan stared out the window and crinkled her nose. She scrunched up her brows and frowned.

"Mario this is not the right place."

"Mi scusi, Signorina Brandt. This is the address I was given to bring you, Via Saverania 31. This is most definitely the correct La Via and numero," Mario replied.

She opened the window to get a better view. "You're right, Number 31. But where's the scaffolding?"

Mario opened the door and glared up at the number with her.

Megan stepped out and stood on the sidewalk. She studied the building. "Mario … I don't understand. This building was covered in scaffolds yesterday."

"Maybe they finished, signorina."

"It looks like the same grey building but it's refurbished with new gothic windows. And that door!"

"What's wrong with the door?"

"It looks new, but how? When did they do all of this? I've never seen anybody working." Megan spotted Robert walking from the opposite direction and waved at him.

"You found your friend," Mario said. "I have another pick-up." Mario handed her his card. "Call me when you are ready to return."

Megan nodded. She stared at Robert. He waved back. As he approached, he stopped walking and gawked at the building.

"What in the world?" Robert said, pointing at the new windows.

"What's going on?" Megan asked. "This is impossible!"

"I just walked past here a minute ago," Robert said, rubbing his head. "I didn't even recognize the place. When I left last night, the scaffolding was still here."

"Alberto will have some answers," Megan said, climbing the stairs. Megan tried the door but it was locked. "Maybe Alberto's not here yet."

"Alberto is always here." Robert grabbed the lionhead doorknocker and pounded on the door.

They stood back and waited. The door cracked open and a familiar voice said, "May I help you?"

Megan looked over at Robert and shrugged.

The door opened wider and the man stepped out. "May I help you?"

"Alberto?" Megan said, laughing. "You shaved off your goatee?"

"Where is your suit?" Robert said, frowning.

Alberto glanced at his casual black pants and light blue sweater. "Pardon? How may I help you?"

Megan sighed. "Quit joking, Alberto. We only have a little more to finish and we'll be out of your hair for good."

"Of course, pardon my ignorance. You're the designers my assistant mentioned. I was not expecting you this early. Come in, come in."

"The designers?" Megan glared at Robert and mouthed, *"What is he talking about?"*

They entered the lobby and gasped. No scaffolding hogged the entryway, and the room was freshly painted and furnished. The room that once housed their tools was now a fully working study. The gardens were immaculate and well maintained, no longer full of dead flowers and weeds.

"How many worked the nightshift?" Megan asked. "And ... where are our tools?"

"We left at nine last night, Alberto —"

"I don't understand." Alberto tilted his head. "Follow me."

Alberto walked through the study and to the anteroom and opened the door. The smaller room held Robert's tools, a crate, and a folded ladder, and … the toiles no longer covered the walls.

Megan stood and held back a scream. "How did all this furniture get in here?"

"My tools and ladder!" Robert said, looking relieved. "Where are the remaining toiles, Alberto? Megan had one more and I had two to take down."

"Those old wallpapers?" Alberto said, pointing across the room. "Please take them off our hands."

Megan's voice raised. "How did you do this and where are the remaining toiles?"

Alberto frowned. "Those old strips of paper are right over here. And what are you talking about? This has always been the office."

"We are here to finish removing the paper," Robert said. "Remember? That was the plan."

Alberto shook his head. "Remove what, exactly?"

"What do you mean?" Megan asked a little louder than she intended. "We have a contract."

Alberto waved his hand through the air. "They are right here." He reached behind a large filing cabinet and pulled out several rolls. "I have tubes if you like."

Megan anxiously inspected each piece. She glared at Robert. "These are in excellent condition. Who could have taken them off the wall, Alberto?"

"I will wait for you in the office," Alberto said.

As they divvied up the remaining rolls, Megan sighed. "I don't get it, Robert. There's a door here and furniture and … this is just nuts!"

"Let me talk to him," Robert said, stepping out of the small storage room.

Megan placed her tubes into her canvas bag. She walked out of the smaller room and shook her head. Standing at the replacement door, she held back a scream. The room was not an office yesterday. Instead of an empty room with their tools, the room was now a fully functional office ... desk, carpet, filing cabinets.

"What's going on, Alberto?" Megan asked. She placed her hands on her hips and took in a deep breath. "Where is the scaffolding? How did you repair everything so quickly? Where did this furniture come from?"

Robert stood behind Megan and laughed. "I know what it is. Alberto is playing a joke on us. You're his twin brother, right?"

Alberto clenched his jaw and almost growled. As his temples pulsed, he said softly, "I am the only living Alberto Montevelli descendent. I am CEO of The Commoner's Bank of Siena. I have no twin brother. This home has been in my family for centuries. Never in disrepair! You have this house confused with another."

"Good acting, Alberto." Robert clapped his hands.

An elderly man with bright white hair entered the study wearing a grey pinstripe suit. "Is everything under control, Signor Montevelli?"

"So glad you are here," Alberto said, stepping closer to the man. "This is my assistant, Giovanni de'Leon."

"Yes, signore," Giovanni replied.

"Do you know who these two are?"

Giovanni studied them before answering. "No."

"Then please escort them out," Alberto said, pointing to the door.

Megan stared at Robert and frowned. They followed Giovanni into the foyer and down the stairs.

"Do you have any paraphernalia?" Giovanni glanced over at Megan.

"Mine was rented," Megan said. "My company will worry about them."

"I see," Giovanni said. "Should I come across any, I will return them. Do you have a card?"

Megan handed Giovanni her business card. "Thank you."

"Good day," he said, running back up the stairs.

"I think I know what's going on." Megan slapped her hands together.

"What?" Robert scratched his head and laughed. "I'm at a loss here."

"We've been hoodwinked," she said, smirking.

"Hoodwinked." He chuckled.

She glared at him. "Are you a part of this?"

"Me?"

"Yes, you," she stomped her foot. "My company never heard of you until I arrived."

Robert shook his head. "As you Americans say, cross my heart." Making an imaginary X on his chest, he added, "And hope to die. I have nothing to do with this. I am as confused as you. On the other side of the coin … as you say."

Megan stared him down. *You and those catch phrases.*

"Are we not left whole here?" Robert asked.

"What do you mean?"

"Our remaining toiles are in excellent condition." He held up a tube. "You said so yourself."

"What's your point?"

"I have my tools and ladder. Nothing is missing and we didn't have to remove the last of the toiles. I'd say it's a win-win. Wouldn't you?"

Megan thought about her sister, Elysse, crossing her heart, and Megan always ended up with the shorter end of the stick. *But can I trust you, Robert?*

Tino pulled the green rickety truck up to the hospital's entrance. The large logo, The Catman and His Amazing Cats, still decorated the sides. Uncle Fabio sat in a wheelchair and a nurse stood next to him.

"Your uncle is very fortunate," the nurse said. "His heart attack was mild. He's on medication and a strict diet." She handed Tino several sheets of paper.

"Ciao, my lady," Fabio said, winking over at Tino. "You do that exercise with your kitty I told you about. Mark my words, she will-a be in your good-a graces again."

"Grazie, Catman," the nurse replied, smiling.

Tino helped Uncle Fabio into the passenger side. His stomach tightened. How would he ever explain the missing cats?

"You taking good care of my children, Tino?" Fabio asked. "I cannot wait until they are in my arms again." He cooed.

"Si," Tino replied.

"Drive a little faster. I am anxious to see them."

"Just taking care of you, Uncle." Tino listened as his stomach churned.

"I appreciate that."

Tino parked the truck and helped his uncle up the stairs. He used his key and pushed open the door. Tino gasped. Belle sat on the arm of the couch staring at him. She meowed and raised her paw.

"Not possible," Tino whispered.

"There's my beautiful Belle," Fabio cooed. Belle jumped into Fabio's arms and purred. "Where are my other babies? Allie? Gigi? Mushmellow? Fabio? Minnie? Trixie? Curry? Harry? Asti? Cherie? Georgie? How I have missed you all. Stop teasing me," he sang out. "Come out, come out, from where ever you are …"

"Uh … there's something I must tell you, Uncle Fab."

Tino's eyes widened. He watched as the cats inched their way out from under the furniture. All eleven meowed and purred.

Belle scooted over to Harry and whispered into his ear. "Where's D'oreo?"

Harry glanced around and shrugged.

"What? That's not possible," said Tino loud enough for Fabio to hear.

"What's not possible, my dear Tino? What else do you have-a to tell me? Good news I hope?" Fabio sat on the floor and hugged each cat. Smiling, he gazed up at Tino. "I can't thank you enough. You took good care of my babies. You took-a such good care of them while I worried so. They are happy and well fed."

Harry nudged Belle and smiled. "Maybe he didn't come back?"

Belle nodded. "We won't say a word. Hopefully, nobody will notice."

Tino gulped. He couldn't believe his lucky stars. Uncle Fab was happy right now. A perfect time to break the news. "I am leaving, Uncle."

"But Tino, where will you go? What will you do?"

"My dream is to open my own tattoo parlor." Tino ran into his bedroom and returned with a pad of drawings.

Fabio studied the inkwork. "Why, Tino. I never knew you had such talent. Perhaps I will help you as a silent partner. I have saved some money throughout the years.

"You would do that for me, Uncle Fab?"

"Of course I would, Tino. Afterall, we are family. Right, my precious babies? But first, we need to do one more show before we find a replacement for you."

Tino shook his head and stared at the cats. *They are still rats. But stupid? No.*

Chapter Twenty-Three

It is said, "It always seems impossible until it is done."
This is not about what is impossible for it is already done ...

"You're staying in Florence?" Robert asked.

"Yes," Megan replied. "Where are you staying?"

"Same. Help me with the ladder and I'll drive. No reason for you to wait for a ride."

"Let me inform my driver."

Megan texted the driver as Robert dragged the ladder to the car. She helped Robert tie the ladder down. She was surprised to discover that Robert's hotel was only a few buildings from hers.

"Let's have lunch," Robert said. "My treat. I'd love to meet your nephew."

"Oh, I don't —"

"I don't want us parting with you not trusting me."

Megan nodded and listened as Robert rambled on about his start-up company in Milan. Every so often, she'd glance over at him and frown. Not sure how much to trust, she wanted to keep her distance. *Who are you really, Roberto?*

Then she thought about Alberto ... *I'm the CEO of The Commoner's Bank of Siena.'* Good acting, Alberto. Was it all show for her benefit? Was Roberto hanging onto her just to confuse the situation? Megan wouldn't be able to confer with her employers to discuss her fears until Tuesday because Monday she'd be on a plane all day.

As she fought off her doubts, Megan looked at Robert and smiled. *He is rather handsome.* As soon as she thought about it, she pushed it out of her mind. Useless thoughts of Robert or Roberto would only waste her time. Before they'd meet for lunch, Megan would warn Tyler of her enemy, Robert.

Megan sat at a table with Tyler that overlooked the River Arno. Glancing at the couples walking in the afternoon sunlight, she laughed. In this so-called *city of love*, no love was available for her … not even Robert.

"Aunt Meg?" Tyler's voice floated through the air. "Aunt Meg?" Tyler said a little louder and tapped on the table.

"Sorry, Ty. Thinking about work."

"Is that your *enemy*? The guy walking over here?"

Robert reached out his hand. "You must be Tyler. Feeling much better?"

Tyler shook Robert's hand and smiled.

"I'm Robert or Roberto, and yes … I'm *technically* the enemy."

Everyone laughed, which seemed to break the tension.

Megan thought about the strange morning. She wanted to talk about it but not in front of Ty. Instead, she tried to disguise her words. Megan felt it important that she knew what actually happened at Via Saverania 31. Nothing was making any sense. She looked over at Ty and smiled. He seemed to be checking Robert out.

"Do you still have that business card Alberto gave you?" Megan asked.

"No, I can't find it." Robert frowned. "Do you have yours?"

"No. I've lost mine too. I just have my drivers' cards and their numbers."

Tyler continued to stare at them.

"I memorized it though," Megan said.

"Tell me. What did it say?"

"It had his name, Alberto Montevelli. Said Rep and not CEO. And that assistant! Giovanni de'Leon was the name of the company he worked for … de'Leon Enterprises. It wasn't a person yesterday."

Raising his brows, Tyler smirked. "Did something odd happen at work this morning?"

Robert looked at Tyler and frowned. "Excuse me?"

"What do you know about space time continuum?" Tyler said.

"Space time what?" Megan repeated.

Tyler leaned in closer and whispered, "Time warp? Time travel?"

"You know the stuffed cat I received when we first checked in?" Tyler asked.

Megan nodded.

"Mine's missing."

"Missing?" Megan asked.

"I asked Vincenzo for another one. And he had no idea what I was talking about. I said, Celestial KittyCat and he said, *'celestial what?'*"

"You mean the legend of the Celestial Cat?" Robert said. "Everyone knows of that legend."

"Apparently, not anymore," Tyler said.

"What do you mean, not anymore?" Megan asked.

"Watch …"

The waiter walked up and placed a glass of water in front of each of them. "Ready to order?"

"Um … first," Tyler said. "What is the legend of Celestial KittyCat?"

"Mi scusi?" the waiter replied.

"Yes," Robert said. "The cat that's supposed to have a tattoo on its side?"

"I know of no tattooed-cat?" the waiter said. "Orders?"

The three ordered their lunch.

"Then, that bank over there." Tyler pointed. "When we first ate here, I remember a flock of birds."

"I remember," Megan said. "We couldn't believe how many there were."

"That building had *Banca de'Leon* on it. Now, it has *The Commoner's Bank of Siena* on it."

"Now that you mention it …" Robert added.

"Okay, Ty, what's going on?" Megan asked.

"Just listen and I'll tell you. And … it might explain some of what you experienced."

"Okay," Robert said. "We're listening."

"It's really … really … really weird."

"Can't be any weirder than this morning," Megan said.

"Or some of the other things I'm noticing," Robert added.

Tyler took in a deep breath and let it out slowly. His heart pounded through his ears as he spoke, "I think you were brought here for a reason and so was I."

Megan smiled.

"There was a girl living in the wallpaper that you took down," Tyler said.

"You mean the girl on the swing?" Megan asked. "I knew I saw her move!"

"The wallpaper moved?" Robert asked.

"No, the girl." Megan nodded.

"Her name is … I mean … her name was CallaLyly Montevelli. She lived over two-hundred and fifty years ago."

"Two-hundred and fifty?" Megan took a sip of water.

Tyler nodded. "She was seventeen. Her parents promised her in a marriage."

"Promised?" Megan repeated.

"Yes," Robert said. "In the past, marriages were arranged. Mostly to make a family financially stable or to stop a feud."

"I think both when it comes to Lyly." Tyler shook his head. "Anyway, she was promised to Agost de'Leon. A real clown. And his father, Giovanni de'Leon, was going to give money to their family bank. The Commoner's Bank of Siena."

"From across the street," Robert added.

"Yes," Tyler said. "Lyly's father was bankrupt. Lyly was so upset over the pending engagement that she ran away and met Patrick. At the giving away party, no one knew that Patrick was from a very wealthy family. He had fallen in love with Lyly and gave her his inheritance." Tyler paused and watched their expressions. When he received no response, he continued.

"Giovanni de'Leon wanted their bank because he hated the commoners. The farmers and such that used the family funds. I think

Lyly's dad gave them a lot of loans. Anyway, Giovanni, who was a really bad man, found another bad man named, Master Joroku."

"Master Joroku?" Robert repeated.

"Yes." Tyler nodded again. "He was a mystic from the orient. And somehow he sucked Lyly into the wallpaper and turned Patrick into an immortal black cat with symbols on his side."

"That's where the legend came from?" Robert asked. "The legend of Celestial KittyCat."

"Time passed," Tyler said, "and de'Leon got the property at Via Saverania 31."

Megan and Robert stared at him. The waiter brought them their lunch and neither moved. Tyler took a bite of his lasagna and smiled.

"Now, for the part you're not going to believe." Tyler chuckled.

Robert took a bite of his food and frowned. "I think I'm following you."

"The wallpaper you accidently left in my room?" Tyler looked over at Megan. Megan nodded. "Lyly pulled me into it. I was sucked through a lantern, which was actually a portal. Then we ran through the papers you were pulling down."

"My God ..." Megan pushed her food across her plate. "I knew I saw something. I thought I just was overtired."

"I remember seeing something move too," Robert said, placing his fork on his plate before winking at Megan. "But I thought I was just working too hard."

"I'm sorry. My head popped out and I was in the room where you two were working. I saw you ... both. Anyway, I figured things out and reversed it."

"Reversed it?" Robert repeated.

"Yea, reversed it. Now, the descendants and the Houses all reversed. Alberto Montevelli is Lyly's baby brother. She introduced me to him. His descendants remained the head of the *Commoner's Bank of Siena,* and Giovanni de'Leon and his descendants were the ones that went broke. And they are working for the Montevellis now. It all makes sense!"

"Right," Megan said.

"Of course," Robert replied.

Tyler took another breath and smiled. "That's why everything you remembered has changed. Time warp!" He smiled widely and took another bite of his lasagna.

Megan touched Tyler's arm. "My God, Ty! I'm so sorry. I blame myself for not staying with you. What you must have gone through and with such a high fever and strong meds. You were clearly knocked out and hallucinating. The doctor said it could happen. I should have believed her."

"What?" Tyler pulled his arm away. "No!"

Robert clapped. "What a wonderful tale, Ty. I love it. You have a great imagination. You should write a book. Be a best seller."

"Aunt Meg, I can tell you about your toiles and in detail. Maybe then you'll believe me cuz I ran through all of them with Lyly."

"Tell me about my toiles," she said, eating her lunch.

"First I fell on top ... I mean ... I met Lyly. It was in the Siena farmlands on a bright yellow background. I looked like a cartoon. Everything was a cartoon. The trees, the houses, the animals. I ran around and played with the blue-green sheep ... the cows."

"Uh-huh," Megan said, taking another bite.

"I tried to open a farmhouse door but only scratched paper. Felt like cloth."

"Okay," Megan said.

"I ran around the circular square, the Piazza del Campo, saw the Mangia Tower and the Duomo ... it was black and white on a crème background. How could I know that if I wasn't in that paper?"

"I'm not sure," Megan said. "But those meds were pretty strong."

Tyler sighed "And I sat in Lyly's bedroom. It was blue and red. That was the bedroom in the house where you were work —"

"Ty, just think about it," Megan said and her voice softened. "I talked to you in detail about my toiles. You pieced your scientific stuff together with what I had said and stuffed them into your dream. All those names you used, with a few exceptions, you heard me say while you were asleep. Maybe I left that business card in your room and you read the address and the names."

"Then where is that card now?" Tyler asked.

"Picked up by one of the staff and tossed out," Megan replied.

Tyler sighed. "Aunt Meg, I was gone. I wasn't in my room. I fell back in time and lived inside your toiles with Lyly. I swear it. Did you actually see me or just talked to me?"

"Of course I saw you, Ty," Megan said. "You were sleeping. I talked to you when you were in the bathroom with your stomach ache."

"But that was the cats ...!" Tyler stared at his aunt. She wasn't believing him. *Just that British guy.* Raising his hands to his head, Tyler frowned. "You're right. It was a dream. But it felt so real!"

"Dreams can be real especially with strong meds," Megan said. "Trust me on that. I'm happy you're looking and feeling better. Just please don't tell your mom any of this."

"I won't." Tyler crossed his heart with his finger.

"Ugh," she sighed.

"Let's finish our lunch," Robert said. "I want to take you on the best tour of Florence. I know the most delicious gelato place in all of the city."

"Considering that we haven't had any yet, and poor Ty spent his time hallucinating, we're in." Megan laughed.

"What is gelato?" Tyler asked.

"The best ice cream in the world," Robert said.

"I'm in." Tyler nodded.

Robert drove them to several places frequented by the locals and coveted by the tourists. Tyler's favorite was the Piazza Michelangelo. A replica of *The David* stood in the center.

"The views are breathtaking," Megan said. "Thank you."

"I knew you'd like it. It's magical," Robert said. He pulled Tyler back from creeping too far over the edge.

"It's so cool," Tyler said.

Turning around, Tyler noticed a crowd chanting, "Catman, Catman, Catman …"

"Those are the cats!" Tyler yelled out. "I have to thank them. They saved Patrick and Dante. Can I go over and watch?"

"You like cats now too? Dogs and cats. I'm learning a lot about you on this trip. Sure, go ahead."

Tyler spotted twelve cats sitting in a row each holding a small cap in their mouth. They were collecting euros for the show. Tyler stepped up to the two in the middle — one orange striped and the other grey.

Patting their heads, he knelt and whispered, "Uh, hi. I have a message from Patrick and Dante … I mean Celestial KittyCat and D'oreo."

The orange cat dropped her cap and meow-ed. The eleven cats dropped their hats and ran closer to Tyler. The crowd clapped.

"Eh?" The Catman said. "What do we have here?"

"Should I stop it, Uncle Fab?" Tino asked.

"No," The Catman replied. "Not yet. This is good for business."

Tyler sat in the middle of the cats. "Patrick and Dante give their thanks. And they said to tell you that their mission was a success. D'oreo, who was really Dante, wanted me to tell you he enjoyed his time with you. I mean really enjoyed it."

Another cat meow-ed.

"I want to thank you too. You did a terrific job impersonating me. We'll keep it our little secret."

The cats bowed to Tyler.

"Now, tha-da boy is-a cat whisperer." The Catman clapped with the crowd. "And si, it takes-a one to know-a one."

Tyler glanced up and saw a familiar face. He waved at the old British man and his wife. The man pointed and said something. She tried to pull him away. Tyler shrugged.

"You see, Lovey," the man yelled. "What did I tell you about *that* boy and those *cats*. See, I'm not crazy!"

"Maybe I owe you an apology, Trevor," the woman replied.

"Where's the black and white one I saw opening the balcony door? And that scraggily black one. Let me ask The Catman."

"I warn you, Trevor. Don't go there," the woman yelled. "You'll open another can of worms. Leave them be."

The old man shrugged and walked away.

Megan stood next to Robert and watched as Tyler ran over to The Catman and his cats. She shook her head and laughed.

Robert cleared his throat. "You have a wonderful nephew."

"Thank you. I think so too. And … thank you for this afternoon. Most fun Ty had since we arrived. Honestly, I'm having a nice time too."

He stared at her and said, "There's something important I need to ask."

"What's that?" Megan smiled.

"I told you a great deal about my company but what I didn't tell you is that I'm in search of a partner. I plan to someday take my company global. I've been thinking about it, and after working with you, I need someone like you with all your expertise and connections. You could help me expand in the United States. What do you think?"

"Sure. Be happy to help you out. I'll think of someone to recommend. When I return, I'll do a little homework."

"No, Megan. That's not what I mean."

"I don't understand."

"I want you." Robert grabbed her shoulders and shook her a little. "You'd make the perfect partner. I'm prepared to offer you a forty percent share. No employment … a partnership."

Megan stepped back and laughed. "You're asking someone who has a trust issue with you … someone who calls you *her enemy* to be your partner? That's taking a leap of faith."

"I don't think so. We make a great team."

Her eyes followed the snaking River Arno through the city below. She looked over at Robert and smiled. "Thank you for your generous offer but my heart is set on starting a new division for my company. I've been there ten years and my employers are promising me a great advancement. I don't want to let them down. It's been my dream for so long."

"I understand." He frowned. "Don't like it, but I understand. I'll tell you what. Should you change your mind …" Robert pulled out a card and placed it in her hand. Then he intertwined his fingers with hers.

Her heart fluttered and she shook her head. "Thank you but my answer is still no. I'll put this in a safe place for now."

"Call me should you change your mind. Better yet, come visit my warehouse in Milan."

"Maybe someday."

Tyler returned and Robert ended their tour at a corner shop in the piazza.

"This is where the locals come. Best gelato in Florence. Always a long line though."

"Can't we wait, Aunt Meg?" Tyler asked.

"We still have the afternoon. Let's get in line," she replied, smiling.

Robert and Megan agreed to part as friends. At the hotel, Megan walked up to Vincenzo and handed him an envelope.

"Don't want to miss you in the morning. Thank you for everything Vincenzo. I couldn't have taken care of business and Tyler without you."

"It was my pleasure, Signorina Brandt. I will probably see you in the morning. Ciao and I hope Tyler had fun today. He has been, as you say, cooped up in his room."

"He said he had a wonderful time. Whatever your staff did, well … most grazie."

"Most prego."

"Now, where is he?" Megan searched for Tyler. "Ah, there you are."

"Look!" Tyler handed her the Palio Record Book. "This lists all the winners since the beginning." Tyler stated. "Yesss!"

"Yes, what?"

"The Pantera Contrada won their first Palio in almost fifty years with the rider Dante Merle, nicknamed, Fuoco, and his horse, Tomassino. And Fuoco won the next fifteen years in a row for the Pantera Contrada." He laughed. "Guess you can't call them Nonnas anymore."

"You're into horses now too?" Megan shook her head.

"Just one." Tyler smiled.

"Let's pack. We leave very early." She patted Tyler on the back. "I need to make sure my toiles are secured. You wouldn't believe how one just kept popping out. Like it wanted to make itself known or something."

You should have believed me, Aunt Meg.

Chapter Twenty-Four

It is said, "Once in a while everyone gets their just desserts." This is not about the sweets but about the things that sour our lives ...

Tyler pulled the cover tighter over his shoulder. Sleeping inside his own bed was just too good to be true. The doorbell rang several times and he sighed. Tyler stared up at the ceiling. The bell rang again. He pulled the pillow tighter over his head and whined.

"Agh!" he stood and stretched.

As he walked downstairs, Tyler glanced into the guest room. No Aunt Meg. She must have already left for work. The doorbell rang again. And again.

"Coming, Aunt Meg!" he shouted, putting on his glasses and running his fingers through his ruffled hair. "Did you forget something?"

Tyler opened the front door wearing just his navy-blue pj's and no shoes. *No Aunt Meg?* The doorbell rang again.

"Darn," he said, closing the door and aiming for the kitchen.

A large red face stared at him through the glass window. Tyler froze. He dropped to the floor and crawled behind the kitchen counter.

"Stop hiding, yah wuss!" yelled that evil and familiar voice. Kevin pounded on the door. "Let's settle this once and for all!"

Tyler popped up from behind the counter and stared out at the husky boy. Kevin was wearing a red t-shirt and tan shorts. Why Kevin Smitters, his arch enemy, on his first day home? Tyler slipped back down and sat with his back against the counter.

"Tyler's not home!" Tyler squealed out in a high-pitched voice. "Go away."

Kevin pounded on the door again. The glass window rattled. "Who yah kidding? I just saw you, and I'm not leaving till we have it out."

Tyler's heart pounded. If he didn't face him today, he'd have to face him tomorrow. Tyler placed his glasses on the counter and slowly unlocked the kitchen door. Glancing down, Tyler stared at the red signature sneakers.

Tyler thought about what Patrick had said about taking down a bully. He ran the examples through his mind. Tyler stepped outside. Kevin backed into the grass and raised his arms. He started hopping around. Tyler stepped off the stoop and chuckled.

"Are you gonna fight or not?" Kevin asked, squinting and hopping around.

Tyler raised his arms and the two circled each other as if two panthers were ready to strike. Kevin Smitters lunged and Tyler stepped to the side. Kevin stumbled and caught himself before falling over. Tyler smiled. Seemed that Tyler could move a little faster than the heavy-set Kevin. Tyler circled behind the angry boy and rammed against his knees. Kevin fell backwards over Tyler and onto his back. Tyler stood and stared down at the wide-eyed boy. He extended a hand.

"Wanna be friends?" Tyler asked.

Kevin's school bag sat on the driveway. Tyler stared at it for a moment and grinned. Kevin never received anything higher than a C on any of his schoolwork.

"Hey, Kev," Tyler said, chuckling. "Summer school?" Tyler motioned toward the bag. "I can help you improve your grades."

Kevin ignored Tyler's hand and rolled onto his knees. He stood and grabbed his bag. "If you tell anyone about this … I'll be back!"

Tyler watched as Kevin limped down his driveway and into the street.

Doesn't want to be friends? He raised his fist into the air and laughed. "Don't come back unless you want more of this!"

Tyler entered the kitchen and locked the door. He grabbed his glasses and climbed the stairs to his room. He fell onto his bed and stared up at the ceiling. He smiled as he closed his eyes.

The sun just started to peek over the tops of the Boston skyscrapers as Megan arrived at the offices of Tighe & Randall on State Street. By nine that morning her crate with the toiles had arrived. Megan's heart warmed as she thought about *the girl in the toile*. She was excited to share everything with the owners and hear about her promotion.

"Good morning, young lady," Mr. Tighe said, standing back and watching her fumble through the crate. "And welcome home!"

Megan stood and smiled. "Thank you. I'm glad to be home."

"Get some coffee and come to my office," Mr. Tighe said. "We'd like an update about your trip."

Megan nodded. She walked to the kitchen and grabbed her old cup. It felt weird holding it again. She filled it with coffee and slowly walked to Mr. Tighe's office.

"Come in and have a seat," Mr. Tighe said, waving his hand toward the couch.

Megan sat and watched as Mr. Randall darted into the room. "You're not going to believe this!"

Mr. Tighe glanced over at his partner and frowned. "Believe what?"

"The funds we transferred to Italy for the acquisition of the paper as well as Megan's travel expense were returned to our bank. Plus an additional ten percent!"

"That doesn't sound right," Mr. Tighe said, raising his brows.

"I've been trying to reach Joroku Enterprises all morning. No one's picking up."

Megan's eyes widened. "What did you just say? Joroku Enterprises?"

"Yes, Joroku Enterprises," Mr. Randall replied. "And welcome home."

Megan nodded.

"Joroku is the third party that brought this deal to our attention," Mr. Randall said.

Megan stared out the window. *Where have I heard that name, Joroku, before?* Then it hit her. Tyler had mentioned the name Joroku when he was telling her of his dream. *Oh, what was it … I remember now.* Megan chuckled. *Master Joroku was the oriental mystic that put CallaLyly into the toile. What a coincidence.*

Together, the partners and Megan pulled out the toiles and examined each one.

"These are exquisite!" Mr. Tighe said. "Great job."

"Thank you." Megan smiled. "It was a labor of love. I appreciate the opportunity."

"I'll have these authenticated," Mr. Randall said. "Thank you, we'll take it from here."

Megan frowned and then smiled. *I've waited this long for that promotion, what's another week?*

"Danny and I cannot thank you enough. First, for taking Ty with you. And second, Ty's come back as a different kid," Elysse said, smiling. "We were hoping the camp would have an impact on him, and instead, he grew quite a bit while in Florence with you. He seems more outgoing and is more eager to make friends."

Megan nodded.

"He's not just sitting in front of that computer anymore."

"You're welcome, sis," Megan said.

"Danny and Ty are going camping ... together!"

"That's great!" Megan said.

"I think it's important for them to have some alone time, don't you?"

Megan nodded. "Speaking of alone." Her eyes widened. "How was your vacation with Danny? Was it everything you had hoped for?"

Elysse sighed. "A little touch and go. He was really surprised ..." Elysse stared up at the ceiling. "I don't mean in a bad way. He was just focused on his presentation and wanted to spend his free time connecting with the other physicists. I was almost a third wheel."

"Oh?"

"Don't get me wrong. We had a good heart-to-heart." Turning away Elysse wiped her eyes. "It'll be okay. It'll work out."

Megan reached for her sister's hand. "You okay?"

"I'm fine." The front door opened and Elysse straightened. "Ty's home."

Tyler walked into the kitchen and Kevin Smitters followed a few steps behind. "Hi, Mom. Hi, Aunt Meg."

"Hi, Ty," said Megan.

"You remember my friend, Kev?"

"Yes," Megan replied. "Hi, Kev."

"Nice to see you again, Kevin," Elysse said.

"Hi," Kevin replied.

"We're going to grab a snack and go to my room." Tyler opened the pantry door.

"Don't ruin your dinner." Elysse sighed.

Tyler nodded. "Can Kev stay for dinner?"

"Sure," Elysse replied. "Burgers and franks on the grill."

"Great," Kevin said. "Ty's helping me with my summer classes. I got an A on my last test."

"That's great, Kevin," Elysse said. "Then we have a reason to celebrate. Keep up the good work."

"Thank you, Mrs. Charles," Kevin replied.

The boys grabbed some snacks from the pantry before running up the stairs.

"See what I mean?" Elysse whispered. "What about you? Anything other than work that happened in Italy?"

Megan shrugged.

"Fess up." Elysse laughed. "I know you like a book."

"Well …" Megan shifted in her chair. "I did meet this Italian guy."

242

Elysee leaned in. "Tell me more."

"We worked together on the toiles." Megan shrugged. "That's about it. But he did offer me a job in Milan."

"What kind of job?"

"Forty percent partnership in his textile company."

"So?"

"So, nothing." Megan laughed. "I'm waiting on my toiles to be authenticated, and then I have my own division. That's the end of the story."

Elysee walked to the fridge and pulled out the hamburgers. She dusted them with a little flavoring and smiled. "When do you find out?"

"Any day now," said Megan, looking down at her hands. "It's just taking a little longer than I expected."

Elysse wanted to give Megan a touch of sisterly advice. She looked up at her and smiled. "If things don't work out maybe it wasn't meant to be. Afterall, it's already written in the stars."

"What did you say?" Megan looked up at her.

"Maybe it wasn't meant to be."

"No, the star thing."

"Ty said it a couple of times." Elysee shrugged. "I like it. It's already written in the stars."

Megan nodded. "I believe he heard it from one of the waiters in Florence. The so-called *city of love.*"

"Italian? Then, tell me … was he handsome?"

Megan threw the newspaper at her sister and walked outside to start the grill.

Chapter Twenty-Five

It is said, "As one door closes a window opens." This is not about a closed door or an opened window but rather a blooming future ...

"Signorina," the taxi driver said. "This is the correct place you say for the address."

Sitting on the back seat, Megan pulled out a few euros. "Thank you, signore." Megan handed him what looked to her like play money. "Can you give me a momento, please."

"Si," he replied, counting the bills. "Change?"

"No, no. All yours."

"Grazie, signorina." He grinned and his crooked, yellowed teeth filled his smile.

"Pre ... go." Megan nodded. She glanced out the window and sighed. *What am I doing here? Must be out of my mind.* Her hands shook and her heart pounded. With her soul still on fire, she thought about Ronald Tighe and how he had smiled at her. How he had been nice to her. Then when he wanted to talk to her in private, it should have been good news.

She'd never forget how embarrassed and depressed she felt as she walked out of his office. Megan glanced down at the report that sat on her lap and frowned. Even just touching the paper gave her the chills.

How would she explain it to Robert? All their hard work and long hours. Not to mention, she had left her nephew in that hotel room alone and sick. Her heart sank as she reread the report.

DuPONT REPORT   Tighe & Randall Wall Covering and Textiles
MULTIANALITICAL   July 13, 2005
NON-DESTRUCTIVE TECHNIQUES   Page 13

further analyses, the resemblance the Siena Toiles provided, possess to the first Christophe-Philippe Oberkampf Toile de Jouy, France, Museum Originals, and they are remarkable. However, of pure coincidence.

We believe the toiles provided, magnificent as they are, precede Christophe-Philippe's first originals by about eleven years. Due to such similarity, the toiles possibly served as an inspiration to Christophe-Philippe as a child when he accompanied his father on his dyeing projects. One trip in particular, Siena, Christophe-Philippe wrote about such in his memoirs:

"I will forever remember, at ten years of age, when accompanying my father on a business trip to Siena, Italy. We were in a district referred to as the Pantera Contrada and visited a house, a splendid travertine structure. There, my father met with a banker in his office study to discuss a loan.

Becoming restless, I, as a child, stepped into an anteroom and there on the floor found rolls and rolls of the most intriguing combination of cloth paper wallcoverings that I could ever imagine.

It was as though the wallcoverings were alive and could speak to me. I studied those coverings in detail for a very long time, and eventually tore a piece of the seafaring sheet to hide on my person.

So fascinated by these, they became my inspiration, to my own Toile de Jouy some eleven years hence, when I formed my own partnership.

However, Father was not able to garner a loan as the banker at the Commoner's Bank of Siena had said he was beyond bankrupt."

They were hoodwinked by Joroku Enterprises, and Ronald Tighe said he had sold her precious toiles instead of suing the bastard! She wanted to cry, scream, or run out of that office. Nothing made any sense. Everything, including Mr. Tighe's and Mr. Randall's attitudes were different. That girl in the toile wallpaper was hers! How dare they?

Now, no new division. No raise. Basically, no job.

Megan rubbed Robert's business card between her fingers. She glanced up at the taxi driver and then back out the window. She stared at the old and rusted warehouse and frowned. *Another hoodwinker?*

"This is really Via Traversa 1, Milan?" she whispered.

The driver turned and stared at her. He reached over and gently tapped her knee. He nodded. "Si, si, signorina. We are at Via Traversa 1. Si."

"Milan," Megan whispered and a tear fell.

"Yes, Milan." The man frowned and added. "Perhaps it is in the stars?"

Megan sat up straight and glared at the man.

"You want we should leave?"

"No!" Megan almost yelled out the word. "I will leave it to the stars."

The driver opened the door and Megan stepped out. Her heart pounded and she felt a little lightheaded.

"It's now or never," she whispered.

"Scusi?" he said.

Megan shook her head. She walked up to the entrance and stared at the single metal door. The small sign read: *Cavelli Textiles & Wallcovering*. The door creaked as she pulled it open. The dimly lit space felt eerie. No windows. She studied the hand-blocking machines that filled her view. They looked authentic and old. Two older women glanced up and stared at her. She searched for Roberto's handsome face.

Maybe he's not here.

Various textiles and wall coverings hung from the rafters. Workers moved about pushing carts or running the machines. As she headed toward the back, the workers ignored her.

Near the back, Megan froze and stared up at the coverings hanging from the rafters. They were the toiles Robert had removed from the anteroom. She smiled. He obviously had taken great care placing them here.

She stepped up to the seafaring toile and stared at the torn corner. The report she held had mentioned a tear. Megan wiped her eyes and whispered, "It's already written in the stars."

Someone tapped her on her shoulder pulling her from her thoughts. A middle-aged man spoke and frowned.

Megan threw up her arms and shook her head. "Scusi. Don't understand. Is Robert Cavelli here?"

"Roberto?" the man repeated.

"Si," she replied.

He pointed across the room.

"Grazie."

Megan walked in the direction where the man had pointed. She stepped through the various toiles hanging from the rafters and stopped when she saw *her* toiles. "Robert Cavelli you jerk!" she whispered. "You're the buyer of the girl in the toile wallpaper?" Megan felt her cheeks flush. *They were to be my future and now they are only a part of my past.*

"Megan Brandt!" Robert stepped out from behind a toile. "You are here." He stepped forward and smiled. "Welcome to my humble warehouse. I hope not for the girl in the toile wallpaper as she is now mine." He chuckled.

"I can see that."

"Please don't be angry. I had mine authenticated and we both know they failed. With my payment, your employers accepted my generous offer. I asked for secrecy. I did not wish to upset you."

"They also accepted my resignation." She stared down at the floor and frowned.

"Megan." Robert took her hand and kissed it. "I'm sorry. Walk with me?"

Megan walked next to Robert and tried to breathe. Her chest ached and her heart was breaking.

"The girl is exquisite," he said. "I have ideas for a CallaLyly's fairytale line along with a Celestial KittyCat. Based on what your nephew told us of course."

"I never told you …"

"Yes?"

"I had a recorder when we first examined the toiles," she said.

"And?"

"And, when I replayed the tape, it was blank."

"Blank?"

Megan nodded.

"Maybe it was corrupted by the airport x-ray machines."

"It was blank at the hotel." Megan stopped and reached out. She touched the paper and smiled. "I like your ideas. May I ask a question?"

"Please."

"In Siena, you once mentioned a third party. May I ask their name?"

"Ru Enterprises," he replied. "Why?"

"Nothing. Never mind."

"That's all you wanted to ask me?"

She smiled. "For now." Megan stood in front of the CallaLyly that was in the medieval house and frowned. She rubbed the deflating report between her fingers. "These toiles are more beautiful and alluring than I remember."

"Yes, the girl is amazing." Robert stared at Megan. "Now, may I ask a question?"

"Why not?"

"Why are you here?" Robert smiled. "In Milan? In my warehouse?"

"I followed a star," she whispered.

Robert chuckled. "I have a secret."

Megan glanced up and grinned. "A secret?"

"I was hoping that if I purchased your toiles, you would eventually come here. By catch or by crook."

Megan giggled. "By hook or by crook." Megan walked over to the girl and studied her. "Did you say *my* toiles?"

Robert's eyes widened. "I bought the girl in the toile wallpaper just for you. You're the only one who can do her justice."

Megan's heart warmed. "You bought her for me?"

Robert reached out and held the toile with the girl and said, "We make great partners, Meg … you and me."

Megan laughed. "If you plan on calling me Meg, then I'll call you Roberto." She looked him in the eyes and liked what she saw. "Has to be 50/50 for it to work for me." She raised her brows.

Robert took her hand and gently kissed the top. "Done. Cavelli and Brandt."

Megan lingered. Feeling her hand in Robert's felt wonderful. "Brandt and Cavelli." She chuckled. "Ladies first. And may I have a contract?"

Robert nodded and smiled.

Megan sipped on the red wine. As she nibbled on the antipasto, her heart raced. *Can I trust him?* Robert moved his hands through the air as he shared his ideas for the girl in the toile wallpaper. He dipped his bread into the seasoned oil and took a bite. "We can have her jump … with a boy … a cat …"

Megan stared at her enemy and smiled. Her heart was melting and she finally felt safe and full of hope.

He bought the toiles for me? "Wonderful lunch." Megan took another bite. "You really are a wonderful cook."

"Thank you." He smiled. "But … can we discuss your recorder and Tyler's story again?"

Megan's eyes widened.

"In the toiles …" he said with a smirk, "… there is an empty swing."

Megan phoned Elysse. She tapped on the table as she waited.

"Hello? Megan?"

"I'm moving to Milan!" Megan laughed. "Robert and I are partners. Fifty percent. He bought —"

"Stop, breathe!" Elysse replied, laughing.

Megan paused and took in several deep breaths. "An unbelievable day, Elysse. Robert … Roberto is simply amazing."

"I'm so happy for you. Sounds like you found your star. Maybe with Roberto? Tell me more. I hear Italian men are handsome."

The sisters talked into the wee hours of the morning. Although Megan yawned and her body ached from the travel and stress, sharing everything was just too exciting.

"Tell Ty to call me, okay?" Megan said just before hanging up. "I'm going to need his fairytale story again. The one of CallaLyly and Celestial KittyCat."

"Excuse me?" Elysse replied.

Chapter Twenty-Six

It is said, "Meeting another after living through a lifetime is inspiring for those who are already friends." This is not about being friends but about the love that some day may bring ...

Present Day

Sunshine peeked through the wispy clouds. Couples strolling on the Ponte Vecchio never seemed to notice the young man wearing a black tux. They didn't seem bothered by the old man clad in linen either. The two leaned silently into the gentle curve of the brick bridge. Taking in a deep breath, Tyler glanced at two lovers who were tossing their keys into the river. The girl wrapped her arms around the boy and they sealed their passion with a kiss.

Some traditions never change. Tyler sighed for he longed for Lyly. From his heart, it was his desire to live inside their make-believe world. It was there where he resided day after day, night after night ... inside the toiles. *I had saved her. I am meant to be there. It couldn't have been a dream. It had to be real.* Tyler stared into the water. The gentle ripples reminded him of his life ... bland and uneven.

"My Aunt Meg and Uncle Roberto married a year later. My cousins, Giuliana and Sofia, are eight and seven now." Tyler wiped away a tear. "I let them down too. They were to be the flower girls."

The old man shuffled from one foot to the other.

"Brandt & Cavelli made the CallaLyly and Celestial KittyCat fairytale line into a huge success." Tyler sighed. "They consulted with me on almost a daily basis." Tyler sighed again. "Unfortunately, my parents divorced when I left for college. Mom has a new boyfriend and Dad's single. He never seems to have time for anyone or anything other than his work." Watching a fish jump out of the water, Tyler frowned. "Bet you're wondering if I ever told him ... the renowned MIT physicist, Dr. Daniel Charles, about any of this ..."

The man released his grip and turned to Tyler.

You don't understand a word I'm saying. Tyler shook his head. "I'll receive my doctorate next year. Metaphysics will soon become my life's work." Tyler took a step back and stretched. He again glanced at the couples and sighed. "I was really there, yah know. Experienced it within time and space. Used the portals, I did. No one'll ever convince me it was just a dream ... just a hallucination." Tyler tapped on the bridge with his hands. "Nope, it was real!"

Now, the old man took in a deep breath.

"Kev is my best man ... correction ... was. I know I left her standing there ... alone. I just couldn't face her or a lifetime commitment to someone I didn't truly love." He glanced at the old Italian. "I was in love with the girl in the toile. I really did love her." Tyler stared up at a cloud and frowned. "Last night at dinner, Aunt Meg saw me staring up at the stars. I was alone on that balcony." Tyler wiped away another tear. "Too alone."

"A penny for your thoughts," Megan had said, stepping up to him.

Tyler was leaning against the railing. He glanced over at her and then back at the stars.

"Beautiful … the stars tonight."

Tyler nodded.

"They're serving dessert. You barely touched your dinner."

Tyler shrugged.

"Are you still looking for your star?" Megan pointed to the night's sky.

"What?"

"For someone who's about to marry, you've never looked happier?" She chuckled.

"I'm sorry. I should probably mingle a little … and smile?"

Megan hugged Tyler around the shoulders and kissed his cheek. "I believe the problem is that you're still looking for that star of yours."

"I remember when I first heard that saying." Tyler smiled. "We were here in Florence."

Megan laughed. "You were so sick."

"Yep, I was."

Megan sighed. "Ty, if you're going through with this marriage because you don't want to disappoint Guiliana or Sofia, don't. We'll find some place for them to toss those petals."

Tyler looked at her and nodded.

"Something is written in those stars for you, Ty. You just have to have patience. Afterall, it was written for me. I just didn't recognize it." Megan stared at her nephew and grinned. She leaned her head against his shoulder and engulfed herself within their love. "Love is a funny thing, Ty. Just depends on what you want to do with it."

A breeze caressed Tyler's face and he sighed. "I told Kevin first. He laughed and slapped me on the back." Tyler lifted his head and allowed the breeze to cool his face. "I did love her. But not in the way a husband should love his wife. She cried. So did I. I ran to the hotel and packed. Then someone knocked on the door. I didn't want to open it. Wasn't sure if it was my mom or dad or …"

The old man rested his arms against the bridge and sighed.

"It was a man dressed in an old-fashioned bellboy outfit." Tyler pulled out a note. "He handed me this envelope. I'm supposed to read this to you. Don't know if you'll understand my English or not."

If you want to change your love life circumstances once and for all, go immediately to the middle of the Ponte Vecchio Bridge. Wear your tux. At 3:13 PM exactly, stand next to a very old man dressed in linen. Tell him everything that happened to you fifteen years ago while in Florence and Siena with CallaLyly of the House of Montevelli of Siena and do not stop until you read him this note. I assure you that you will finally find true love of the kind you seek.

The old man pulled out a piece of paper and grinned. He handed it to Tyler. The paper and handwriting were the same.

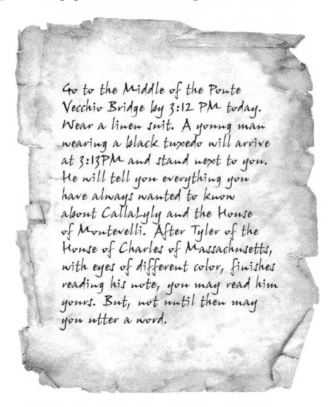

Go to the Middle of the Ponte Vecchio Bridge by 3:12 PM today. Wear a linen suit. A young man wearing a black tuxedo will arrive at 3:13PM and stand next to you. He will tell you everything you have always wanted to know about CallaLyly and the House of Montevelli. After Tyler of the House of Charles of Massachusetts, with eyes of different color, finishes reading his note, you may read him yours. But, not until then may you utter a word.

Tyler smiled and nodded. "You did understand what I said."

"Every word," the man replied.

Tyler shook his head and handed the man back his note. "May I ask your name and is this a joke? Who put you up to it?"

"Walk with me, Tyler," the man said. "I will explain what you need to hear." The man waved to the right of the bridge.

Tyler glanced at his watch. "I have a little time." Tyler removed his jacket and flicked it over his shoulder.

"My name's Domenico Montevelli. I'm ninety years old next week."

"Congrats." Tyler nodded.

"I'm a great-grandson of CallaLyly's younger brother, Alberto. My son, Alberto Montevelli, is named after him. He's the CEO of the banking empire you saved all those years ago. Alberto still lives in that very house you visited when you were twelve."

"I know but —"

"Please, allow me to continue." The man nodded. He held his hands behind his back as he walked. "CallaLyly was an amazing woman. She was the first to study banking at the Universita of Florence. She and her father turned their dream into a reality — loaning to the commoners. Eventually they expanded to other parts of Italy." He chuckled. "She made Patrick a very wealthy nobleman in the process. They were kind and generous to all. A few years after you left, they married. Named their first son Patrick Domenico Tyler Barrett."

"She remembered me then," Tyler whispered.

"Yes," Domenico replied. "During those years, only a male could inherit the family business. Therefore, once her brother came of age, CallaLyly and Patrick moved to England where they began their own financial business under the name of Barrett. About a decade ago, the Commoner's Bank of Siena merged with Barrett Financial. Now known as CB & Barrett."

"What does any of that have to do with me and my wedding?"

Domenico laughed. "Keep walking, Tyler. I'm getting there. Upon her deathbed, CallaLyly wrote down everything that happened with you. She left her legacy to the Montevelli House. It was her last request that her legacy be guarded by the Montevellis and their descendants along with a lock and key."

Tyler laughed and a tear rolled down his cheek. "Then she kept it."

Domenico nodded and continued his story. "Just before she passed …"

"Help me to my bureau," CallaLyly said to her nursemaid. "I've not much time."

"Yes, ma'am."

With each step, Lyly moaned.

"Careful, ma'am." The nursemaid guided her by the arm.

Lyly winced as she sat. The nurse fluffed the pillows behind her. She placed the parchment with the Barrett insignia on the desk. With her hand shaking, Lyly slowly and cautiously dipped her quill into the ink.

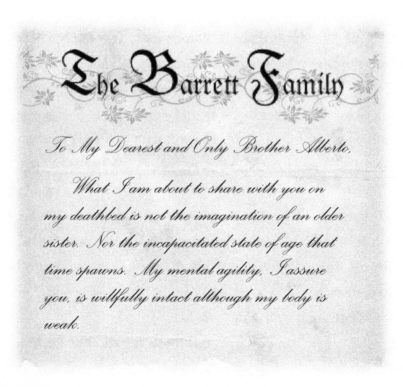

The Barrett Family

To My Dearest and Only Brother Alberto,

What I am about to share with you on my deathbed is not the imagination of an older sister. Nor the incapacitated state of age that time spawns. My mental agility, I assure you, is willfully intact although my body is weak.

I have purposely bided my time and now it beckons. My words are truth. A truth that blew life back into our family's name. I met a boy with different colored eyes who changed my world.

I beseech you to listen with an open mind, and to honor my wish of passing our legacy to each of our descendants until the end of time. My wish then shall be fulfilled. The following explains all in detail.

I told Father and he believed everything that I shared. My story will read to you as a fairytale and this very story haunted our father for years. He said that it felt as if he was living another life. A life where I no longer lived, where I had disappeared.

It began with the dawn of The Gala, my age seventeen. Father had negotiated my marriage to this evil man's son ~ ~ ~

Lyly placed the lock and key along with the parchment into an emerald box engraved with the name *English House of Barrett*. She glanced over at the frame with a portrait of Patrick and smiled. *I will be with you soon, my love.* Lyly glanced up at her nurse and whispered, "Please call my horseman."

The nurse nodded and left the room. After a few moments, she returned with a young man who bowed and smiled.

Lyly handed the legacy box to the young man and whispered, "As wings in flight, please deliver this into the hands of Alberto of the House of Montevelli of Siena. Only to my brother!"

The young man nodded.

"Then return with his response."

As the days turned into night and the nights into day, Lyly waited for the young horseman to return. One afternoon when her legs ached and her head pounded, he returned with a note.

> To My Beloved Sister, Your truest desire shall be fulfilled. Your Loving Brother Alberto

Lyly closed her eyes and a tear ran down her face. "I shall request the *StarWriters* to write a personal wish onto my star. To ensure a meeting between friends who will one day become more than just friends."

CallaLyly closed her eyes and stepped forever into the wonders of the other world to walk again by the side of her lover and husband, Patrick.

"Lyly knew the power of her last few words," Domenico said.

"I was always happy for Lyly and Patrick," Tyler replied. "Still, what does this have to do with me?"

"We're almost there, Tyler." Domenico laughed. "A couple more shops past Tino's Houses of Incredible Tattoos."

"Tattoos?" Tyler glanced into the window as they passed and smiled at the large picture of The Catman and his amazing cats.

"No, no. Here we are."

Domenico stepped into a small book store and Tyler followed. The window was decorated with various types of toile wallpaper. Domenico pointed to a stack of books and smiled.

Tyler picked up a book and read off the title. "The Boy with Two Different Brown Eyes Who Saved a Banking Empire, by CaLy Montevelli."

"It's a fairytale for teens," Domenico said with a large smile. "My granddaughter, CaLy Montevelli." Domenico picked up another copy and rubbed his hand down the cover. "Not all the Montevellis are believers on our success." He smiled. "With the exception of myself and my granddaughter." He patted Tyler on the back and laughed. "Thanks to you. We are forever in your debt, son."

"No need to thank me." Tyler sighed. "Lyly was the one that was successful in her endeavors. Makes me happy that your family is secure and together." Tyler glanced around. "I should be going. There's a flight to Boston I must catch." He extended his hand to Domenico. "Nice to have met you."

"Don't leave just yet, Tyler." Domenico walked over to the young attendant. She wore jeans and a white t-shirt. As she arranged a few books on a large table, Domenico patted her on the shoulder. She turned and smiled.

"I wish for you to meet someone," he said.

The young woman turned around and Tyler froze. He stared at the ornament that hung around her neck.

"Tyler, I wish for you to meet CaLy. My granddaughter."

"You could pass as Lyly's twin!" Tyler said, nodding. "Nice to meet you CaLy."

With the exception of a few blonde highlights, CaLy was the spitting image of CallaLyly of the House of Montevelli of Siena.

"CaLy," Domenico said, softly, "This is *the* Tyler."

"Hello, Tyler …" CaLy looked closely into Tyler's eyes and blinked several times. "Your eyes are a different shade of brown!"

"Sorry, born that way," Tyler replied. "And … you have my lock and key."

CaLy nodded. "Passed down through the family."

The two stared at each other without talking.

Domenico chuckled and said, "CaLy, I need to use the toilette. I'll be just a moment."

CaLy nodded without removing her eyes from Tyler.

Tyler pulled out his wallet and removed a small, folded sheet of paper. He carefully unfolded the paper and CaLy watched his fingers move and it looked as if he was unwrapping a long-lost secret. Tyler picked up a small key and held it up to CaLy's lock.

"They match," he whispered.

"I always dreamed of meeting you one day, Tyler of the House of Charles of Massachusetts."

Her gaze penetrated deeply into Tyler's soul. He shivered and nodded. "Call me, Ty?"

"She smiled."

"May I buy you a drink? Would love to talk more about —"

"I'm on the clock," she whispered.

"I'll stand in for you." Domenico, her grandfather, chuckled. "Go have a coffee or something."

Tyler and CaLy strolled toward the piazza. Tyler would glance at the path and then back at CaLy and smile.

"I'm sorry," Tyler said. "It's just …"

CaLy giggled. "Grandfather says I'm CallaLyly reborn. He's shown me portraits. I agree, I do resemble her."

Seating themselves at a table near the fountain in the center of the piazza, Tyler motioned for a waiter. "The book … you believe the story?"

"Ever since I was little, grandfather would tell me about her and you. I could never hear it enough. My father is a non-believer." She sighed. "Most in my family regards our history as a fairytale."

"Crazy as it may sound, I was there with Lyly. We lived inside the toiles. It was real."

"I don't always understand how, but I believe."

"Time and space came together." He shook his head. "It's my doctoral thesis. I'm a physicist." He placed his hand over hers. "I believe you believe."

"I'd love to hear your whole story, Tyler."

"Ty," Tyler replied.

For the first time since he was twelve, Tyler felt at home in CaLy's presence. Was he confusing two realities? CaLy was not Lyly. There were two centuries separating them but he somehow felt drawn to CaLy just the same.

"Cin, cin," CaLy said, raising her glass.

They toasted Lyly and her fairytale as they shared stories and ate dinner. When the sun slowly fell behind the historical Duomo, CaLy shivered and rubbed her arms. Tyler swung his jacket over her shoulders.

"How about some gelato?" he asked, remembering the time he spent with Roberto and Aunt Meg. "I know the best place in all of Florence."

"Lead the way." CaLy giggled.

A few blocks away, they entered a small shop. After staring at the various flavors, Tyler chose vanilla and CaLy chose cherry.

Tyler smacked his lips. "What did I tell you?"

"Not bad." She laughed.

Walking and laughing with CaLy, Tyler felt as if he had finally arrived home. It was odd, but Tyler suddenly wished that everything were a blueish-green. He chuckled and said, "I don't want the evening to end. And I would very much like to see you again."

"I would like that too," CaLy replied.

He pulled the key from his pocket. He smiled and touched the lock that hung around her neck. He inserted the key and turned it. The lock popped open. He laughed and handed CaLy the key.

CaLy smiled and pulled the chain over her head. She unhooked it and slipped on Tyler's key. Tyler placed the lock and keys back over her head. He held her shoulders and smiled.

"This is crazy. We've only just met but this feels so right."

CaLy smiled and nodded. "I feel like I've known you forever, Ty."

Tyler leaned in and gently kissed CaLy on the lips. He pulled back and smiled. Then CaLy leaned in and kissed Tyler. After several moments, they held hands and walked past a man standing near a tent.

Tyler stopped and stared at him. He looked Asian and wore a long red robe with a multi colored hat and his gray mustache draped down to his torso. Tyler watched as the man used his long golden finger nails to cut a silhouette from a white sheet of paper.

The man glanced over and winked at Tyler.

Tyler frowned. "Let's walk this way." Still holding CaLy's hand, Tyler pulled her away from the Asian wizard who continued to stare at them.

Joroku watched as the young couple walked away. He glanced into his copper pot and frowned. Through the slivers of the torn paper, the sorceress glared back at him.

"Have you taken care of business?" the sorceress asked.

"Yes, Mother. The letters were delivered by Ru. From what I just saw, quite successful."

"I am proud of you my son, Joroku. How is your new assistant, Ru? And your love potion business?"

"Neither are well."

Every fifty years or so, Joroku must train someone new. The love potion business was tough with all the new social media craze. Seemed that most preferred to never leave their couch. Joroku preferred the old-fashioned way.

"I see a new assistant in your future," the sorceress said. "A female this time."

"And is that written in the stars, Mother?"

"You still have a little matter you must deal with first."

Joroku groaned.

"It is time, my son."

Joroku fashioned his last silhouette to the black paper using his spit. An elderly man dressed as a bellhop walked up. The couple kissed as they walked away.

"Did all go as expected, Master Joroku?" Ru asked.

"Yes. Thank you, Ru. Our time in Florence is finished. Gather our belongings. We will return to New York shortly."

"In our usual manner?" Ru asked.

Joroku squinted at him.

"Remember when we traveled on the cruise ships?" Ru asked. "You placed us into scrolls and then tucked us inside the luggage."

Joroku laughed. "How could I forget. We mingled with the rich and slept comfortably inside our wallcoverings."

"Unfortunately, air customs no longer allows baggage to travel alone," Ru said.

Joroku nodded and placed himself, his beloved copper pot, and their belongings into a paper scroll. Ru cautiously placed the tubes into a suitcase.

"Don't worry, Master Joroku," Ru whispered. "I shall place you safely under my cushioned seat."

Sometime later, in the Chinese Province of Yung, at the National Museum of the People's Palace, the 13th Century Emperor took his customary seat of power. He reveled in the applause. A vacant portrait lay at his feet.

"He is truly the best actor portraying the emperor of that time," the female museum's director said, clapping. "We've never had better."

"He's definitely living the part!" her assistant replied. "He looks so real!"

Epilogue

It is said, "Evil looks to exist." This is not about just existing but about the coming evil...

"Scat, you vermin, this meal is mine!" The man with the pure white hair yelled as he sorted through the daily garbage. He slapped the two fat and furry rats with his walking stick. "I'm not sharing."

The rodents darted into the shadows.

More than once, the white-haired man had listened to the nobles yell those same exact words at him. *'You rat! Nothing but a vermin. May you crawl into the shadows and never re-surface.'*

He used a dirty cloth to hold the stale bread. Giovanni of the House of de'Leon of Florence was now blind in one eye and the other was nothing more than a misty blur. He was once known as *All Eyes* — all knowing and all powerful. Now, he was known for nothing. Over the last decade his banking empire had collapsed, which forced him to sell his lands and belongings. He was only allowed to keep his deteriorating house. His grand home with a loving wife and three sons was now just an old estate that was crumbling in around him.

He spat on the road and sighed. He'd been coughing up blood for over a year now. Late into the darkened nights, he often spoke to his deceased wife.

"My dear, oh, how our sons have failed us," Giovanni whispered into the howling winds that soared through the broken and cracked panes.

"They have disowned me, my love. Left me alone and abandoned. I arranged a wonderful marriage for Agost with the daughter of the House of Montevelli. He rewarded me by disappearing … the fool!"

Carrying his table scraps as if they were a feast, Giovanni dug his stick into the damp soil. He walked with a gait and needed the stick to pull himself forward. His stomach growled. He passed a horse drawn carriage and scowled. Elegantly clad nobles glared out their contempt for the elderly beggar.

"Damn you all!" Giovanni cursed. "I wanted to maintain our feudalism in this town. It was my right to rule!" He raised his walking stick and shook it as the coach wobbled down the dirt road. Giovanni shook his head and sighed. "Evil doers!"

A second coach ambled up the road. The horse neighed and nodded as it passed.

"You shall pay. You shall all pay." He mumbled through his cracked and rotting teeth. "Those Montevellis are digging into your fortunes and promoting peasants and commoners!" He laughed again. "One day … you shall all suffer as I."

Limping into his cold and damp home, he placed his cracked stick against the crumbling plaster. Giovanni lit his only lantern and sat at his broken bureau. Giovanni smiled at the thought of afflicting revenge while eating his evening's feast.

From inside his jacket pocket, he pulled out a piece of toile. As a rat scurried across his feet searching for the fallen crumbs, Giovanni stared at the seafaring motif.

"Not much time," he whispered.

Within the rays of the candlelight and with a quill pen in hand, Giovanni pondered. Something had happened that reversed his reality, and his heart now pounded at a tune that no longer seemed to flow.

"I need to somehow reverse my destiny."

Giovanni wrote on the torn parchment his ill-fated tale.

> I, Giovanni of the House of de'Leon of Florence bequeath this house and all its contents to my descendants.
>
> To the powers that can become you: Follow my words and your life shall change for the better.
>
> His powers rely on the copper pot that is always by his side. Steal it and he will pay all his wealth.
>
> Giovanni of the House of de'Leon of Florence

Using his walking stick, Giovanni pried open a small panel on the wall. He reached inside and felt along the bricks.

He laughed. "There you are."

The golden talon he had made from smelting gold coins weighed heavily in his hands.

"You citizens are nothing but fools!"

Giovanni smashed the talon against the wall and a claw broke off. He laughed and picked it up. He ran his fingers over the sharp object and smiled. After rolling the toile within the parchment, he tied them together around the remaining talon. He placed them behind the hidden panel and laughed again.

"I never lose!" Giovanni screamed and his words echoed into the night's darkness.

Giovanni sat the broken claw on the bureau with a note stating that the funds were to be used to pay any future taxes. He stared at the shiny gold and shook his head.

"Always about the money."

The following morning, the authorities found Giovanni behind a deserted building. His eyes were staring into the sky and his walking stick rested only a few feet away. Several rats had already feasted on his eyes and lips. As he died, Giovanni understood that he would never again walk upon the face of the Earth.

A special thank you to Indignor House,
And with utmost heartfelt thanks to Lynn Yvonne Moon,
my editor, extraordinaire.

An abundance of thank you's to Katherine Savarese for
her never ending assistance on my projects.

And thank you to Brianna Jaro for Social Media.

I would like to mention additional appreciation to all
who worked the long hours behind the scenes —

Thank You!

Mary K. Savarese is the award-winning author of *Tigers Love Bubble Baths & Obsession Perfume (who knew!)* Koehler Books April 2019. *Tigers*, her debut novel, won the 2021 prestigious First Horizon, Eric Hoffer Book Award.

Born in Brooklyn, New York, Mary K. Savarese holds a Bachelor of Arts in accounting from City University, NY. Her career centered within the insurance and financing community. Mary spent thirteen years as a religious education teacher working with young adults. She now lives in Florida with her devoted husband. Mary is a Catholic Eucharistic minister enlightening the residents of local community nursing homes. She now spends her spare time writing her enlightening and fun stories to entertain those brave enough to turn the pages.

https://www.maryksavarese.com

Lightning Source UK Ltd.
Milton Keynes UK
UKHW011845100921
390383UK00008B/422/J